S0-CFT-940

SWEET TEMPTATION

Some might call Enrique Espiritu Esperanza kooky for offering cookies to the voting public, but they were gobbling it up. To Chiun, though, the dark-horse candidate offered something even better. Money.

Still, the Master of Sinanju had an important question. "How much money?"

"Billions," said Esperanza.

Chiun considered. He thought of duty. He thought of honor. Then he thought of the beauteous Cheeta Ching and what billions could buy.

"I accept," said the Master of Sinanju, bowing deeply.

If this meant severing his sacred contract with the U.S. government . . . if it meant breaking up the team that had struck terror into evildoers the world over . . . if it meant putting himself and Remo on opposite sides of a fight to a great many deaths . . . well, that was the way the Oreo crumbled. . . .

⊘ SIGNET   (0451)

THE HEART-STOPPING ADVENTURES OF REMO AND CHIUN
created by Warren Murphy
and Richard Sapir

- [ ] THE DESTROYER #74: WALKING WOUNDED   (156005—$3.50)
- [ ] THE DESTROYER #75: RAIN OF TERROR   (157524—$3.95)
- [ ] THE DESTROYER #77: COIN OF THE REALM   (160576—$3.95)
- [ ] THE DESTROYER #79: SHOOTING SCHEDULE   (163583—$4.50)
- [ ] THE DESTROYER #80: DEATH SENTENCE   (164717—$3.95)
- [ ] THE DESTROYER #81: HOSTILE TAKEOVER   (166019—$4.50)
- [ ] THE DESTROYER #82: SURVIVAL ZERO   (167368—$4.50)
- [ ] THE DESTROYER #83: SKULL DUGGERY   (169050—$4.50)
- [ ] THE DESTROYER #84: GROUND ZERO   (169344—$4.50)
- [ ] THE DESTROYER #85: BLOOD LUST, Special 20th Anniversary Edition
                                                  (169905—$4.50)
- [ ] THE DESTROYER #86: ARABIAN NIGHTMARE   (170601—$4.50)
- [ ] THE DESTROYER #87: MOB PSYCHOLOGY   (171144—$4.50)
- [ ] THE DESTROYER #88: THE ULTIMATE DEATH   (171160—$4.50)

Prices slightly higher in Canada.

Buy them at your local bookstore or use this convenient coupon for ordering.

NEW AMERICAN LIBRARY
P.O. Box 999, Bergenfield, New Jersey 07621

Please send me the books I have checked above.
I am enclosing $_____ (please add $2.00 to cover postage and handling).
Send check or money order (no cash or C.O.D.'s) or charge by Mastercard or
VISA (with a $15.00 minimum). Prices and numbers are subject to change without
notice.

Card #_____ Exp. Date _____
Signature_____
Name_____
Address_____
City _____ State _____ Zip Code _____
        For faster service when ordering by credit card call 1-800-253-6476
Allow a minimum of 4-6 weeks for delivery. This offer is subject to change without notice.

The Destroyer

#89

DARK HORSE

CREATED BY
WARREN MURPHY & RICHARD SAPIR

A SIGNET BOOK

SIGNET
Published by the Penguin Group
Penguin Books USA Inc., 375 Hudson Street,
New York, New York 10014, U.S.A.
Penguin Books Ltd, 27 Wrights Lane,
London W8 5TZ, England
Penguin Books Australia Ltd, Ringwood,
Victoria, Australia
Penguin Books Canada Ltd, 10 Alcorn Avenue,
Toronto, Ontario, Canada M4V 3B2
Penguin Books (N.Z.) Ltd, 182–190 Wairau Road,
Auckland 10, New Zealand

Penguin Books Ltd, Registered Offices:
Harmondsworth, Middlesex, England

First published by Signet, an imprint of New American Library,
a division of Penguin Books USA Inc.

First Printing, July, 1992
10 9 8 7 6 5 4 3 2 1

Copyright © Warren Murphy, 1992
All rights reserved

 REGISTERED TRADEMARK—MARCA REGISTRADA

PRINTED IN THE UNITED STATES OF AMERICA

Without limiting the rights under copyright reserved above, no part of this
publication may be reproduced, stored in or introduced into a retrieval system, or transmitted, in any form, or by any means (electronic, mechanical,
photocopying, recording, or otherwise), without the prior written permission
of both the copyright owner and the above publisher of this book.

PUBLISHER'S NOTE
This is a work of fiction. Names, characters, places, and incidents either
are the product of the author's imagination or are used fictitiously, and any
resemblance to actual persons, living or dead, events, or locales is entirely
coincidental.

BOOKS ARE AVAILABLE AT QUANTITY DISCOUNTS WHEN USED TO PROMOTE
PRODUCTS OR SERVICES. FOR INFORMATION PLEASE WRITE TO PREMIUM MAR-
KETING DIVISION, PENGUIN BOOKS USA INC., 375 HUDSON STREET, NEW YORK,
NEW YORK 10014.

If you purchased this book without a cover you should be aware that this
book is stolen property. It was reported as "unsold and destroyed" to the
publisher and neither the author nor the publisher has received any payment
for this "stripped book."

For Mark DerMarderosian, and twenty years of friendship. (Give or take a month.)

And for the Glorious House of Sinanju,
P.O. Box 2505, Quincy, MA 02269.

1

It was called "the Buddy Holly rule."

It applied to the President of the United States and the Vice-President. It was strictly observed by sports teams. Rock bands adhered to it religiously, as did corporate officers.

It was inflexible, unbreakable policy wherever it applied. And it applied to every business and political situation. And, on occasion, social situations.

It should have applied to the Governor of California and his lieutenant governor.

Technically, it did. They were, under no circumstance, to fly on the same plane, travel in the same vehicle, or even ride the same elevator. That was unshakable policy.

Unfortunately, unshakable policy applied only to political trips, arranged for by political aides and handlers.

This was social.

The governor of California didn't know that his lieutenant governor was going to attend the concert at Los Angeles's Music Center.

He discovered this amazing coincidence shortly after the flight attendant had shut the 727's big door.

Almost immediately, someone began pounding on it.

The governor, seated in first-class, smiled thinly. He knew how the airlines worked. If the door was closed, you missed your flight. There was no second chance, no appeal. The jetway passenger bridge was about to be retracted from the jetliner's aluminum skin. This particular airline was plagued by recurring schedule problems. They were not about to add to them, the governor was sure, simply for a single passenger who couldn't even make check-in.

The governor settled back to see what the editorial pages of the *Sacramento Bee* were saying about him today.

Suddenly, a harried voice could be heard in between spasms of pounding.

"Let me in! Let me in!"

This guy just isn't going to give up, the governor thought, wondering how he had managed to get onto the jetway in the first place. The late ones were usually intercepted beforehand.

The flight attendants began to buzz among themselves. One knocked on the flight deck door, and slipped in.

She returned after a very brief consultation with the captain and went directly to the exit door, where she undogged the locking latch. She gave the door a shove.

And in stomped a face the governor of California knew only too well.

"What are *you* doing here?" he asked, taking his brief-case off the empty seat beside him.

The lieutenant governor flopped onto the seat, ex-tracting a white handkerchief from his coat pocket. He ran this across his bedewed forehead, while he caught his breath. His face was flushed.

"Damn cab ran out of gas!" he huffed. "Can you be-lieve it—a cab running on empty? Only in California."

The jetway ramp was retracted, while the two highest-ranking officers in the State of California shared a rueful laugh. With a rising whine, the jet slithered out from its berth.

"You're lucky they relented," the governor said as the 727 turned into its takeoff position, wishing they hadn't. The lieutenant governor was a Democrat.

"I kept telling them I was the damn lieutenant gover-nor," the lieutenant governor muttered. "Wasn't sure they heard me."

A pleasant voice over the intercom called on the flight crew to begin a cross-check in preparation for takeoff.

In a moment, the engine whine rose and the wheels under their feet began to bump and rumble.

As the jet started to pick up speed, pushing them back into their seats, the governor remarked, "You know, we shouldn't be doing this."

"Doing what?"

"Flying together. It's the old Buddy Holly scenario."

"Huh?" asked the lieutenant governor, who had been born in New Zealand.

"You know, the Crickets. Everybody got on the same plane, it crashed, and rock and roll took a mortal blow."

"Didn't one of them take the bus?" asked the lieutenant governor, as the wheels left the runway.

"Search me. Back then, I was listening to Guy Mitchell."

The jet climbed steeply, and their stomachs sank. The sound came of the wheels toiling up into their wells.

Only after the engine roar had settled down to the familiar whine of horizontal flight did they resume speaking. By that time, the flight attendants were offering martinis and smiles.

"Well," the governor said ruefully, "if anything happens to us, there's still the secretary of state."

This thought sobered both men until the drinks were set before them.

"What's your business in L.A.?" the governor asked, when the first very-dry sip had gone down.

"I'm attending a concert," the lieutenant governor said. "Nana Mouskouri, or something like that."

The governor started. "Really? Those are my plans!"

"How about that?"

"I didn't know you were a fan of her music."

"I'm not," returned the lieutenant governor.

"Then why?"

The lieutenant governor shrugged. "The tickets were free."

In the act of swallowing a gulp of dry martini, the governor of California felt his mouth go dry. Something of the fear he felt must have showed up in his eyes, because the lieutenant governor took one look at his paling face and blurted, "What's wrong?"

Slowly, the governor of California withdrew an envelope from his suit. He displayed a ticket. His next words were little more than a croaking.

"Came two days ago. Anonymous."

"Mine contained airline tickets, too," the lieutenant governor said, in a voice drier than his drink.

"Mine, too."

The two highest elected officials in California—*over*

California, now—digested this startling coincidence in silence.

"Someone," the lieutenant governor said thickly, "must really want us at that concert."

"Or maybe," the governor croaked, "on this flight."

Their eyes were already wide. They had been widening all through the conversation. They could hardly have grown wider, but they did. A child could have run a Magic Marker around the outer edge of the irises and not touched or discolored an eyelash.

They were both thinking the same thing. They were thinking how unpopular their administration had become in less than two years. How many special-interest groups despised them. How unpopular recent gubernatorial vetoes had been.

The governor shot up in his seat.

"Turn this plane around!" he demanded harshly, his voice like something that had been torn off bleeding muscle.

The flight attendant hurried up the aisle. She presented a concerned face, and a smile that promised reassurance but jittered around its lipsticked edges.

"Sir, is something the matter?"

The governor used his finger to point. "This is the lieutenant governor sitting next to me."

The attendant looked, said, "Yes?"

"We're not supposed to be flying together!"

"It's the Buddy Holly rule," the lieutenant governor chimed in dutifully. "And you know what happened to them."

"Was he an actor?" wondered the flight attendant, who looked all of twenty-two.

The governor cleared his throat and mustered up his best oratorical voice. "Please inform the captain that the governor of the state sincerely requests that he turn this flight around and put us down at LAX," he said, giving each syllable a tight, steely enunciation.

"I'm sorry, but that's against the airline's rules."

"Please do this."

"Yes, *please*," the lieutenant governor pleaded, moist-eyed.

The flight attendant hurried off. She was gone for a while.

Eventually, a stone-faced man in airline black stepped into the first-class cabin. He wore his years in the cockpit on his regular, seamed face.

"Are you the captain?" the governor said tightly, trying to keep control of himself.

"Copilot. The captain sends his regrets."

In terse words the governor presented his case, ending with, "This can't be a coincidence."

The copilot gave an aw-shucks laugh and tilted back his uniform cap.

"Sir . . ."

"Governor."

"Governor, what I think you got there is a pair of tickets from Miss— What did you say the lady's name was?"

"Mouskouri."

"It's clear to me that you're both being treated by the little lady herself. I don't see what the fuss is."

"You don't understand!" the lieutenant governor put in frantically.

The copilot's face hardened. "Maybe it's the other way around," he said flatly. "We held up the flight to let you on board, sir. Now, the captain has the discretion to do that. But turning the plane around without an on-board emergency?" He shook his head. "No. I'm sorry."

They harangued the poor copilot, demanded to see the captain, but the man stood his ground.

Eventually, with mumbled apologies and a stiff face, the copilot returned to the cockpit.

The flight attendants refreshed their drinks and made a point of showing off their legs.

The governor and his lieutenant soon settled down. The drone of the jet engines became routine, putting them off their guards.

"Maybe it *was* Miss Mouskouri who sent the tickets," the lieutenant governor said hopefully.

"It's the only explanation that makes sense," the governor agreed.

"Still," the lieutenant governor said wistfully, "I wish I had taken the bus. Just in case."

They shared a laugh that rattled in their throats like old bones. It was an unpleasant sound that squelched further conversation and provided absolutely no reassurance up at twenty thousand feet, in a jet buffeting through clouds and air pockets like a shaky rollercoaster.

The jet rattled. The overhead luggage compartments jiggled uncertainly. The seats, although bolted to the cabin floor, shook and bounced them on their plush, roomy cushions.

The governor and lieutenant governor started to grow nervous all over again.

"Is this plane shaking worse than usual?" the lieutenant governor muttered.

"I can't tell. I'm shaking too much myself."

"Why are you shaking?"

"I'm thinking of how many death threats I've been getting since I vetoed that Gay Rights bill."

"Well, I didn't veto it. I was for it. But you—you wouldn't listen to me."

"That's right. If it was the Gay Rights people, they wouldn't be after you." A flush of relief raced up the governor's boyish features.

At that exact moment, the 727 went into a steep dive and the overhead compartments popped, like topsy-turvy jack-in-the-boxes.

A yellow oxygen mask slapped the governor of California in the eye. An identical one dangled before the lieutenant governor's suddenly bone-white face. They might have been hangman's nooses from the sick, incredulous way the two politicians stared.

The captain's drawling voice came over the intercom, saying, "Nothing to be concerned about, folks. We're experiencing a little problem with our pressurization, so we're just gonna descend to ten thousand feet while we check it out. If you start feeling light-headed, that's what the yellow oxygen masks are for."

"Oh my God! We're going to crash!" the governor said, voice twisting.

"But he just said—"

"I don't care what he said!" the governor snapped, pulling the plastic oxygen mask to his face and hyperventilating wildly.

The lieutenant governor grabbed his mask with one hand and his stomach with the other. As he inhaled deep lungfuls of cold, plasticky oxygen, he prayed to God to keep him from throwing up in the mask and blocking the air line.

On the flight deck, Captain Del Grossman had his flight chart in his lap, as scraps and wisps of cloud whipped by the windshield.

The copilot was guarding the throttles. The captain looked up from his chart and peered out the side window.

Below, under the lower edge of the cloud layer, he saw a city-sprawl that looked like a transistorized circuit board.

"Looks like Fresno," he muttered.

"Can't be Fresno," the copilot said. "It's not possible that we could have wandered this far off-course."

"That's why I said, 'looks like.'" The captain took another look at the flight chart. "According to our heading," he said, "we should be on Low-Altitude Airway Number 47."

"Right," the copilot said, as a hanging hump of cloud swallowed all forward visibility.

"But if we're following that route," the captain added, "we should be seeing the San Joaquin River beneath us."

"Huh," the copilot grunted. They were barreling through a world of gloomy stratocumulus now. "Wanna go lower?"

"No," said the captain. "I want you to check your flight chart."

The flight chart came out of its compartment, and the captain took the throttles.

The copilot checked his chart, frowned, and compared it with that of his senior officer.

"Everything I see tells me we're on-course," he said, with almost no conviction in his voice.

"And everything I see," said the captain, "tells me we're off-course."

"Charts don't lie, you know."

"And I trust the evidence of my eyes."

They were silent while the jet nosed through seemingly impenetrable cloud. The pressurization problem, which had forced them down to this perilously low altitude, was forgotten.

"I'm going to try to get under this damn weather," the captain grumbled.

He reached for the throttles. And his hand froze.

"Jesus H. Christ!"

There was no time to react. No time for anything. They both understood that with complete and utter clarity. They had each logged over twenty-six thousand hours in the air and knew the limitations of their aircraft.

Visibility was less than an eighth of a mile. The 727 was slamming along at about three hundred and seventy miles per hour.

By the time the stone face of Mount Whitney broke the low-hanging clouds and filled the windshield like an implacable idol, there wasn't even enough time to become afraid.

The cockpit crew were snuffed out with an appalling finality that could only have been equaled if they had taken seats in a high-speed trash compactor.

First-class got it from both directions. The foot-thick wall of tangled steel and human detritus that the cockpit and nose had become rammed back, while the rest of the airframe, still under power, drove it toward the collapsing forward bulkhead.

The governor and his lieutenant had a heartbeat's notice. That was all. Then they were both inextricably intertwined, in a roaring metallic entanglement that was almost instantly awash in the poisonous stink of Jet-A fuel. The plane careened and broke up as it made its absolutely final descent.

Down the side of the mountain that shouldn't have been there.

2

His name was Remo, and he had a dilemma.

Should he do the hit before, or after, the target was baptized?

It was, Remo had to admit, a first.

Remo had done hits many times. Too many to count. Big shots. Small fish. This particular fish was big. And ugly. There would be no mistaking him amid the small army of Federal marshals, FBI agents, press, and invited observers that, according to Upstairs, were due at any moment.

It couldn't be too soon for Remo Williams.

He was crouched in a thicket on a spongy isle in the heart of the Florida Everglades. It was hot. The air steamed. Love bugs danced in the heat. Remo showed barely a trace of sweat on his cruel face and bare arms. Still, that did not mean he was comfortable—only that he was the master of his own body.

For twenty years he had not felt cold, or heat, or pain or any ordinary discomfort that he was not able to will his body to ignore. For twenty years he had breathed not merely with his lungs, but through his entire body: nose, mouth, unclogged pores. For two decades he had been Sinanju. A Master of Sinanju. The latest Master of Sinanju in an unbroken line that stretched back to the dawn of recorded history. A line that had begun in a ramshackle fishing village on the West Korea Bay where men hired themselves out as assassins and bodyguards in order to feed the village, and now continued in Remo Williams, the first white Master of Sinanju, who served the newest empire on earth, the United States of America, as its secret assassin.

On a nearby hump, a heron flew up.

Remo had heard it unfold its wing preparatory to flight. The sudden upflinging of colorful feathers did not take him by surprise—although it startled an alligator into slithering into the water.

Why would anyone pick the Florida Everglades to be baptized in? Remo wondered, not exactly for the first time.

It was probably the least of the questions hanging in the humid Florida air.

Remo had been assigned the job of eliminating General Emmanuel Alejandro Nogeira, the deposed dictator of the Central American nation of Bananama. Snuffing out General Nogeira was something the Medellin drug cartel, assorted political enemies, and even the U.S. Rangers had attempted over the years.

Ever since he had risen up from rent-a-colonel in the Bananamian version of the CIA, to the day he was seized by U.S. forces as they liberated the country he had bankrupted through greed and corruption, Emmanuel Nogeira had proven immune to assassination.

The former general and self-proclaimed Maximum Chief had grinningly attributed his longevity to Voodoo—specifically to the red underwear he wore to ward off the Evil Eye. He ascribed his continual survival to a wide array of charms, friendly spirits, and ritual sacrifices—usually involving beheaded chickens. In actual fact, he had simply found the perfect—if somewhat inconvenient—sanctuary from his numerous enemies.

A United States federal prison.

The U.S. government had proclaimed a great victory on the day they captured General Nogeira. American servicemen had lost their lives in the effort to bring him to justice. He had been spirited into the U.S. and charged with violating American law through a pattern of drug-smuggling activities. The evidence against him was overwhelming.

Then General Nogeira proceeded to turn the tables on his captors, making a mockery of the American judicial system. He demanded—and got—prisoner-of-war status, a private cell, and privileges usually reserved for criminals serving time in corrupt Mexican jails. Not to mention the unfreezing of his assets.

Despite this, Nogeira had been convicted of drug trafficking, and sentenced to life without parole. But no sooner had that happened than the appeals began. It was estimated that the appeals process would not be entirely exhausted until the year 2093.

Since he had time to kill, General Nogeira announced that he had given up Voodoo, and was now a born-again Baptist. Or would be, once, as he put it, the "gringos" allowed him to be baptized.

Naturally, the prison authorities to whom he had put this unusual request had denied his petition, citing security risks.

Dipping into his seemingly limitless legal fund—the product of his voracious drug dealings, which he had managed to safeguard from confiscation by claiming it represented his income from the days when he was a CIA informer—General Nogeira enlisted the American Civil Rights Collective in his attempts to embrace his newfound religion.

It had taken nearly a year, but the ACRC had taken the issue all the way to the Florida Supreme Court. The Justice Department had caved in at that point. Not on principle, but because the appeals process was threatening to devour their entire operating budget.

General Emmanuel Nogeira had won—once again.

This time he publicly thanked Jesus Christ, whom he had claimed as his personal savior.

General Nogeira asked to be baptized in the Florida Everglades, claiming that it was the environment most like that of his native country, which he missed very much.

For the first time in nearly two years, General Emmanuel Alejandro Nogeira would be outside the walls of the maximum-security federal prison in Miami.

There were rumors that the Medellin Cartel would hit him then. There was other intelligence that they actually planned to liberate Nogeira and reinstall him in Bananama, which he had single-handedly turned into the major coke transshipping point between Colombia and the United States.

That was when Upstairs had ordered the hit on Nogeira.

"Not that I mind," Remo had said at the time, "but

why? He's going to rot in prison until the next century. Why not let him rot?"

"Because," he was told, "the man is costing this country thousands of dollars a day in legal fees. He's a common criminal, yet he has been declared a prisoner of war, entitled to wear his uniform and to an allowance of seventy-five Swiss Francs a day. He has his own private cell, and two adjoining ones for his shredding machine and a safe that contains classified U.S. documents the CIA was compelled to surrender to him in the name of a fair trial." Upstairs thinned already thin lips. It was clear that Remo's superior was offended by all this. Deeply offended.

Remo had to admit that Upstairs had a point. He didn't care if there were hit teams sent out to interrupt the baptism. He just wanted to get the hit over with and get out of the Everglades.

So the question remained: Before the baptism, or after?

It was a serious dilemma. If he hit Nogeira before he was baptized, then the general would probably go straight to hell. After, and maybe the guy had a chance to do penance. Spend a few centuries in Purgatory. Remo wasn't sure about that part. He had been raised Catholic. The Baptists might as well have been Jains for all he knew of their theological rules. Did they even have confession?

Crouching on the spongy isle, Remo frowned. The frown made his cruel face harden into angular lines. He was neither handsome nor ugly. Certainly not as ugly as Emmanuel Nogeira, who looked like a comic-book depiction of the Incredible Toad Man.

Remo's eyes were set deep into his skull, and his cheekbones pronounced. His body was lean, almost skinny, and unremarkable, except for his wrists. They were as thick as door posts, as if some mad surgeon had implanted steel rods where his ulna and radius connected with his metacarpals.

Except that the wrists were Remo's own. The two decades of training in the discipline that was Sinanju, the sun-source of the martial arts, had produced this freakish side effect.

Remo tried to imagine what his mentor, the Reigning Master of Sinanju, would say about his dilemma.

He could hear the squeaky voice in his mind's ear after only a moment's reflection.

"Do the House of Sinanju proud. Leave no trace."

Not much help there. Remo thought back to his orphanage days, and Sister Mary Margaret.

Remo wasn't quite sure what Sister Mary Margaret would have said, but it probably would have entailed calling off the hit. Not an option for America's secret assassin.

Finally, Remo considered the counsel of his superior, Dr. Harold W. Smith.

It was easy to figure out Smith's hypothetical advice. "Just do it quietly," Smith would say.

That went without saying. Smith, who ran the supersecret government organization for which Remo worked, had a mania for secrecy. And with good reason. The agency officially did not exist. It was known only as CURE. CURE was no acronym. The letters had no individual meaning. CURE was the symbolic name for the agency's function. That is, a prescription for American society, which criminals such as Emmanuel Nogeira had made sick by twisting constitutional guarantees to serve their own criminal purposes.

Remo had dealt with a great many people who made a mockery of the Constitution, but few did so as blatantly as General Nogeira, who wasn't even a U.S. citizen. This, perhaps more than anything, Remo decided, had offended the proper Smith.

The more Remo thought about it, the more it offended him, too.

He made his decision.

"Screw the baptism," he murmured. "Let him burn forever."

Just then the sound of approaching air-boats sent birds fleeing, and brought on a spasm of splashing in the cypress roots. Remo counted eight splashes. The identical number of alligator heartbeats his sensitive ears had detected pumping in syncopation with reptilian lungs.

Maybe, Remo thought with a fierce grin, the gators will enjoy a nice Banamanian snack.

Remo parted a thicket of yellow-green leaves that felt like cardboard cutouts, and got a good look at the noisy procession.

There were six air-boats in all. The lead boat was choked with Federal marshals, and a few others in blue windbreakers emblazoned with the stenciled letters FBI. They brandished machine pistols.

The occupants of the second boat were too well dressed to be law-enforcement officials. Unless gold Rolexes and hand-tooled leather briefcases had become standard-issue. Remo decided that they were Nogeira's lawyers. He counted twenty. The rest must have had the day off.

There was no mistaking General Emmanuel Alejandro Nogeira, as the first two air-boats rounded a twisted oak dressed in Spanish moss, and the third came into view.

The general wore his fawn-colored military uniform, with its row of three bronze stars on black shoulder boards. His uniform was impeccable—no doubt dry-cleaned at U.S. taxpayer expense.

The general stood in the blunt bow of the air-boat, unfettered, because the ACRC insisted that it was unconstitutional to manacle an individual while he practiced his religion. The Florida Supreme Court had agreed to that—by a narrow margin.

He was, Remo saw, even uglier in person than on TV.

The general was short and squat, like a repulsive frog. Remo recalled reading that in his native country he was called *El Sapo*—the Toad—because of his bestial brown face and heavy-lidded serpent's eyes. He was also sometimes called *Cara Piña*, or "Pineapple Face." He had more acne scars than Tom Hayden.

Remo decided right then and there that the alligators probably would not touch the man. Unless alligators practiced cannibalism.

The first air-boat turned, and Remo saw that the three boats trailing in the rear were filled with reporters. There were a lot of reporters, burdened with minicams and camera equipment. They were busy interviewing a man and a woman. The man was dressed in minister's black. The woman he couldn't see clearly.

This presented Remo with a fresh dilemma. Since officially he no longer existed, he would have to figure out a way to take out Nogeira without getting his latest face on nationwide TV. Every time that happened, Upstairs insisted he go under the knife. Remo had had so much plastic surgery over the years the only change Upstairs hadn't made was to turn his face inside out.

There was a big hump of dry isle nearby, and one by one the air-boats throttled down and glided up to this. Their prows beached with gritty hissing sounds.

General Emmanuel Nogeira stepped off the air-boat like Napoleon onto Saint Helena.

He lifted his hands into the air, fists clenched—a gesture that would have been familiar to anyone who had watched television in the months before the U.S. intervention that had turned Nogeira into a prisoner of war. His thick, blubbery lips peeled back into a dazzling smile. It was the only thing about General Nogeira that was not inherently repulsive. The smile was dazzling. It belonged on someone else's face.

The baptist minister stepped forward, open prayer book in hand.

"Shall we begin?" he inquired.

A throaty female voice cut in. "Not until the speech."

This brought a glower from one of the Federal marshals, who said, "We are here to allow the prisoner to exercise his freedom of religion, not to give a speech."

"Not him," the throaty voice snapped. "Me."

"No time," the marshal said.

"If I am not allowed to exercise my constitutional right to free speech," the voice growled, "then I fully intend to sue you, your superiors, and the entire United States government."

The Federal marshal turned red. An FBI agent stepped forward. They conferred briefly.

Finally the Federal marshal said, "Make it short." He did not sound happy about the delay.

The woman came into view. Remo recognized her then. Rona Ripper. The ACRC lawyer who had single-handedly spearheaded the legal drive to get General Nogeira baptized. She looked like Elivra, plus forty pounds.

Rona Ripper stepped up to General Nogeira and put her arm around his shoulder. The general's smile gained at inch at either side of his mouth as he placed his arm under hers. His hand came to rest at the small of her back, above the belt line.

"This man," she said loudly, "stands before you a victim of U.S. imperialism!"

Camera flashbulbs popped. Microphones rose. Pencils scribbled furiously in lined note pads.

"This man, this patriot in his country, was exercising his right to rule his nation as he saw fit, when murderous U.S. killer-soldiers descended from the skies and virtually kidnapped him out of his lawful seat of power!"

Remo wondered if Rona Ripper was talking about the same General Nogeira who had nullified an election, and had his goons stone the duly-elected president and vice-president of Bananama in full view of television cameras.

From his vantage point, Remo had an excellent view as the general's hand slipped down over the woman's right buttock. He gave her a playful squeeze. Rona Ripper went on as if she hadn't noticed.

"They accuse this man of all kinds of barbarism!" she thundered. "None of it true!"

General Nogeira pinched experimentally.

"This man is neither a criminal nor a torturer nor a murderer. He is kind, gentle, and loving. Children write him letters, and he answers every one of them."

General Nogeira took a fistful of buttock and gave Rona Ripper a hard squeeze.

Rona Ripper turned bright red. It was impossible to tell if the coloring was the result of blushing, or the passion aroused in her by her speech. She plowed on.

"He is a great man, a man who—"

General Nogeira's straying hand went up to the top of Rona's skirt and slipped down inside it.

This produced an immediate reaction. Rona Ripper shoved him away and simultaneously slapped him in his pocked face.

Remo took this as his cue.

He withdrew into the water. It smelled. Remo drew in a deep breath and his head went under. He struck out in the general direction of the isle where the baptism was to take place.

Even though it smelled, the water conducted sound perfectly. It brought to Remo's alert ears the slither and splash of an alligator entering the water.

Remo changed direction. He scarcely had to turn his head in the direction he wanted to go, and his body followed. That was Sinanju, which unified every cell in the body into a single responsive organic engine.

The alligator was long and greenish-black, like a mutant glob of snot, and it had hooded eyes that reminded Remo very much of General Nogeira's. Sleepy, yet as creepy.

The gator was working in his direction by kicking and pawing the water with its feet. Its mouth yawned open, disclosing rows of yellowed needle teeth

Remo knew little enough about alligators. He did know they could grab hold of a man's arm and literally saw off the limb. He got that from a *Leave it to Beaver* episode. Their muscular tails could lash out and stun a man senseless, perhaps kill him. Remo wasn't sure where he'd picked up that morsel of information. He might actually have read it somewhere, but the "where" escaped him, and there was no time to think about it because the alligator had suddenly shot forward, his jaws distending.

For a wild moment, Remo wondered if it was going to attempt to swallow his head. Did alligators do that?

Remo made a half fist that left his lower palm exposed and drove the hard heel of his right hand into the alligator's snout

Limp-legged, the reptile shot back as if equipped with reverse thrusters. And why not? It had just been struck by a blow that carried as much force behind it as a steam-powered pile driver.

Remo shot ahead, catching up to the reptile.

He took hold of its jaws and closed them like a crude suitcase. Then, twisting, he took hold of the creature's forelegs, aligning his body with that of the reptile's.

Remo allowed himself to float upward. The feel of the alligator's knobby stomach against his back was like a pebbled beach. Although he was certain the creature had been stunned, he reached up and gave the slick stomach a tickle. He had heard that that made alligators go to sleep. He didn't believe it, but what could it hurt?

When the alligator's ridged back and protuberant eyes popped above the water's surface, there was no sign of Remo Williams.

The alligator started moving forward, looking for all

the world like any ordinary alligator swimming through
the Everglades—except that this one's legs did not kick
and his long tail, instead of trailing behind, drooped for-
lornly in the brackish water.

Because he wanted the reptile to look as natural as
possible, Remo made more splashings with his feet than
he needed to pilot the alligator to his destination.

Remo's plan was simple. He was going to push the
alligator along like a horny torpedo, toward the baptis-
mal site, then slip away.

While everyone—and more importantly, every camera—was focused on the reptile, he would slip out of the
water, deal with the target, and slip back. A single heart-
stopping blow would make it look like Nogeira had suffered a heart attack.

The unexpected crackle of gunfire made Remo abandon the plan, and the alligator. At first Remo thought
they had spotted the gator too soon, and had opened up
on it.

He pushed against the beast, seeking the water bottom. His idea was to get as deep as possible. Most bullets
lost force and direction upon entering the water.

As soon as Remo touched bottom, he realized the gunfire was not directed toward him or the gator. There
were almost no sounds of bullets plunking into water.

Remo took a chance. He thrust his head above the
waterline.

He saw pandemonium.

The phalanx of beached air-boats was coming apart in
a storm of automatic weapons fire. The protective steel
cages over the pusher propellers seemed to be melting,
the firing was so fierce.

The Federal marshals and FBI agents drew weapons
and dived for cover. The media, however, simply stood
their ground, busily recording every bullet strike and
sound as if they had papal dispensations to protect them
from harm.

The sources of the firing were the approaching air-
boats and cigarette boats. Brown-skinned gunmen lined
the rails. Assorted Uzis, Mac-10s, Tec-9s and other vicious weapons were pouring out concentrated hell.

Everyone seemed to have a role to play in the sudden

drama—except General Emmanuel Nogeira. He stood frozen, bestial face going from the converging attackers to the federal agents digging in for cover. His wide mouth hung open like a greedy frog's.

It was clear the general didn't know whether he was being attacked or rescued.

In the act of pulling the general's groping hand from her skirt, Rona Ripper went white as a sheet.

General Nogeira grabbed her and wrestled her around and in front of him. Bullets chopped moss off cypress tree branches and made plinking sounds in the water.

Remo submerged.

The attacking boats were not far from his position. He laid his palms on his thighs and gave a great double kick.

Remo became a human arrow. As he passed under a pair of boats, he poked holes in the careening hulls. If any of the cameras had been underwater, they would have recorded a casual tapping. Remo used one finger. It was enough.

Perfectly round finger-sized holes perforated the hulls. Water surged in. Then the crafts began to wallow and slow down.

Remo veered toward an air-boat. Its flat bottom surged over him.

He took hold of the dangling rudder and made a fist. The fist went through the aluminum hull as if the fist were aluminum and the hull mere flesh.

Kicking back, Remo got out of the way.

The air-boat, being shallow, simply dropped. Mud began stirring up when the great spinning fan dropped below the water line.

Remo moved among the floundering passengers, pulling them down by their legs and breaking their spines at the neck like a farmer harvesting chickens.

Through the nicely sound-conducting water, Remo caught the shrill scream of panic.

"Gators! Look out! Gators!"

Remo grinned, letting a solitary air bubble escape through his teeth. If they thought he was an alligator, so much the better. He continued with his work.

He got a glimpse of brown faces as he pulled the attackers down. Bananamian or Colombian? He couldn't tell. It didn't matter. They were bad guys. Dealing with bad guys was his job.

Remo quickly brought most of the boats down. He didn't come up for air once. He didn't need to. If necessary he could hold his breath for hours, releasing only a little carbon dioxide at a time.

Keeping submerged, Remo swam around to the other side of the isle, away from the tumult.

When he stuck his head back up, he saw that the press had retreated for cover. All except one man, who lay screaming, clutching his minicam with one hand and his bleeding leg with the other. He was crying, "Medic! Medic!" and the look on his face was one of disbelief.

The FBI and Federal marshals had staked out firing positions. They were returning fire in a steady, methodical way, not wasting ammunition or firing recklessly.

A shrill voice carried over the concatenation, crying, "I'll sue! I'm suing everyone for violating my civil rights."

It was Rona Ripper. She was crawling on her stomach for shelter.

An FBI agent in a blue windbreaker started out to assist her. His head disappeared in a fine crimson mist as a dozen machine pistols sought his head.

Rona Ripper instantly started crawling backward, crying, "I surrender! I surrender!" Her face dragged in the sand because she was trying to crawl with her hands raised.

"Damn!" Remo growled, seeing no sign of General Nogeira.

A surviving cigarette boat veered off from the rest of the attacking flotilla and rounded the isle on the opposite side.

Remo figured it had gone after Nogeira. He jackknifed under and began swimming at high speed.

His ears picked up a clumsy splashing and he popped out of the water like a dolphin.

General Nogeira was stumbling out of the back side of the island. His pocked face was a picture of ugly fear.

He saw the churning boat, and his expression became ludicrous. He doubled back.

The cigarette boat piled up on the isle, and its passengers jumped off and gave chase. Some of them wore fawn-colored uniforms not much different from General Nogeira's. One, wounded, had to be helped along.

They all disappeared into the thick foliage.

Hanging back in the water, Remo wondered if he shouldn't let nature take its course. The way he saw it, the Bananamanian armed forces had dibs on the man who had ruined their country.

The decision was made for him. A scream rose up in the close, humid air.

A few seconds later, a man came stumbling back into the water. He ran blindly, his hands clutching his eyes. His fingers and lower face were slick with blood. The blood was coming from his eyes. The five bronze stars on his shoulder boards more than identified him.

The general was screaming in Spanish, a language Remo didn't understand. But the horrible tones told him all he had to know.

The man had been blinded. Probably by a knife across his eyeballs.

He proved this by stumbling over a twisted cypress root and falling face-first into the water.

Remo was wondering if he should put the suffering brute out of his misery when an alligator came charging out of the thicket.

"Charging" was the only word for it. The reptile erupted into view and ran like an absurd, clumsy dog for the water's edge. Its jaws snapped open and shut with every clumsy step.

The alligator plunged into the water and snapped up the general by one flailing arm. It wasted no time. It dragged the screaming man, pounding against its greenish hide, below the water.

After that, Remo decided to tread water and count bubbles.

When the bubbles stopped, Remo had counted forty-two. The water had become a diffuse color resembling pink lemonade.

Remo climbed onto shore with the intention of taking care of the assailants. They must be pretty dumb, he thought, to let the general get away from them like that. Or maybe not so dumb—since he hadn't actually gotten away.

The gunfire had died down.

It started up again, more ferocious than before.

Remo went through the saw grass like a lawnmower through hay. He got to the high hump and looked down.

The FBI and Federal marshals were pinned down in a crossfire. The withering fire was coming up, from the surviving boats, and down, from a line of fawn-uniformed attackers not a dozen yards below Remo's position.

Maybe he was wrong. Maybe this was a Colombian hit team, after all.

Remo slipped down to the line and began relieving the assailants of their weapons. He did this in a novel way. He literally disarmed them.

The first man to be disarmed was down on one knee hosing the low ground with his Uzi when it happened.

Remo slipped up behind him, took him by the hard balls of his shoulder bones, and separated his hands. He seemed to exert casual effort. But five thousand years of accumulated knowledge were behind the gesture.

The shoulder joints went *pop*!

The man's arms came away in Remo hands. He threw them in two directions.

The man jumped up and, squirting blood from each shoulder like a human lawn sprinkler, began to dance and caper until blood loss had turned him into a squirming pile on the ground.

By that time, Remo was flinging arms in all directions with joyous abandon.

This spectacle didn't exactly go unnoticed. Gunmen scattered, firing to cover their retreat. Remo was forced to waste time evading the crossfire. He could dodge bullets as if they were spring rain, but this was a slashing rain.

Remo was forced to drop to his stomach and let the storm pass over him.

When the firing finally had died down, Remo stood up in time to see the remaining attackers pile into the water under a hail of FBI return fire. The attackers were stubborn: They did not desert their comrades. A few died in the attempt to rescue the others who had fallen.

This forced Remo to revise his opinion yet again. No drug-killer worked this way. This was a military operation.

Then, under harassing fire, they waded up on a single air-boat and blasted away at the grassy isle that had been chosen for a baptism but instead had become a baptism of fire for a number of federal agents.

Hearing the FBI getting itself organized, Remo faded back to the back end of the isle and the water.

He swam past the bloated body in the fawn-colored uniform. The alligator had hold of it by the head and was vigorously attempting to crack open its skull.

As Remo, swimming underwater to avoid detection, left it behind, his ears were rewarded by an ugly *crack* of a sound.

He hoped Upstairs would be satisfied with the way things had turned out. The target had been taken out, even if Remo had had help. As for the attackers—whoever they turned out to be—they would have a hard time getting out of the country once the FBI had alerted Washington.

The last thing Remo heard as he put the day's work behind him was the throaty voice of Rona Ripper, threatening to sue everyone from the FBI to the President of the United States.

It annoyed him—but the thought of General Emmanuel Alejandro Nogeira, roasting in Hell, unbaptized, more than made up for that.

3

Dr. Harold W. Smith received the first report on the deaths of the governor of California and his lieutenant governor directly from the President of the United States.

There was a red phone on one corner of Smith's desk, in an office that overlooked Long Island Sound. The phone had no dial. It didn't need one. It was a dedicated line. On the other end, hundreds of miles south of Washington, D.C., an identical red instrument nestled in an end table attached to the bed in the Lincoln Bedroom of the White House.

When the phone rang, Harold Smith brought the red receiver to his gray, bitter face. He cleared his throat and said, "Yes, Mr. President?"

He held his breath. He always held his breath at these moments, because if the next voice Dr. Harold W. Smith heard was not that of the current President of the United States, Harold W. Smith was obligated to swallow a coffin-shaped poison pill he kept in the watch pocket of his gray vest. After shutting down CURE, the organization that officially did not exist.

The parched Texas-by-way-of-Massachusetts voice came as an imperceptible relief to Smith. The news did not.

"The governor of California has just perished in an airline crash," the President said, dry-voiced.

Smith recalled the governor. Like the President, he was a Republican. He could not recall the name of the next man in line, the lieutenant, and whether or not California's lieutenant governor was a Republican or not. Not that it mattered to Smith. He no longer voted. It was the price he was forced to pay to remain above national politics.

The President's next words made Smith's unspoken question moot.

"The lieutenant governor was on the same flight," the President said.

Smith sat up. His cracked leather chair, his personal seat of power for as long as he headed CURE, creaked in protest.

"Isn't that against all protocol?" Smith asked. A frown creased his pale forehead. Or rather, the permanent lines of worry that rode his face deepened.

"It is. That's why I'm calling you. The FAA will naturally be investigating this, but I thought, given the bizarre circumstances, that you might look into this—discreetly."

"I understand," Harold Smith said. "Discreetly" meant that Smith was not to send in Remo. When Remo went in, bodies piled up. This was not that kind of situation. Yet.

"Do you have any idea where the two men were bound when the plane crashed?" Smith asked.

"It didn't actually crash. It flew into the side of a mountain."

"That *is* unusual. I will get on the matter directly," Smith said.

"Remember. Be prudent."

"Always."

Smith hung up. When the President had interrupted his workday, Smith was going over the overtime logs for the institute whose management was his day-to-day responsibility—and CURE's cover.

The brass plate on Smith's closed door read: HAROLD W. SMITH, DIRECTOR. There was a larger brass plate on one of the brick posts that framed the wrought-iron gates to the institution. It read: FOLCROFT SANITARIUM. Smith headed Folcroft. But Folcroft business could wait.

He slid the overtime logs into a desk drawer, and his thin hand paused over a bottle of Maalox. It was his habit to take a tablespoon of this every day at this time, in the normal course of events. On bad days, he took Zantac. On hectic days, children's aspirin. A triple dosage. Then there were his Alka-Seltzer days, and his mineral-water days, and his warm-milk days.

Today, Harold Smith felt like none of these things. He wondered if this had anything to do with the recent ordeal he had undergone—in which an ancient enemy of the Master of Sinanju had ensnared them all in his web. It had been a disturbing experience, which Smith only dimly recalled. Smith had not been himself. The doctor had pronounced it a virus. Both he and Chiun had been infected. It was invariably fatal.

Smith might have died but for a quirk of fate.

He had suffered a heart seizure. Only quick action by the Folcroft staff, and the electrical restimulation of his diseased heart muscle, had pulled him back from the brink.

Miraculously, it had also burned all trace of the virus from his bloodstream.

Now, months later, Smith was back to normal. No, he was more than normal. His stomach no longer bothered him. His blinding headaches had abated. He no longer needed his Zantac, or Maalox, or Tums, or Flintstones-brand aspirin, or any of those common remedies.

Another man would have been relieved. Smith was worried. He was a chronic worrier.

He decided against taking a tablespoon of Maalox, just in case, and closed the drawer. Pressing a concealed stud on the other side of his shabby oak desk, Smith watched a panel drop and slide away. An ordinary computer terminal hummed up and clicked into place.

It was no more ordinary than Smith. It connected to a bank of mainframes deep in the Folcroft basement. These in turn fed off virtually every computer in the country that could be accessed by modem. Their memory banks contained a vast reservoir of raw data on people, companies, and organizations that could conceivably be of use to Smith in the performance of his secret duties.

Smith got to work. He was relieved that he would not need Remo and Chiun on this one. They invariably brought results—but also problems.

Smith logged on to the wire service news-feeds. He got the preliminary bulletins that were now breaking all over the nation.

These told him the bare facts. The airline, flight number, and confirmation that the governor and lieutenant governor were on the passenger list—although the bodies had yet to be recovered.

This scant information was enough. Smith logged over to the airlines reservation data banks, using the access code of a mythical travel agency.

The governor's ticket had been purchased by a third party, Smith discovered, through a Sacramento travel agency. He called up the purchaser's name.

Behind his rimless eyeglasses, Smith's puritanical gray eyes blinked.

The name was Emmanuel Nogeira.

"This must be a joke," Smith muttered.

Smith next went to the lieutenant governor's ticket file. It, too, was a third-party purchase, charged to the same Mastercard number.

This time Smith gave vent to a gasp as dry as the New England soil that had nourished him.

An "Emmanuel Nogeira" had purchased that ticket as well. He had also paid for the Federal Express shipping cost to the recipient ticket holder's name.

Smith switched off, and called up the Mastercard file after a brief tapping of keys and the press of a hot key. Smith had set up his system so that by pressing the hot key marked F4 on his keyboard, whatever computer system he had called up would be immediately attacked by the proper password, kept on permanent file in the mainframe.

The Mastercard system surrendered in a twinkling.

The file showed that the "Emmanuel Nogeira" in question currently resided at the Metropolitan Correctional Center in Miami, Florida. His occupation was given as "Displaced Dictator and Prisoner of War."

Reflexively, Harold Smith reached for his drawer of pharmaceuticals.

He pulled it open, looked inside, and realized that, despite the horrific discovery he had made, he felt no need for medical support. Slowly, he closed the drawer.

The card file showed that Emmanuel Nogeira was carrying six months' worth of debt. He was just a hair under his credit limit.

It also showed that he had purchased two front-row tickets to a Nana Mouskouri concert at the L.A. Music Center for eight P.M. on this very night.

Smith swallowed what little saliva remained in his rapidly drying mouth. The fatal flight had had a Los Angeles destination.

Harold W. Smith was a man who believed in order. He understood that he lived in a mathematical universe, one ruled by variables and constants. Coincidence abounded, but unbroken chains of coincidences did not.

In a rational universe governed by mathematical principles, the green alphanumeric symbols that wavered before Harold Smith's eyes told of a clever plot to lure the governor and lieutenant governor of California to their deaths.

Smith did not yet know how. He was a long way from understanding why. But he had a working model of the problem—and he had pulled it all together in just under five minutes.

Smith sat back in his chair, his gray eyes still on the screen, but no longer seeing the displayed data, except as abstract green lights. His eyes were focused inward.

Smith was a gray man. He was thin and pinch-faced. He might have been a stern headmaster out of the nineteenth century. His clothes, although twentieth-century, had that flavor too. His lanky, angular frame was swathed in a three-piece gray suit of conservative cut. His hair was white and thinning. His school tie bore Dartmouth stripes. It was the only splash of color on his otherwise colorless person.

No one looking at Harold Smith could imagine his burdens, or grasp the fact that, next to the President of the United States, he was the most powerful man in the U.S. government, which of course meant the entire world.

Through his nondescript computer, Smith ran CURE. He enjoyed full autonomy. Although he reported directly to the President, just as he had to the current President's predecessors going back to the one who had died in office after creating CURE, a victim of an assassin's bullet, Smith was not answerable to the Executive Branch. He took requests, reported concerns. That was as far as it went. Smith was empowered to take whatever action he deemed necessary to deal with internal problems and external threats.

Technically, this arrangement made him more powerful than the President. But there was one presidential directive Smith was obligated to accept: the shutdown command. If invoked, Smith would, without hesitation, erase his massive data banks, put into motion a plan of action that would take his sole enforcement arm, Remo Williams, out of the picture. And when that was accomplished, and only then, he would swallow his vest-pocket pill and go to his reward—whatever that might be.

Right now, Smith wasn't thinking about any of that. He was wondering what plan General Emmanuel Alejandro Nogeira had in mind—and for the first time, he was worried that his enforcement arm might succeed in an assignment.

Because right at this moment, Harold W. Smith wanted General Emmanuel Nogeira very much alive. And only hours before he had sent Remo to Miami to liquidate Nogeira.

"Damn."

The curse was barely a breath. Smith rarely cursed. He was of taciturn New England stock. Vermont Smiths didn't curse, although sometimes they kicked the furniture.

There was no way to contact Remo in the field. He was the perfect field agent in some respects. He almost always came through. But a dismal failure, insofar as carrying communications equipment was concerned. In desperation, Smith had simplified his contact phone number to an unbroken succession of ones. Even Remo could not forget that code.

If only he would call in, Smith thought, his weary eyes going to the blue contact telephone.

They were still on the blue instrument, several minutes later, when it shrilled suddenly.

Smith grabbed the receiver, said, "Remo! Have you completed your mission?"

"Yes and no," Remo said guardedly.

"Please do not burden me with evasions. I want a direct answer. Did you terminate your target?"

Remo's voice was abashed. "I'm sorry, Smitty. I kinda screwed it up."

"Thank God," Smith said.

"Huh?" Remo grunted.

"Nogeira is alive then?"

"Not exactly."

"What do you mean?"

"An alligator got him."

"Got? By what do you mean, 'got'?"

"Got, as in 'turned into a human Tootsie Pop,' " Remo said flatly. "What other kind of 'got' is there, where alligators are concerned?"

"Then he is dead," Smith said woodenly.

"I think his toes may still be twitching, but his head was definitely dead," Remo said dryly.

"This is unfortunate. I very much wanted Nogeira alive."

"Yeah? Then why'd you send me out to take him out? Was this some bullshit field test that I screwed up by not screwing up?"

"No, Remo," said Smith in a tired tone. "In the last hour both the governor and lieutenant governor of California have been killed in a plane crash. According to my computers, they were on their way to a concert. The tickets—both airline and concert—were provided by Emmanuel Nogeira."

"But he's been in prison for two years," Remo said.

"A prison in which he had unlimited access to a telephone, and full use of his credit card," Smith pointed out.

"Some prison," Remo remarked.

"Remo, I need a full report on the assignment."

"Okay," Remo said. "Put the scrambler on top speed. Here goes."

Remo rattled off his report. At the end of it, he added, "There is one consolation."

"And that is?"

"Nogeira never did get baptized."

Smith was silent a moment. "You say you are not clear on the identities of these assailants?"

"Take your pick," Remo said. "Either they were Colombians out to kill him, Bananamanian Army forces out to kill him, or his own people out to kill him. Whoever they were, they were out to kill him. And they definitely contributed."

"I think we can leave the Bananamanian Army out of this," Smith mused. "It was in their interest to let American justice run its course."

"If that means they wanted to see Nogeira punished,"

Remo inserted, "I'd say they go back to the top of the list. Because American justice was being run into the ground by this guy, not the other way around."

"Point taken," said Smith, his voice losing its distant, reflective quality.

"You think Nogeira was behind the plane crash?" Remo asked, after the pause on the line had grown lengthy.

"I am certain of it."

"Well, whatever he was up to, the secret died with him."

"He may have had confederates."

"The guys who wasted him?" Remo suggested.

Smith's response was thin. "Perhaps."

Remo asked, "What do you want me to do?"

"Nothing. I will have Federal agents cover the airports, highways, and train stations."

"I think you can save your breath."

"Why is that?"

"From the way those guys shot up the FBI down there, I think the word's already been put out."

"Of course. Then I must confer with the President."

"Before you do, do me a favor, Smitty?"

"What is that?" Smith said, wincing at that bit of familiarity. He hated to be called "Smitty"—the more so because it usually meant Remo was about to ask a favor.

"Call Chiun first and tell him that even though I didn't do the hit, I did right."

"You did neither," said Harold Smith, who was too busy now to bother with trivial disputes between his field operatives.

He hung up the phone without another word and took hold of the red telephone, wondering what the President's reaction to his discovery would be.

4

In the lobby of the Fontainebleau Hotel overlooking the Miami waterfront, Remo hung up the pay phone.

He glided to the bank of elevators. "Glided" was the perfect word to describe the way Remo moved. He wore a white T-shirt and tan chinos. His feet were encased in hand-made loafers of Italian leather. Quality shoes. Still, they should have left impressions in the deep nap of the lobby carpet. But they did not. His soles seemed just to caress the nap, like constantly moving brushes.

Remo's casual attire should have gotten disapproving looks from the lobby staff. It did not. He might have been invisible. In a way, he was.

The elevator door dinged and opened. Remo stepped aboard, punched the seventh-floor button, and folded his lean arms. His deep-set brown eyes were clouded with worry.

Maybe Chiun won't ask me how it went, Remo thought.

Yeah, and maybe he'll have cooked dinner for us both. Neither was very likely, Remo knew.

He came off the elevator with his hands in his pockets and his mouth an unhappy downward curl on his face.

He pushed open the door to his room.

Instantly, his nostrils were greeted by the fresh, sweet smell of boiled white rice—his favorite—and the tang of baked fish.

Remo grinned. Maybe the day would be saved, after all. Something had caused Chiun to break down and cook dinner.

He started toward the kitchenette of their suite of rooms.

"I smell good eating," Remo said.

"And I smell failure," came a squeaky, querulous voice.

"Uh-oh," Remo muttered. In a brighter voice he said aloud, "Do I smell dinner?"

"No, you do not."

"No? Why?"

"Because I smell failure."

This time, Remo's "Uh-oh" was audible.

He paused on the threshold of the kitchenette. The Master of Sinanju was in the act of pouring the contents of a stainless-steel pot into the sink. He reached down and touched the garbage-disposal button. It rumbled. The steam emanating from the sink was quickly drawn from sight. The fresh smell of steamed rice went away with it.

"You're throwing away perfectly good rice," Remo pointed out.

"I am no longer hungry," said Chiun, next taking a tray of baked fish from the oven.

This, too, was consumed by the garbage disposal.

Remo could only watch helplessly, his saliva glands—just about the only physical part of him he did not fully control—working overtime.

"Who said I failed?" Remo asked unhappily.

"Your feet."

Remo looked down. His feet looked like they always did. His shoes shone. Not that he ever bothered to shine them. Whenever they got dirty or picked up a scuff, he simply threw them away and bought new ones. Sometimes in that order.

"What about my feet?"

"They stink of failure."

Remo sniffed the air. "I don't smell anything."

"This odor is not smelt, but heard," Chiun said, thin-voiced. "Your every footfall reeks of shame, and failure."

"I did not fail," Remo said stubbornly.

"You did not accomplish your mission?" asked Chiun, turning to face him for the first time.

Chiun, Reigning Master of Sinanju, stood no more than five feet tall. In his kimono, he resembled a frail cone of scarlet. The front was a swirl of calla lilies, stitched in silvery thread.

Eyes the color of steel regarded Remo, giving off cold, brittle sparks. They were set in a face that might have been a resin mask, yellow and lined with age. The bald head shone under the overhead light. Over each ear, wispy white hair made a gentle puff. His chin, resolute despite its unquestionable frailty, boasted a curl of a beard that was like smoke frozen in eternity.

Slowly, long-nailed hands rose and the fingers, thin and the color of eagle talons, came together. Fingers grasped the opposite wrist and the scarlet sleeves came together then, hiding the old Korean's hands.

"Speak," he intoned.

"Okay," Remo said quickly. "I didn't complete my mission."

"Then you failed."

"I did not fail," Remo repeated.

"You lie. This was the most important mission Emperor Smith has given you, and you botched it like the clod-footed amateur that you are."

"Who said it was so important?"

"I do. Smith asked you to do a simple thing: to dispatch a former head of state. A minor thing—for Sinanju. A major thing, in our Emperor's eyes."

"Smith said nothing of the sort."

Chiun cocked his head. "You did not kill this man?"

"No. But he is dead."

"*Aiiee!*" Chiun wailed, his hands springing into view. They took hold of the puffs over his ears and tugged in consternation. He did a little circle dance in his sandaled feet. "You let competition steal the food from our babies' mouths!"

The reference was to the children in Sinanju—who were fed by the work of the Master, as they had been for five thousand years. It was the reason the men of Sinanju had first hired out their services to the emperors of ancient Asia.

"Actually, an alligator got him," Remo admitted, folding his lean arms.

"Who saw this?" Chiun asked quickly.

"No one, as far as I know."

"Then you will tell Smith that you dispatched this evil warlord yourself," Chiun snapped. "Use flowery phrases. He will not detect the deceit in your tones."

"I think that when the autopsy results come in and show that Nogeira died from having his head chewed off his shoulders, we'll have a hard time keeping that story alive."

"I will inform Emperor Smith that you are employing a new technique—designed to fool the gullible into believing wild alligators were at fault. We will tell him that this was done in Egyptian times."

"They have alligators back then?"

Chiun gestured with a lifted finger. "Crocodiles. A minor difference no one will discover, if we keep our wits about us."

"I can't lie."

"Why not?"

"Because I already reported to Smith."

Chiun's slit eyes widened in shock. "Before conferring with me? Who did you think you work for?"

"Smith."

"No! A thousand times, no! You work for the village. Smith is merely a middleman. The emperor is not important, only the emperor's gold."

Remo smiled thinly. "I'll tell Smith that next time I see him."

"Don't you dare!"

"Fine. Then get off my back."

"Never. Through you, my House survives. I will never get off your back until you are perfection."

"Never happen," said Remo, going to the cabinet over the stove. He began rummaging for something to eat. A feast awaited him—if a rice smorgasbord was his idea of sumptuous dining. Virtually every kind of rice was available to him, from domestic whites to exotic browns that smelled like popcorn.

He pulled off the shelf a clear plastic bag, heavy with hard, white grains, and grabbed up the still warm pot.

The Master of Sinanju watched this with grim mien.

"What did Smith say when you broke the terrible news of your abysmal failure?"

"He said he didn't want me to kill Nogeira, after all. So there."

Chiun's pale eyebrows drew together. "He changed his mind?"

"It was changed for him."

"Ah. The so-called 'President,' exerting his will. Perhaps this will impell Smith to see the light."

"If by 'light' you mean overthrow the President, I doubt it."

"What exactly did Smith say? We may yet salvage our honor in this sordid matter."

"I forget," Remo said cagily, drawing tap water and filling the pot.

"Come! Speak! You are hiding something."

"Okay," said Remo. "Turns out he wanted Nogeira alive."

"Unbelievable!" cried Chiun. The single word was a keen of anguish. "Even in your failure, you have failed."

Remo looked up from the sink. "How's that again?"

"You failed to eliminate your target," Chiun spat. "That is one thing. Your emperor changed his mind and desired that the evil one survive. You had a golden opportunity to demonstrate that you anticipated your emperor's unspoken wishes, and you allowed a mere alligator to come between you and glory."

"Since when is Smith *my* emperor?"

"Since you have piled failure upon failure."

"The way I see it," Remo retorted, going to the tabletop refrigerator, "I'm a victim of Smith's not knowing what he wants."

Chiun nodded vigorously. "Yes. Good. Now you are thinking. We will blame Smith."

Remo looked back. "We will?"

"In our histories, of course. This way our ancestors will understand that no blame will attach itself to us, and become something they will be forced to live down in later times."

"Now might be a good time to get it down in the ol' scrolls," Remo suggested. "While it's still fresh in your mind."

"You begin to show glimmerings of intelligence," said Chiun, who then swept away in a flourish of Christmas-red kimono skirts.

Remo returned to picking through the refrigerator, his unhappy mouth brightening into a self-satisfied grin.

With luck, Chiun would spend the next hour telling his future descendants how Mad Harold, the Emperor of

America, had blown the mission. That would be plenty of time for Remo to cook up a mess of rice and fish.

His grin went away by degrees, when he discovered that there was no more fish to be had. There was plenty of duck, though. All kinds.

The trouble was, it took a lot longer than an hour to cook a duck properly.

Remo hurriedly pushed the smallest duck he could find into the oven and turned on the burner. With luck, it would be ready before Chiun was finished.

Just to be safe, he turned the heat up as high as it would go. After all, luck was something Remo had encountered little of today.

The oven started smoking immediately, but smoky duck would be a hell of a lot better than no duck at all, Remo reasoned. And who knew? He might discover that he liked smoked duck.

Remo never found out. When the smoke got thick enough to attract the Master of Sinanju's attention, Chiun swept in, and threw open the kitchen window to let in fresh air.

He also threw the smoking duck out the open window. Without a word, he tossed the boiling rice water after it, and returned to his labors.

Remo settled for yesterday's cold rice.

5

Harmon Cashman had hope in his heart. For the first time in almost four years, since the last presidential election, he had hope in his heart.

Back in those halcyon days, Harmon Cashman had been chief advance man for the then Vice-President and now current President of the United States. He had served the man well. Got him through the minefield of the Iowa Caucuses. Helped shape his presidential image. Distanced him from his predecessor, the incumbent President.

It was true that they had come to New Hampshire trailing in the polls. The campaign was on the ropes. No other way to describe it. There, the governor of the state had stepped in. A real bulldog. No finesse about him at all. But he had single-handedly turned the New Hampshire primary and the fortunes of the Vice-President around.

Harmon Cashman had to hand it to the New Hampshire governor. Even now. Never said any different.

What Harmon Cashman had never understood was how the governor had ended up White House Chief of Staff. That job was supposed to have gone to Harmon Cashman. True, there had been no such agreement, written or oral. But it was understood. At least, it had been understood by Harmon Cashman.

After the election, the President-elect had broken the news to Harmon Cash, gentle but direct. He explained that he owed his office to the governor, who had turned everything around for him. Snatched victory out of the jaws of defeat, the man had. Harmon Cashman took it hard. He declined any lesser appointment. It was Chief of Staff or nothing.

It ended up nothing. To be more precise, a handwritten thank-you note from the new president was forthcoming. A two-pager. Believing himself humiliated, Harmon Cashman, the most seasoned advance man in national politics, withdrew from electioneering, telling himself there would be other elections, other candidates.

Now, four years later, with the presidential primaries in full cry, he found this was true. But not for Harmon Cashman. No one liked a sore loser. The GOP shunned him. The Democrats, who this year more than ever all looked and sounded alike, like some extended family with matching hair, wouldn't have him on their teams. They figured he was some kind of Republican Trojan horse.

Harmon Cashman had made overtures to certain state campaigns, but in every case the boat had already left the dock. There was no place on any campaign—unless he wanted to stuff envelopes in some stuffy storefront campaign headquarters in East Treestump, Nebraska.

This all changed the day hope came into Harmon Cashman's life.

Hope came up to the front door of Harmon Cashman's Manassas townhouse, carrying a paper sack and bearing a beatific smile that made Harmon Cashman instantly want to help the face behind the smile.

"I am called Esperanza," said the smile.

Harmon Cashman understood the name to be Spanish. He frowned. "I had a maid named Esperanza once," he muttered, looking over the face behind the dazzling smile.

It was a round, cherubic face, the color of toffee. The skin was as smooth as molasses, as if poured into a mold; perfect and without blemish.

The eyes were a liquid, like melting licorice. They gleamed with a I-want-you-to-like-me gleam.

The man was some kind of ethnic. But he had such a nice face that Harmon Cashman was instantly lulled into swallowing his surpise.

"Esperanza," the man said, "is my last name." His voice reminded Harmon of honey, sweet, and golden clear. It was the perfect radio voice. An alto. With a

trace of fire under it. "Esperanza means 'Hope.' " He
lifted the paper sack. "I bring you hope."

Brown fingers pulled open the bag. Harmon Cashman
looked inside. He saw vaguely familiar hard, black,
round shapes mixed with curls of white. Like thin smiles.
They seemed to be smiling at him, those round black
shapes. The smiles were familiar. They reminded him
somehow of Virginia, where he had grown up. And
Grandma Cashman's kitchen.

He reached in and pulled one of the hauntingly familiar smiles out of the bag. It was sandwiched between two
serrated wafers of black chocolate.

He sniffed it. The odor brought back powerful childhood memories.

"This is an Oreo cookie," he said, blank-voiced.

"Yes, you may have another," said the man who called
himself Esperanza.

Blinking, Harmon Cashman succumbed to an urge that
had been suppressed since childhood. He took another
cookie. Grandma had always allowed him two. Sometimes three.

He bit the dry, crumbly edge off one. It tasted as sweet
as he had remembered. And he had not eaten an Oreo
sandwich cookie in a long, long time. He wondered how
the man knew he used to gobble these things up by the
boxful when he was in short pants.

"My full name is Enrique Espiritu Esperanza," said
the cherubic man.

"I'm Harmon Cashman," Harmon Cashman said,
through lips to which clung black crumbs and flecks of
white creme filling. He licked them clean, but with the
next bite they collected more chocolaty Oreo bits.

"I know. That is why I have come to converse with
you."

"Say again?"

"I am running for governor of California, and I need
you to manage my campaign. I understand that in what
you do, you are the best."

"I never heard of you," replied Harmon Cashman, his
mouth full.

"That is why I have come to you. You will help me
to become known."

The man had such a pleasant way about him that Harmon Cashman immediately stepped out of the way and said, "Let's talk."

They ate as they talked. Harmon Cashman somehow ended up with the bag of Oreos. The man took another out of the inner pocket of his suit. This was a small roll of Oreos. Lunch-box size.

As they munched away happily, Enrique Espiritu Esperanza talked of his vision.

"As you know, there has been a tragedy in California."

"They broke the most basic rule of political travel," said Harmon Cashman, gobbling his cookies. "You know, these are the best Oreos I ever tasted," he murmured. His eyes gleamed with pleasure.

The liquid eyes of Esperanza shone like those of a doe.

"They have called a special election. It is wide open. To anyone."

Harmon shook his head ruefully. "Only in California."

"It is a fine place. It is my home."

"Never been there more than three-four weeks."

"You will like it there—if you accept my offer."

Harmon Cashman extracted the last Oreo from the bag. He nursed it, as if afraid that when it was gone there would be no more like it in the world. Now he understood what some people meant by "comfort food." And he wondered why he had stopped eating the things. He thought it was around the time he had discovered beer. And girls.

"Are you familiar with those who are running to take the late governor's place?" asked the smooth, pleasant voice of Enrique Espiritu Esperanza.

"Yeah. The last Democrat to hold the job. Since he washed out of the Presidential race, he's claimed he had a conversion. He's a Republican now. And the state committee can't do a damn thing about it."

"The Democrat is just as strange."

"There's no way Rona Ripper has a shot," Harmon Cashman snapped. "She's a woman, and thirty pounds overweight, so the camera makes her look obese. And she's a card-carrying ARCRer. No chance."

"Her campaign theme is a good one. Anti-smoking."

"Hell, California's the biggest anti-smoking state there is. She's preaching to the converted."

"And Barry Black is promising Republican results with Democratic ideals."

"Mixed message," Harmon Cashman scoffed. "They don't sell. He's just splitting the vote."

"Precisely. That is why Enrique Esperanza has an exceptional chance."

"How come I never heard of you?" Harmon wondered.

"Before this, I was a simple farmer. Growing grapes."

"There's good money in grapes."

"But there is greater satisfaction in governing. I would like to be the governor of my state and help it prosper again."

Harmon Cashman ticked off points on his finger. "Good business background. Your smile's photogenic. Nice voice. You got the goods for a media blitz. But you're a dark horse."

Enrique Esperanza looked blank. "I am a what?"

"Dark horse," Harmon explained. "It's a figure of speech. It means a candidate who nobody has ever heard of and who has almost no chance. A long shot."

"A dark horse is like an underdog?"

"You got it," said Harmon Cashman, swallowing the last morsel of cookie.

"Then I will be the dark underdog," said Enrique Espiritu Esperanza. "I will carry this name proudly."

"You need a slogan."

"My name is my slogan."

"Huh?"

"Hope. I represent hope. I am Esperanza."

"Hmm. A lot of Hispanics in California. You know, it's so simple, it might fly."

"You are on board then?"

Harmon Cashman hesitated. "You got any more Oreos?" he asked, looking at the remaining cookies in Enrique Espiritu Esperanza's soft brown hand with open greed.

"Here," said the dark-horse candidate for governor. "You may have the last of mine."

"It's a deal," said Harmon Cashman, snatching up the Oreos. They were tiny, so he took smaller bites, knowing that he would have to make them last.

They were long gone by the time Enrique Espiritu Esperanza had outlined his plan to take the governorship of California. It was a brilliant plan, or so it seemed to Cashman, who didn't know the ins and outs of the California political scene.

As Esperanza explained it, the California population was gradually shifting. The influx of new blood from the Central and South American nations, from the Pacific Rim and other places, was inexorably pushing the state's demographics into completely uncharted territory for an American state. In such an uncertain climate, anything was possible. Even his election.

After he had explained it all, Enrique Espiritu Esperanza leaned forward and let the full beatific radiance of his smile wash over Harmon Cashman. His dark, liquid eyes were imploring. Harmon Cashman understood the nature of personal power. He understood that the simplest, most effective and direct way to cultivate personal loyalty was not to do a person a favor, but to ask one. Somehow, this cemented the wielder of personal power with his adherents.

He had seen it work a thousand times. And for all his savvy and cynicism, it was working on him.

"I accept," he said sincerely. "And proud to do it."

"What do you need to begin?"

"More Oreos," Harmon Cashman said without skipping a beat. "These baby ones just don't have the kick of the big ones."

Enrique Espiritu Esperanza threw his round head back and laughed like distant church bells. The sound reminded Harmon Cashman of Sunday morning back in Virginia, for some reason. But he was scarcely aware of it.

For he had everything he wanted in life: a candidate he could believe in, and a campaign to wage.

But most of all, he had hope again.

He spelled it "Esperanza."

6

The days that followed were heady ones for Harmon Cashman.

The election was scheduled for six weeks hence. In national electioneering terms, that might as well have been next Tuesday. On the state level, it was the equivalent to a hundred-meter dash.

"We'll need signatures to get on the ballot," Harmon Cashman had said during the flight to California.

"I have been collecting them," replied Enrique Esperanza, who insisted on being called "Rick."

"It is a good American-sounding name, no?"

"Only in front of the right audience. In the barrios and out in the fields, you're Enrique."

"I am Enrique. And Enrique will have for you all the signatures you will need."

And he delivered. They came, in a torrent of paper. Mostly signed by Hispanic names.

"Looks to me like you got a pretty good field organization to start," Harmon Cashman had said delightedly, as they spread out the petition sheets in the storefront in Los Angeles, their main campaign headquarters.

Enrique Espiritu Esperanza smiled broadly. "I have many friends who like me and wish that I succeed."

"These guys are documented, aren't they?"

Esperanza smiled, "Of course."

"We'll need a hell of a lot more than these to put you over the top, Rick."

"I have a strategy I have devised for this."

"Yeah?"

"It is Amnistía."

"What is that—Spanish?"

Enrique Espiritu Esperanza laughed heartily, and with a total lack of self-consciousness. He patted Harmon's knee.

"Yes, *mi amigo*. It means 'amnesty.' I am referring to the Federal program which runs out soon. It provides that all illegal aliens, migrant workers—what some call crudely 'wetbacks'—be allowed to petition for citizenship. With citizenship comes American rights. Such as the right to vote."

Harmon Cashman blinked. "How many migrants in California?"

"Not just California. But in all of America."

"Only the ones in California count."

"Not if they come to California for their Amnistia."

Harmon's eyes widened. "Is this legal?"

Enrique Espiritu Esperanza's cherubic face became placidly confident. "There are no restrictions on where they may settle as citizens," he replied. "Is this not a free country?"

"It is not only free," Harmon Cashman said joyously, "it is the greatest country in the world. But how will you get them to come here?"

"Leave that to me."

"Will they vote for you? Most of them, that is?"

Enrique Espiritu Esperanza spread his generous arms like the statue of Christ on a Brazilian hilltop. "Look at me: my skin, my eyes, my voice. Do you think they could vote for any of the others if I am on the ballot?"

"Let's get you on the ballot, then!"

They got on the ballot. With signatures to spare.

"Now we need campaign workers," Harmon Cashman said. "Lots of them."

"Let us go for a ride," said Enrique Espiritu Esperanza.

Harmon Cashman drove the tasteful white Mercedes that seemed to be the perfect vehicle to convey Enrique Espiritu Esperanza from place to place.

"You must sell a lot of grapes," Harmon said, noting the custom interior.

It was early morning. All along Mulholland, brown-skinned men with sad faces and tattered blanket rolls under their arms stood waiting, their eyes watching the passing traffic with expectation. A faint, uneasy light, like tiny bulbs, could be seen deep in their dark eyes. From the first day he had arrived, Harmon Cashman had seen this phenomenon all over Los Angeles. He figured the bus system must be very, very bad.

They parked. A pickup truck rumbled up and the driver called out a summons in Spanish. Harmon didn't catch the words. He wouldn't have understood them if he had.

But the Hispanic men with sad faces piled onto the open bed of the pickup until they were spilling off the sides. There was room for perhaps thirty men, and near to fifty were scrambling for a place. A fistfight broke out. It was brief. The winners found places in back of the truck and the losers ended up sitting on the asphalt, tears streaming down their unwashed faces.

"They will be paid twelve cents an hour to break their backs in the fields," said Enrique Esperanza, his voice for once sad.

"It's a hard life," said Harmon Cashman glumly.

"We will pay them a decent wage, and they will work for us."

"You don't pay campaign workers!" Cashman said in horror.

"We will change the rules. While others are playing by the old rules, we will win."

"But—but it's un-American!"

"Exactly. I intend to run the most un-American campaign ever."

At that, Enrique Esperanza stepped from the white Mercedes and walked up to a Mexican man who sat on the gutter, crying tears of shame because he had been too slow and now he and his family would not eat.

Enrique knelt beside the man and laid a hand on his shoulder. He whispered a few words. The Mexican's eyes went wide. He took up the man's toffee-colored hand and kissed it. Lavishly.

Enrique Esperanza helped the man to his feet, and lifted his arms. His voice rose, clear and bell-like. It called up and down the length of Mulholland.

It's like watching a modern Pied Piper at work, Harmon Cashman thought with admiration.

"Drive slowly," said Enrique Esperanza, after he had returned to the car.

At the wheel, Harmon Cashman craned to see out the back window. Mexican migrant workers had formed up behind the white Mercedes in lines three deep.

"Why?" he asked.

"So they can follow," Enrique said simply.

And follow they did. Others were picked up along the way. As they trailed behind the white Mercedes, their voices rang out joyously.

"Esperanza! Esperanza! Esperanza!"

"What did you tell them?" Harmon whispered, his eyes wide with awe.

"What I told them cannot be expressed in words. It is what I gave them."

"Yeah?"

"Hope, Harmon. I gave them hope."

"I getcha," said Harmon Cashman, fingering an Oreo cookie out of his vest pocket. He had taken to carrying them that way. One never knew when a person might need a pick-me-up. It was going to be a hectic six weeks. . . .

The white Mercedes pulled up before an empty storefront, the first they came to.

"What's here?" Harmon wondered.

"Our second campaign headquarters."

"Do we need two in L.A.?"

"Yes. One where the white people will feel comfortable, and one for the brown people. This will be the brown people's place."

"Good strategy. I never did think that 'Rainbow Coalition' stuff made any sense."

Within an hour, they had the rental agent opening the front door with a key. The storefront had been unrented for eight months. The haggling was brief. It ended when Enrique Esperanza offered the rental agent a second Oreo. The man also promised to vote for Esperanza. His eyes shone with admiration.

By afternoon they had phones installed, castoff desks and chairs in place.

"We have our new headquarters!" Enrique Esperanza announced in a pleased, infectious voice.

Harmon looked around. "Can these guys speak English?"

"English will not be necessary this first week. They will reach out to their friends, their relatives, their brothers of brown skin in far states. They will tell them of Amnistia, and the opportunities to have their voice heard in California. To elect one of their own."

Harmon Cashman frowned. "It's a good start, sure. But what about the Anglos?"

"We call them *blancos*. As for them, I have a message for them too."

"What's that?" Harmon Cashman asked, nibbling on an Oreo.

"That cookie you are eating. Do you know what the tax on it is?"

"No. Why should I care?"

"The tax is eight and one quarter percent. It is called the snack tax. A terrible outrage."

Harmon Cashman looked at his Oreo, the innocent Oreo of his Virginia childhood.

"You know, you used to be able to buy one whole box for thirty-five cents when I was a kid," he said wistfully.

"Now it is two dollars. Plus tax. How can they tax such a thing?" Enrique Esperanza asked morosely. "Children eat these."

"Damn it, that's ridiculous!"

"We must repeal this terrible, unjust tax," said Enrique Espiritu Esperanza.

"Ricky," Harmon Cashman said, his voice trembling with righteous indignation. "I *know* this is an issue we can make real to people."

"And we will. All we need do is hand these cookies out at rallies."

Harmon Cashman almost choked. "Are you sure there'll be enough to go around? These babies are expensive now."

Esperanza grinned broadly. "Of these cookies, there will be more than enough to win the election, I assure you."

"You've sold me," said Harmon Cashman, separating the two black wafers and scraping the white creme filling onto his tongue with his lower incisors.

*   *   *

Within two weeks, two hard-fought combative weeks, Enrique Espiritu Esperanza had himself a statewide network of staff. They came in all colors, brown, yellow, white.

It shouldn't have surprised Harmon Cashman as much as it did. This was California, after all. People didn't vote color or race, they voted issues. The snack thing, which had festered for a year, suddenly erupted.

Harmon first saw evidence of this at a Burbank rally.

White staffers stood at the door of a rented hall, handing out glassine bags of cookies to everyone who walked through the doors.

The post-bills plastered all over town said FREE COOKIES in big letters and RALLY FOR HOPE in somewhat smaller but still prominent letters.

The legend, "Sponsored by the Campaign to Elect Enrique Espiritu Esperanza for Governor" was in small print.

The people who came out were not patronage hounds or sycophants, but a cross-slice of the California electorate. Some had agendas. Others were simply looking for a trendy cause, or a free snack.

"Tax-free as well as free," the staffers said, as they passed out the glassine bags. Ricky had coined that particular slogan. He was good at slogans. The man was a natural.

When the house had settled down, Enrique Espiritu Esperanza stepped up to the podium. No applause greeted him, just respectful attentiveness. In the back of the hall, Harmon Cashman was worried. The audience had not been salted with campaign workers, whose job it was to fire up the crowd. Ricky had insisted it was not necessary. This could be a disaster.

Enrique Espiritu Esperanza was attired in a white suit, shirt, and tie. These made his benevolent brown face stand out, starkly beautiful.

He began speaking, his tone steady, his words a velvet purr. He spoke of a change for California. Of the recession. Of unemployment. Of unfair taxes, and the public's growing distaste for the politics of recent years. The backstabbing, the bickering.

"I stand for what I am," said Enrique Espiritu

Esperanza. "I am Esperanza. I am hope. Hope for a better future."

It was sincere, polished, and said nothing risky. In short, it was a perfect campaign speech. High on homilies, lean on substance. Harmon Cashman had heard such speeches thousands of times in his career. But coming from the charismatic Esperanza, this one sounded fresh, clear as spring water—even brilliant.

At the end of it Enrique Espiritu Esperanza said, "I ask that you vote for me on election day. I will make you all proud that you did so."

There was silence. It was punctuated by the dry snap of Oreos breaking under the pressure of biting teeth, and thoughtful chewing sounds.

"If you have any questions, I will be happy to answer them," added Enrique Espiritu Esperanza.

A hand went up. A young woman. Her eyes shone with what seemed to be innocence.

"Yes?"

"Do you have any more cookies?"

Enrique Espiritu Esperanza allowed a sad look to come over his wide, cherubic face.

"I am sad to say, no. We have used up our budget for this rally."

"Aww . . ." said the bright-eyed young woman.

A forlorn sigh ran through the audience. There were a few "darns" and "drats," sprinkled with more pungent curses.

"There would have been more," Esperanza added, "but you understand. . . . The tax."

"That damned tax!" a man howled.

A man jumped to his feet. "Somebody ought to do something!"

Esperanza raised his smooth brown palms. "This is exactly what I propose. To repeal this detestable tax that deprives the open-minded people of this state of the small comforts of life."

A shout of encouragement went up. Others chimed in.

At first, Harmon Cashman thought that the crowd had been salted behind his back. He realized this was unlikely. Maybe it was the cookies. Maybe *everyone* went wild for Oreos. After all, this was America. What child had not eaten them by the carload? And how many of those had stopped eating them as adults? Sure, Harmon Cashman decided, it was their taste buds getting nostalgic. Using Oreos to create loyalty—it was a masterstroke. Brilliant.

Then, they began to chant, "Esperanza! Esperanza! Esperanza!"

And Cashman realized that the migrants had fallen into the same chant. And no one had slipped *them* any cookies.

"This guy," Harmon Cashman muttered over the swelling chanting, "must have the greatest pheromones anybody ever saw!"

In rally after rally, it had been the same. The guy just got up on the podium, sometimes without benefit of a microphone, and no sooner did he start to speak than the crowd was with him.

For Harmon Cashman, the campaign was like a vacation in Heaven. He hardly had to do a thing. The press got wind of the Esperanza fever, and suddenly they were running a press campaign. Without so much as lifting a telephone.

At the end of two weeks, the name "Enrique Espiritu Esperanza" had appeared at the bottom of the polls. His speeches were leading the local newscasts. By the middle of the third week, the dark horse nobody had ever heard of was edging up to be in striking distance of the front-runners, Barry Black and Rona Ripper.

Their campaign staffers were smart. They simply ignored the upstart. That gave the Esperanza campaign a clear field to sprint éven further ahead.

Besides, what was there to criticize? Oreo cookies and hope?

"We're in trouble," Harmon Cashman confided to his candidate over a working lunch that very afternoon.

Enrique Espiritu Esperanza looked at him with his doe-like eyes. "I am shooting up in the polls. How is this terrible?"

"We were doing great as an underdog. Nobody bothered to attack us. We were running a guerrilla campaign, and if we'd kept it at the pace we were going, by the time the polls had you in a dead heat it would have been a week before the election, and too late for the other campaigns to do anything about you."

"It is better to win big and win early," said Enrique Esperanza without hesitation.

Harmon Cashman stook his head. "Not if they score any hits. They're going to dig up all the dirt on you they can."

"They will find no stain on my honor. Enrique Espiritu Esperanza is as pure as the driven snow."

"And this appeal to the ethnic vote. It's going to bring the hate-mongers out. You know that?"

"Let them emerge into the light. One cannot step on a hiding cockroach, and the only way to draw out a cockroach is to turn off the light, wait, and turn it on again. I have turned off the light. Now the cockroaches will come. Let them. Let them."

They came.

It was at a Sacramento rally. An indoor rally, this time.

Esperanza was in the middle of his speech before a packed house, when two men jumped up from either side of the front row and shouting "Down with Esperanza!" opened fire with machine pistols.

An X formed on the white wall above and behind the unflinching figure of Enrique Espiritu Esperanza. One bullet track made a slashing diagonal from the left. The other showed up as a wavering line of punch holes coming down to the right.

They should have crossed at a point exactly between Enrique Espiritu Esperanza's black eyes.

Except the percussive stuttering sounds went suddenly quiet.

On the podium, Enrique Esperanza stood blinking, as if unable to comprehend that he had come as close to having his head blown off as the bullet capacity of a Tec-9 machine pistol clip.

In the front row, the gunmen were fumbling empty clips out and attempting to get fresh ones out of their coat pockets.

"Get them!" Cashman shouted.

The hall turned into a sea of panic.

On the podium, Enrique Espiritu Esperanza called for calm.

Belatedly, Harmon Cashman lunged for his candidate, threw him to the floor.

"Stay down!" he hissed, surprised at his own personal courage.

"I am not afraid," said Enrique Espiritu Esperanza, his voice as calm as a sultry breeze. "Those *asesinos* cannot harm Esperanza. Esperanza is hope."

It sounded corny, but coming from the lips of his candidate, it brought proud tears to Harmon Cashman's eyes.

The police got the crowd under control. The gunmen had escaped in the confusion. After the situation had stabilized, and people had been questioned, the weapons were found taped to the undersides of a pair of folding chairs.

"They are very clever, these men," Enrique Esperanza said, when he was shown the weapons. "Without these incriminating tools, they were able to blend with the crowd and simply walk out the doors unchallenged."

"They'll be back," Harmon Cashman said, when the police were through with their questions and had left. "Guys like them never give up."

"I am not afraid," said Enrique Espiritu Esperanza, who sounded as if he meant it. "I am Esperanza."

7

Harold W. Smith received the report of the attempt on the life of gubernatorial candidate Enrique Espiritu Esperanza the same way most of America did. Through the media.

Smith was driving home when the bulletin broke over the radio. Smith had been listening to a classical music program on National Public Radio. Smith liked National Public Radio—when they broadcast music. The minute someone who was not an announcer spoke for more than ninety seconds, he either turned off the radio or switched stations.

The bulletin was brief:

"UPI is reporting that an attempt was made on the life of the Hispanic dark horse candidate for governor of California, Enrique Espiritu Esperanza, within the last hour," the metallic announcer's voice said. "Details are sketchy at this time, but initial reports are that Esperanza was unhurt. The unidentified assailants are believed to have escaped in the confusion."

In the darkness of his battered station wagon, Harold W. Smith voiced a question:

"Who is Enrique Espiritu Esperanza?"

There was no followup, so the question went unanswered.

Smith pulled over to the side of the road and turned on the dome light. A well-worn briefcase, its edges peeling and thus unlikely to be stolen by a casual thief, sat on the seat beside him. Smith threw the safety latches, so the briefcase would not detonate a gram of plastique embedded in the lock, and opened it.

Revealed was a minicomputer with a cellular telephone handset attached.

Smith brought the system up and dialed into the Folcroft mainframes. He had not been following the California race for two weeks now. Once the uproar over the deaths of the governor and lieutenant governor had subsided, and there had been no activity that seemed suspicious, Smith had concluded that whatever had been General Nogeira's motives in assassinating the officials, the plan had died with him.

The President of the United States had agreed, and pending the National Transportation Safety Board crash report, they decided to let the matter rest.

And now this.

Smith had been completely unaware of the existence of a candidate by the name of Enrique Espiritu Esperanza.

Smith punched up the name. The liquid-crystal display began emitting a brief file. Smith's gray eyes absorbed the data with interest.

He learned that Esperanza was an independent candidate for the governorship. A Napa Valley wine-grower by profession, he had become wealthy and had entered the race as a dark horse. He was barely a blip in the polls, which were dominated by Barry Black, Junior and Rona Ripper.

His message was not so radical that someone was likely to attempt to do him in, Harold Smith concluded. Yet obviously someone had tried.

Smith called up Remo's current contact number. Normally, it was something he would simply have committed to memory, but Smith's memory was not as sharp as it once had been, and lately Remo had been changing residences so often that it was harder to keep track of his whereabouts.

As Smith hit the autodial key, he thought wistfully that there had been advantages to having Remo reside here in Rye, near Folcroft. But recent events had forced Remo and Chiun back into the nomadic lifestyle they had once practiced. It was a situation not to anyone's liking.

The phone rang once. The receiver was lifted, and a squeaky voice said, "Speak."

"Master Chiun. It is I."

"Hail Emperor Smith, the Infallible," Chiun said in an excessively loud voice. "Your wisdom exceeds that of the pharaohs. Sinanju lives to serve you well—despite certain embarrassments that have occurred of late."

Smith cleared his throat. "If you are referring to the Nogeira incident, once again, I do not hold it against you."

"As you should not. It was Remo's blunder."

"Nor do I hold it against Remo," Smith added quickly. "It was just one of those things."

Chiun's voice grew conspiratorial. "The true perpetrators. You have their names at last? I will attend to them myself, so as to atone for my pupil's blunder."

"No," Smith admitted. "Washington gave up on that angle weeks ago. The perpetrators have melted into the shadows. It is possible they never left the country at all, which would explain why they have not been intercepted at the usual international points of departure."

"Obviously they are cunning beyond words," Chiun mused. "Otherwise they would not be hiding within your very borders after their brazen, cowardly attack."

"Er, yes," said Smith uncomfortably. "That is all in the past now. I have an important assignment."

"Your generosity knows no bounds."

"Excuse me?" said Smith, for a moment wondering if it was once again contract-renewal time. Chiun tended to speak of America's generosity only on those annual occasions.

"Your faith in Sinanju must be great indeed to give Remo a second chance," Chiun went on. "It is not misplaced. Whoever must be dispatched, Sinanju vows his hours are numbered."

"I don't want you to, ah, dispatch anyone. There is a gubernatorial candidate who is in peril."

"I will let you speak with Remo," Chiun said, his tone noticeably cooling.

The sound of a hand covering the mouthpiece came to Smith's ear. Still, Chiun's squeaky voice could be heard, although muffled.

"It is Smith," Chiun said.

"What does he want?" Remo's voice, very distant and not at all happy.

"I am not certain. He has lapsed into that patois of

his that is not English. I think he wants you to take out the garbage."

"Garbage?"

"Gubernatorial," Chiun said. "Is that not the same as 'garbage'?"

"No," Remo said.

"Whatever it means, it is beneath my dignity as Reigning Master to deal with it. Since you have yet to atone for your recent misdeeds, I give Smith to you."

The sound of the hand coming off the microphone was like a suction cup popping free of window glass. Remo's voice, clear and filled with acid, came again.

"Thanks a bunch, Little Father." Into the telephone, he said, "What's going on, Smitty?"

"One of the candidates for governor of California has survived an assassination attempt tonight."

"Ripper or Black?"

"Neither. Esperanza."

"I never heard of Esperanza."

"Nor had I," Smith admitted frankly. "He is barely registering in the polls, yet someone is trying to kill him. I want you and Chiun to look into it."

"Any suspects?"

"None. There is an outside chance that this attempt might be some repercussion from the Nogeira scheme, perhaps some sleeper hit team that has activated in spite of the death of its mastermind, Nogeira."

"I still have a hard time believing that toad-faced ogre could have caused that plane crash from jail," Remo muttered.

"The FAA investigation continues," Smith replied crisply. "We may know something soon. In the meantime, I want you to look into this event."

"How?"

"Join the Esperanza campaign, to start."

"Hold the phone, but isn't he the victim?"

"I want you and Chiun in place if there's another attempt. If one comes, you know what to do."

"And if there isn't?" Remo wondered.

"By that time," said Harold Smith, bathed in the pale radiance of his station wagon dome light, "I hope to have developed some concrete leads for you to follow."

"Great," Remo said dryly. "And here I was just getting settled in sunny Seattle."

"I am not aware that Seattle is particularly sunny."

"Funny," Remo said acidly. "Neither am I. It hasn't stopped raining since we hit town."

"I will expect progress reports every twelve hours," Smith said thinly.

"You can expect them," Remo returned. "But getting them is another thing. You have to make progress to report on it."

"We shall see," said Smith, hanging up.

Closing up his briefcase, Harold Smith shut off the dome light and resumed his drive home. He was in his third week without medication of any sort and, while he did not feel like a new man—his burdens precluded such a renewal of spirit—it was good not to have his stomach churning with excess acid, and his brain throbbing with persistent headaches.

He wondered how long it would last. In this job, he thought ruefully, probably not very long.

8

The first thing Remo did upon disembarking at LAX airport was to buy a newspaper from a vending machine.

"You have no time to read the comic strips," Chiun sniffed as they walked toward the cab stand. He wore a royal blue kimono.

"I'm not," Remo said, tossing the business and entertainment sections into a trash can. "I want to read up on Esperanza."

"Esperanza," said Chiun thoughtfully. "It is a worthy name."

"It is?"

"In the Spanish tongue, it means hope."

"I guess he knows it too. Because it says here he's holding a 'Rally for Hope' tonight. Maybe we should catch it."

"I would prefer to catch this man today," Chiun retorted.

"What's the rush?"

"The air smells bad. I would not linger in this so-called 'City of Angels.' "

The Master of Sinanju said this as the automatic glass doors slid apart and they were hit by a wave of dry heat and smog.

Remo, feeling his lungs begin to rebel, said, "This is worse than Mexico City."

"Nothing is worse than that foul place," Chiun sniffed, his hazel eyes looking to the brownish layer of clouds.

The first cab in line, they discovered, was not airconditioned.

"No thanks," Remo said. "We'll take the next guy."

"You gotta take me," the cabby said. "It's the rules."

"Whose?"

"The Drivers' Association."

"We don't belong," Remo pointed out in a reasonable voice.

"Then you don't ride."

The Master of Sinanju took this in without a change of expression. He drifted up to the rear tire, pretending to scrutinize the low-lying smog.

One sandaled foot bumped the rear tire.

The rubber popped a rip, and air hissed through the ragged eruption.

The cab settled at its southern corner.

"It is okay, Remo!" Chiun said loudly. "We will ride with this man!"

"We will?" Remo blurted.

"He is desperately in need of our business." Chiun pointed. "Look. His wheels are in a sad state."

The driver came out and looked at his tire.

"A flat?"

"It is too bad," clucked Chiun, "but we will wait for you to repair it." He beamed. Remo looked at him doubtfully.

The cabby shook his head. "Can't. The rules say you take the next one in line."

"Then my son and I will take the next conveyance in line with sorrow in our hearts," the Master of Sinanju said magnanimously.

"Yeah, yeah," the driver grumbled, popping his trunk and removing a tire iron and jack.

The second cab—this one air-conditioned—took them out into traffic. They got all of sixty yards out before they hit a traffic jam. It didn't last long. It was just that they encountered so many on the way into the city.

As they drew cool, filtered air into their lungs, Chiun folded his kimono skirts delicately and said, "Remo, tell me of this assignment."

Remo shrugged. "What's to tell? Someone killed the governor and lieutenant governor. Now there's a special election to replace them."

Chiun nodded. "Typically debased," he said.

"What is?"

"The American approach to democracy. Not that the Roman brand was any good. It lasted but four centuries."

"A mere tick of the Korean clock," Remo said, smiling.

Chiun's button nose wrinkled up. "Koreans did not have clocks until the West introduced them as a form of slavery."

"Slavery?"

"When one is watching clocks, one is not attending to one's proper business."

"I won't argue with that," Remo allowed, looking out the window. They were approaching the city. He saw business signs in an amazing variety of languages, including the modern Korean script called *hangul*.

"In Roman times," Chiun went on, "the governors were appointed by the emperor."

"Well, we elect ours."

"The Romans voted for their consuls. That was in their early primitive period, before they came to embrace the sweet serenity of rule by emperor."

"Like Caligula, I suppose?"

Chiun frowned, transforming his wizened face into a dried yellow apricot. "He has gotten bad press," he sniffed, watching the palm trees whip by. "It is no wonder the trees grow as they do here," he added.

"How's that?"

"The bad air. It makes the trees grow naked, except for their heads. Trees should not possess heads. It is unnatural. Like elections."

"Look, Chiun. Since we're going to volunteer our services to the Esperanza campaign . . ."

Chiun's head whipped around. His thin eyes went wide.

"Volunteer? Sinanju—volunteer!"

Remo nodded. "That's how it works. People who support a candidate volunteer their services."

"Then they are fools and worse," Chiun said harshly. "I will dispatch no enemies for no gold."

"Sounds like a cute campaign slogan," Remo remarked. "But volunteers are what Smith wants us to be. So we do it."

"We do not!"

"We who are loyal to our emperor do," Remo pointed out dryly.

The Master of Sinanju absorbed this example of white

logic without comment. His eyes narrowed. Perhaps, at the next contract negotiation, he would find a way to make Smith pay for any enemies of Esperanza he was forced to dispatch without pay. With interest, of course.

They finally pulled up before a Wilshire Boulevard hotel, where Remo understood from *The Los Angeles Times* Enrique Espiritu Esperanza had taken the penthouse suite for his protection.

Remo paid the cabby, after a brief argument over the tip. The driver insisted the tip was insufficient. Remo pointed out the undeniable fact that it was ten percent of the fare.

"But it was a two-hour ride because of traffic," the cabby complained. "How can I make a living at these rates?"

"Drive in another state," Remo said, turning away.

They entered the lobby. Remo noticed a single dollar bill sliding up one of the Master of Sinanju's voluminous sleeves.

"Don't tell me you were planning to chip in on the tip?" he asked incredulously.

"No, I surreptitiously relieved the driver of one dollar."

"Why?"

"You provided him valuable career advice, therefore overtipping him. I merely balanced accounts."

"Then you can catch the next tip."

Chiun's tiny mouth expressed disapproval. "Perhaps," he said.

There were three LAPD police officers standing guard at the elevator bank, and also being besieged by press. Microphone and micro-cassette recorders were pushed into their faces. Questions were snapped. Remo was reminded of a pack of hounds yapping at a cornered fox.

"Has candidate Esperanza requested police protection?" one reporter asked.

"No comment."

"Who is behind this attempt, and what is his motive?" another demanded.

"That is still under investigation."

"I insist upon being allowed upstairs," a sharp-voiced

woman said, in a screeching voice that could have sharp-
ened razor blades at fifty feet.

Remo, hearing that voice, said, "Uh-oh."

The Master of Sinanju, hearing that same voice,
squeaked, "Remo! It is Cheeta!"

"It is not," Remo said quickly, taking Chiun by the
arm and attempting to pull him out of the lobby.

The Master of Sinanju looked no more sturdy than a
sapling. Yet all of Remo's efforts couldn't budge him. In
fact, when Chiun breezed toward the elevator, Remo
found himself being dragged along. He let go, barely
finding his feet in time.

Horror on his face, Remo got in front of the Master
of Sinanju, blocking him.

"Look, you'll blow our cover!" he said urgently.

"But it is Cheeta Ching!" Chiun squeaked. "In
person."

"I know who it is," Remo hissed. "And that barracuda
represents one of the biggest TV networks in the country.
You cozy up to her and our cover will be blown. And
we know what that means, don't we? No more work. No
more Emperor Smith. And no submarine full of gold
offloading in Sinanju every November."

The Master of Sinanju drew himself up proudly. "I
am not a babbler of secrets. I will tell her nothing, of
course."

"That's good. That's good. Tell her nothing. Period.
Because if she gives you the time of day, she will ask
you a zillion questions, none of them her business."

At that moment, Cheeta Ching's voice rose again.
"I'm going to stay here until someone from the Esperanza campaign agrees to come down to talk to me!" she
screeched.

Chiun's eyes narrowed. For a horrifying moment,
Remo thought he was going to rush in and announce,
prematurely, that he was the official assassin of the
Esperanza campaign.

Instead, the Master of Sinanju turned in place and hurried out into the street. Hands disappearing into his kimono sleeves, he floated around to the back of the
building and gazed upward.

The hotel was California modern. Not much in the way
of gingerbread, ledges, or handholds.

The Master of Sinanju stepped up to one corner and laid hands on each joining wall, then began rubbing them in small circles, as if drying his palms. Abruptly, his sandals left the pavement.

It was one of the most difficult of Sinanju ascent techniques: the employment of converging pressure to gain purchase. His spindly legs working, the Master of Sinanju pulled himself up like a poisonous blue spider.

Remo let him get a few floors ahead and followed, thinking that Chiun was obviously showing off on the rare chance that Cheeta Ching might spot him. Remo knew that the Master of Sinanju had been infatuated with the Korean anchorwoman ever since he had discovered her when she was a mere local anchor back in New York.

Once she had gone national, she had become Chiun's obsession. No amount of common sense, such as their undeniable age difference and Cheeta's subsequent marriage to the cadaverous middle-aged gynecologist Chiun had dubbed "that callow youth," could dissuade the old Korean from his delusion that Cheeta was fated to be his one true love.

"I'm glad you see things my way!" Remo called up, as he drew under the Master of Sinanju's scuttling form.

"It is better this way," Chiun answered.

"Absolutely."

"Once I have gained the confidence of this 'Esperanza,' I will convince him to grant Cheeta a special audience."

"Maybe," Remo said cautiously.

"And she will be eternally grateful to me," Chiun added.

"Not likely," Remo muttered.

"And so will consent to have my child," Chiun finished. "Which is her great destiny."

"What!"

Chiun halted at the twelfth floor. His stern face peered down and his voice was cold.

"It is her destiny, Remo. I warn you not to interfere."

"Little Father," Remo said sincerely. "I would not get between you and Cheeta Ching for any amount of money."

"Good."

"Especially," Remo murmured, "when she's in heat."

Chiun resumed climbing. Remo followed, his face worried.

They expected the penthouse to be guarded, and they were right.

The wide patio promenade surrounding the penthouse itself was patrolled by security guards. They could hear their feet crushing the gravel. The sound was specific enough to tell Remo what kind of weapons they carried. Most had sidearms. From the sound of his swaggering, wide-legged walk, one toted a rifle openly. Since it was designed for long-range use, that weapon represented the least threat to them.

"We will take the rifle first," said Chiun.

"You got it," Remo said.

They got to a narrow strip of ornamental metal and, using it for a tightrope, worked their way to the north side of the building, where the rifle-toter was walking back and forth and sounding anxious.

Carlos Lugan was *muy* anxious. He had joined the Esperanza campaign only two days ago, walking off his security guard job without even bothering to turn in his uniform. The march of migrant workers shouting "Esperanza! Esperanza!" had been like the summons of some smiling siren. Carlos was from El Salvador. His mother still lived in San Salvador—and only because Carlos Lugan sent her a check every month. Without it, she would starve like her friends, whose family could not get to America.

So when Carlos followed the chanting migrants to a Rally for Hope, and heard that the Esperanza campaign was paying seven dollars an hour for help, he did not hesitate. That was two dollars more than his job paid. He became a loyal Esperanza supporter.

Carlos was not disappointed to find himself, in the wake of the failed assassination attempt, performing much the same menial tasks as he had in his previous situation. He was proud to be a servant of Esperanza. In truth, he hoped someone *would* make another attempt on his life. That way, Carlos Lugan would gladly throw himself in the path of the bullet. He fantasized about the moment. About martyring himself for the man who had offered him such hope, and provided him with the where-withal to increase his monthly check to his mother by an incredible twenty dollars.

Unfortunately for Carlos Lugan, it was not a bullet he had to face in the defense of his candidate. It was something older, more accurate—and virtually indefensible.

Carlos was standing at the edge of the parapet, which was waist-high. There had been a time he was afraid of heights. But working for Esperanza, he was afraid of nothing.

He failed to see the hand that reached up for his rifle muzzle.

In fact, he did not notice the absence of the rifle, even though he had been holding it firmly in both hands. Carlos was staring out at the Los Angeles skyline—what he could see of it in the smog—and his chest burned with intense pride.

A creeping numbness came over his hands. He looked down at them. And blinked. Blinked several times rapidly.

There was no understanding it, at first. He had been holding his rifle. Now it was no longer there. Had he, in his passionate fantasizing, dropped it? He turned around to look . . .

. . . and the gnarled yellow hand that had casually relieved him of his weapon reached up and seized the exposed back of his neck. The hand—Carlos did not know it was a hand—exerted such force that Carlos had the weird impression of a vise seizing his neck. This, of course, was impossible. He decided he had been shot. That was the only explanation. A bullet had struck his magnificent body, forcing him to drop the rifle. Now a second bullet had entered his neck from the back, severing his spinal cord and paralyzing him with cruel finality.

The anti-Esperanza devils were attacking!

Carlos fell face-first into the gravel. The fact that it did not hurt convinced him his spinal cord had been severed. Not that there was any doubt.

Out of one eye, he saw a pair of white sandals pad past. They were followed by a pair of feet encased in ordinary shoes. There were only two of them—two assassins.

Carlos tried to shout a warning, to alert his patron of danger, but no words came. Only tears coursing down the humiliated face of Carlos Lugan, the loyal.

He saw, as if dreaming, his *compadres* succumb to the pair, an Anglo and an Asian. The Asian meant his worst fears were true. There was bad blood between Hispanics and Asians in Los Angeles.

The Asians were out to stop Esperanza, fearing him.

They carried no weapons. They simply deployed, slipping up stealthily behind the other guards and bringing them to the same humiliation that had visited Carlos Lugan, by taking them by the backs of their necks and lowering their faces into the gravel.

Then, like ghosts, they slipped up to the sliding glass doors of the penthouse suite, where Esperanza was plotting strategy with his campaign manager.

Certain he was dying, Carlos Lugan said a silent prayer. Not for himself, but for Enrique Espiritu Esperanza.

Remo paused at the sliding glass door. He turned to the Master of Sinanju, whispering.

"Okay, Little Father. Here comes the tricky part."

"I will handle this," Chiun said, girding his blue kimono skirts.

"Remember," Remo cautioned. "We are just good citizens out to help a candidate."

Chiun gave the sliding door a firm tug. It shot along its track and shattered into a thousand pieces.

Seated around a coffee table on which a map of L.A. County was laid out, Enrique Espiritu Esperanza and Harmon Cashman looked up. Their mouths dropped open at the sight of a tiny wisp of an Asian man followed by a lean, unhappy Caucasian, stepping through the suddenly open door.

Harmon Cashman bolted from his chair and flung himself across the body of Esperanza.

"Assassins! Stop them!" he shouted to the guards.

From an inner room, two hulking Mexicans came charging out. They resembled a pair of Lou Ferrignos, with extra coats of tan. They brought up Uzi machine pistols while vaulting over the furniture.

The Asian and the Caucasian separated. The pair

didn't appear to move. Yet suddenly they were five feet apart, utterly unconcerned and outwardly not seeming to hurry. Their movements appeared casual, even slow. Except they were unexpectedly in places far from their earlier positions, without, apparently, having crossed the intervening space.

The phenomenon befuddled the two bodyguards. They continually repositioned the muzzles of their weapons. Each time they were about to fire, the targets floated out of their sights.

One man beheaded a lamp, because his brain had been too slow in translating the image his retina had picked up: the image of empty space where a skinny white guy had been an instant before.

The two Mexicans quickly became so used to the utter confoundedness of their targets that they were too surprised to be surprised when the pair, synchronizing their actions to the nanosecond, simply swept in from their blind sides and rendered the weapons useless.

They used their hands. They floated up and around the Uzis unseen, and the two ringing claps came as one.

The Anglo and the Asian stepped back, joined up once more. The white man folded his arms defiantly, a cruel smile tugging at his lips. The Asian simply tucked his hands into his wide blue sleeves. He looked unafraid.

And the two bodyguards lifted flattened and useless weapons to firing position and depressed the triggers. The triggers refused to pull. They looked down.

It was then and only then that they comprehended the intriguing fact that their weapons were much, much thinner than they had been. In fact, they resembled gray palm leaves studded with rivets.

"Let me give you a hand," the Caucasian told Harmon Cashman, reaching out with his hands.

Before Harmon could respond, he was lifted to his feet. The other hand pulled Enrique Espiritu Esperanza to his feet.

"To what do I owe this intrusion?" Enrique asked blankly, his liquid eyes taking in the bizarre sight of his guards attempting to brain the tiny Asian.

The old man—all five feet of him—turned to bow in Esperanza's direction. The bow coincided with a strenuous attempt to brain him, with strangely wide and flat Uzis, on the part of the two Mexican bodyguards.

"I am Chiun, Master of Sinanju," said the old man in a low voice.

When he straightened, the weapons were coming down again.

Esperanza raised broad palms to quell the violence. He might have saved the energy. His towering guards had missed again. One fell on his face. The other, rearing back for a third attempt, suddenly dropped his useless weapon and grabbed his left foot, howling. He hopped on his right foot, as if the left had been hit by a jackhammer.

He hopped right out of the room and never hopped back.

"I have heard of Sinanju," said Esperanza quietly.

Remo, standing beside the white-coated man, blinked.

"I have been sent by a person I cannot name to safeguard your life," Chiun said placidly.

"I see."

"I have vanquished your guards to show the superiority of our services."

"I accept," said Enrique Esperanza. "Name your price."

"Grant the gorgeous creature named Cheeta an audience, and no further payment will be necessary."

"Done."

As Remo watched, his mouth dropping with each syllable spoken, the Master of Sinanju bowed gravely. Enrique Esperanza returned the gesture with the elegance of an Aztec lord.

Harmon Cashman sidled up to Remo.

"You with him?"

"Yeah," Remo said unhappily.

"Can you explain anything of what I just heard?"

"No."

"I didn't think so," Harmon said glumly.

Enrique Espiritu Esperanza turned to Harmon Cashman.

"Harmon, these men will form the nucleus of our security force from now on."

"Are you sure about this, Ricky?"

"As certain as I am of my ultimate safety," replied Enrique Esperanza.

Frowning, Harmon Cashman walked up to the Master of Sinanju. He offered his hand, saying, "I'm Ricky's campaign manager."

Chiun nodded. "I will allow you to remain in his presence then," he sniffed, ignoring the hand.

"You . . . you . . ." Harmon sputtered.

The Master of Sinanju turned to the dark-horse candidate for governor.

"Is it this man's function to assist you in your work?"

Esperanza nodded. "It is."

"Then he should be about the business of escorting the wondrous Cheeta to our presence, should he not?"

Esperanza gestured. "Harmon. Have Miss Ching brought up here."

"You're giving her a statement?"

"No, I am granting her an interview. On our terms."

Harmon Cashman looked at the Master of Sinanju. "What are you?"

"Korean."

"Okay, you might be able to help us in Koreatown." He turned to Remo. "You. What's your name?"

"Remo."

Harmon nodded. "The Italians aren't much, demographically speaking, but we can use all the help we can get with the minority crowd."

"Since when are Italians in the minority?" Remo asked.

"Since this is California at the end of the twentieth century," replied Harmon Cashman in a smug voice, as he went to the elevator.

9

Cheeta Ching was furious.

There were those who claimed that Cheeta Ching had been born furious. Certainly she had been born ambitious. In newsrooms from Los Angeles to New York, she was known as "the Korean Shark." Other reporters had hung this nickname on her. It was hardly an affectionate coinage.

Nobody, but nobody, got between Cheeta Ching and a story.

Right now, a trio of LAPD police officers stood between her and her goal, a one-on-one with the most charismatic local candidate for governor since Barry Black's last run.

Cheeta, who had family in Los Angeles, had first heard about Esperanza from her sister-in-law. The stories were intriguing. A spectacular orator, who cleverly dispensed indescribably tasty cookies at his rallies and played to minority aspirations.

Cheeta had a lukewarm spot in her frosty heart for candidates who played to minorities. Being a member of minority groups herself, she felt oppressed on two fronts. One, because she was a woman, and more importantly, because she was Korean.

Nobody seemed to understand what unique beings Koreans were. People lumped her in with the Chinese and the Japanese, and the other Asians who were pouring into this country by the thousand, threatening Cheeta Ching's unique standing as the premier Asian-American anchorwoman of renown.

In fact, she was proud to say, Koreans didn't even belong to the same racial family as those other so-called minority Asians. Ethnically, Koreans were closer to Turks and Mongols.

The trouble was, Turks weren't considered a true minority in America. Minorities enjoyed strength in numbers, and had political-action groups looking out for their interests. If you were a Turk or a Mongol or, God forbid, a Finn, no one cared about you.

So Cheeta bit her tongue every time some fool referred to her as "Asian." Someday she would come out of the closet as an Altaic Mongoloid. When it was politically advantageous. Or when she finally became pregnant. Whichever came first.

At the moment, it was more effective to shout, "I'm an oppressed Asian-American female person, and I demand my rights!"

The police officers looked away, their faces stony. The other media had dropped their camera equipment and were using their index fingers to protect their eardrums. The screech of Cheeta Ching in full cry had been known to shatter wineglasses. This was so well known that several cameramen were pressing their minicam lenses to their chests, to protect them from the sonic assault.

"I happen to be the number-two anchorperson on my network!" she added shrilly.

To which a voice in the media pack added, "Yeah. In the dead-last-in-the-ratings network."

Cheeta whirled on the others. They recoiled at the blazing fury they saw crackling in her predatory eyes.

"I hope every one of you ends up at my network one day!" she hissed venomously. "I'll have you for lunch, with kimchee."

No one said anything in reply. They knew Cheeta was sincere. And they also knew that if they did end up at her network, Cheeta would make their lives miserable.

Having cowed her colleagues, Cheeta Ching returned to hectoring the police detail.

"I used to be an important reporter in this town. Don't any of you remember that?"

"Yeah," one cop said, his voice gravelly. "We remember. Especially that twelve-part series on police insensitivity."

That tack having proved fruitless, Cheeta let her perfect brows knit together. Her flat face—the term "pancake makeup" had a double meaning when applied to her—attempted an unsuccessful frown. She wondered if her hair spray was wearing off. Usually, the estrogen-impaired half of the human race was easier to handle than this. She wondered if it had anything to do with the Rodney King videotape, which her network broadcast, on average, once a week, to illustrate stories on police forces all over the nation. Even positive ones.

At that moment the elevator door separated, and a flustered man Cheeta recognized as Harmon Cashman, campaign manager to the Esperanza campaign, appeared.

Grabbing the handiest minicam, Cheeta knocked over two of the police officers and successfully eluded a third to get to the elevator. She might have saved herself the trouble, because as soon as she had stepped aboard, thrusting a hard elbow into the Door Close button, Harmon Cashman said, "Ricky will see you, Miss Ching."

"Of course," said Cheeta Ching dryly, taking a tiny canister of hair varnish from her purse and applying it generously to her glossy black hair. "I'm Cheeta Ching."

On the way up, Cheeta examined her face in a small compact. To her horror, she saw that her makeup was flaking. They were almost to the penthouse level, so she closed her eyes, steeled herself, and shot a blast of sticky hair varnish directly into her own face.

When she opened her eyes, the compact revealed that this carefully guarded professional secret had once again saved the day. She looked flawless. Professional. Perfect.

And why not? she thought to herself, as she stepped off the elevator. I am Cheeta Ching, the most famous Korean woman on the planet. If that isn't perfection, what is?

Remo Williams was saying, "I'm a campaign aide, not a freaking maid."

Chiun rushed about the room, straightening cushions and blowing dust off the window drapes, squeaking, "Hurry, Remo! She is coming. Cheeta is coming!"

Remo stood his ground. "No. You broke the glass door, you pick up the shards."

"I will grant you anything you desire!" Chiun pleaded.

"Peace of mind," Remo said instantly. "And a boon to be named later."

"Done!" Chiun crowed. "Now hurry! The great moment is about to arrive!"

Grinning, Remo found a corn broom and swept the door glass out of sight. He hid the bullet-shattered lamp and piled the unconscious Esperanza bodyguards in a back room.

He returned to the living room just in time to hear the elevator doors roll open.

Chiun, his eyes wide, swept in on Remo, saying, "Back! She must not see you!"

"Why not? I'm part of the team."

Chiun raised a warning finger. "Remember Emperor Smith's admonition. Your face must not be seen."

"Oh, yeah," Remo said. Smith was still upset because Remo's original face—the one he had worn in his former life as a Newark patrolman—had inadvertently been restored through plastic surgery. He retreated to the back room and listened.

The sound of Cheeta Ching entering the room was unmistakable. Her high heels sounded as if she were using them to drive railroad spikes.

Chiun's voice came then—the low, grave tone he affected on important occassions, completely the opposite of his usual high, squeaky one.

"I am Chiun."

"Great," Cheeta said. "You're just the person I need."

"Of course," Chiun replied. "How could it be otherwise?"

"Here. Take this."

"What is this?" came Chiun's voice, taken aback.

"It's a minicam. It's very simple to operate."

"Why would I wish to operate such a contraption?" Chiun asked, his tone injured.

"Because I left my cameraman down in the lobby and I need my hands free for the interview," replied Cheeta Ching, as if explaining why the sky is blue.

There was a pause. Remo, who was not ordinarily gifted with second sight, knew exactly what was coming next.

"Remo!"

"You rang?" Remo said, grinning as he stepped out into the living room.

The Master of Sinanju gestured carelessly in Remo's direction. "This is Remo, my lackey. Instruct him, and he will obey your every whim."

Remo looked at Cheeta Ching. Cheeta Ching looked at Remo. Cheeta's almond eyes widened in twin explosions. Her too-red vampire lips softened. Her whole face softened. It seemed to be melting. Like a butterscotch sundae. A patch of pancake base cracked loose from her chin and fell to the rug.

"Romeo," she said in a breathy voice.

"Remo," Remo corrected.

"You could change your name," Cheeta cooed. "For me."

"I'm outta here," Remo said, retreating as if from Typhoid Mary.

"Wait!" Cheeta called out. "Don't go!"

The Master of Sinanju, his expression stricken, said, "Go, Remo. You are no longer needed."

It was too late. Cheeta got between Remo and the door. She put her back to the door and threw out her chest. There wasn't much to throw out, but Remo got the message. So did Chiun.

"Remo!" he said hotly.

"This isn't my idea," Remo protested.

Cheeta Ching took Remo by the arm. Her nails dug in experimentally, as if testing his muscles. "Come with me," she said warmly. "I'll show you how to operate the camera. I bet you'll be wonderful at it. Perhaps you might like to become my personal cameraman. The last one had terrible reflexes."

"He will not!" Chiun blazed.

Cheeta said, "Hush, grandpa. And tell Esperanza that Cheeta Ching is ready for him."

The Master of Sinanju stood as if quick-frozen. His hands became fists and his cheeks became red. They puffed out in exasperation.

"Remo!" he hissed. "Do something!"

Remo asked Cheeta Ching, "Aren't you married?"

"Oh, him. You're probably heard about our little problem. I've been trying to get preggers for ages."

"I am much more virile than that round-eyed, big-nosed, ape-footed clod!" Chiun shouted.

"Anybody would be," Cheeta said dryly, not taking

her dark eyes off Remo Williams. "He's a gynecologist. Takes a lot to start his engine."

"I'd better get Ricky," Harmon Cashman said uneasily. "He's on the phone."

"Yes, you had better," Chiun said bitterly, his hazel eyes boring into Remo.

Because it meant getting Cheeta Ching's nails disengaged from his bare arms, Remo agreed to operate the minicam.

"You just point and shoot, right?" he asked.

"No, it's much more complicated than that," Cheeta said sweetly. Her voice was like butter warm from the microwave. "Make sure you pan over to my face every time I ask a question."

"Isn't this interview about Esperanza?" Remo wondered.

"No. It's an interview with Cheeta Ching." She winked. "Stick around, and I'll show you why that's such a big deal."

Remo hefted the camera onto his shoulder, found the eyepiece, and experimentally roved the lens around the room. The face of the Master of Sinanju appeared in the viewfinder. It was very, very angry.

Remo took the camera away from his face and mouthed the words, "Not my fault."

"Humph," said Chiun, flouncing around, presenting his cold, austere back to his pupil.

The sounds caught Cheeta Ching's attention. "You. Grandfather. Yoo-hoo." She was still in her buttery mode. "Why don't you run out and get us some coffee?"

"I am no servant," Chiun said huffily.

"Well then, don't you have something you could be doing? This is a major, major interview for Mr. Esperanza. Only important people should be here. We cannot have any distractions. I'm sure you understand?"

"I," said the Master of Sinanju, in a voice that was like ice cracking in a glass, "do not."

Chiun stormed from the room out onto the patio promenade, where he could pretend to suffer in silence yet keep his eyes on Remo and the fickle Cheeta unobtrusively.

Enrique Espiritu Esperanza made his entrance a moment later. He came bearing a silver tray, which he placed on the coffee table before Cheeta Ching, who didn't deign to rise at his entrance.

"For you," he said smoothly.

"Thank you," said Cheeta, casually taking an Oreo cookie from the tray. As Enrique Esperanza sat down, she shook the cookie in his face. "Before we get to the story behind your brush with death yesterday, tell me about these."

"They are very good," Enrique invited. "You should try one."

Cheeta held up the confection so that Remo could get a close-up of it in her hand. He zoomed in eagerly. Cheeta's face in the viewfinder made him feel like an extra in *Jaws*.

"I'm given to understand that the Oreo cookie is the symbol of your campaign. Can you explain your position on the snack-tax controversy?"

"Gladly, Miss Ching."

Remo switched the lens over to the cherubic face of Enrique Esperanza. Remo's finger was on the trigger—or whatever they were called. The thing was whirring. He hoped that meant it was recording and not rewinding. He'd always had trouble with mechanical stuff.

"I am against all hurtful taxes," said the dark-horse candidate for governor.

"You can't be serious. That's boilerplate."

"But I am. Taxes are wrong when they hurt people."

"Would you mind expanding on that?" Cheeta Ching asked, lifting the cookie higher. The dark chocolate aroma wafted into her nose, tickling nasal receptors, which in turn triggered long-dead memory cells. Somehow it brought her back to her teen years, when she'd had a weight problem, and cookies had made her feel so good.

In the middle of an exclusive interview, Cheeta Ching almost did an unspeakable thing. She almost ruined her lipstick by biting into an Oreo sandwich cookie.

As the aromatic dark chocolate floated like some fragrant genie to her lips, she thought that maybe her tiny transgression could be edited out in production.

The Oreo never made it to her blood-red lips.

Instead, it exploded into black chocolate powder and flecks of partially hydrogenated soybean oil creme filling,

as a high-powered bullet pulverized it before burying itself in the fabric of the leather sofa behind her.

Cheeta Ching was rarely at a loss for words. But now
she found herself staring dumbly at her numb forefinger
and thumb, which had been holding the confection.

They stung. And there was a little blood on the ball
of her thumb, which had been scraped in passing.

"I . . . uh . . . oh . . . I . . ." she gulped through
bloodred lips.

Then the room seemed to explode all around her.

10

Before the second bullet shattered the panoramic glass window on the west side of the penthouse, everybody in the room reacted to the first shot.

Everyone, that is, except Cheeta Ching.

Remo Williams helped Cheeta to react by jamming her face deep into the sofa cushions. Cheeta yelped. Remo gave the back of her neck an extra squeeze and she promptly went to sleep.

The second bullet came, bringing with it a shower of plate glass like sharp, crystalline hail.

Harmon Cashman had already thrown himself across the body of Enrique Esperanza. He grabbed the silver tray of Oreos off the coffee table and cradled them from harm as well.

While he waited to die, he used his tongue to soak up cookie crumbs that had fallen like chocolate snow on his coat sleeves.

Remo grabbed both men up, and, tucking them under each arm, rushed to an inner room.

The Master of Sinanju burst in from the outside, crying, "Cheeta! My beloved!"

"I just put her down," Remo called back.

Chiun fell upon the limp anchorwoman, carried her inside in spindly arms, gently placed her on the bed. He turned to Remo.

"Why did you do that?" he demanded, eyes flinty.

"Put her to sleep? So she wouldn't see anything that would get on the news!"

The Master of Sinanju stamped a sandaled foot. "But you have deprived me of my moment of glory! I have rescued the one and only Cheeta, and she does not know!"

"Little Father," Remo said earnestly. "I promise to put in a good word for you when she comes to. Okay?"

Glass shattered in the outer room. It was followed by a snapping, ricochet sound.

"Come on. We have a sniper to slay," Remo urged.

Chiun turned to Esperanza. "Have no fear."

"I have none," said Enrique Espiritu Esperanza. "For I know I am protected by the best."

Chiun, bowing formally, breezed from the room. Remo followed.

"Who is that guy, that he knows all about you?" Remo asked.

"Esperanza is a great man," Chiun said.

"Bulldookey," said Remo.

They weaved their way through the furniture. No bullets struck them. No bullets came at all.

Moving low, they reached the parapet and peered up over the edge.

There was only one sniper. He was crouched on the roof of a high-rise office building, directly across Wilshire. They could see the color of his face. It was as brown as a cashew.

"He looks Latino," Remo whispered.

Chiun stood up and shook an angry fist, which was mostly bone covered by yellow parchment-skin.

"Hear me, O villain!" he called. "I am the Master of Sinanju, and I say that your minutes are numbered!"

The sniper brought his weapon up to his cheek and put an eye to the sniper scope.

It was a mistake. The Master of Sinanju cracked a piece of parapet off the roof combing, and with a flicking motion sent it screaming on its way.

The sniper had no sooner laid the cross hairs onto his target than the scope filled with stone. The stone, moving at terminal velocity, drove the scope into the man's eye socket, shattering it, so that the tube buried itself for half its length in the soft cheese of his brain.

"Scratch one sniper," Remo said, coming to his feet.

"He will never threaten Cheeta again," the Master of Sinanju intoned.

"Not to mention the inspiring Esperanza," Remo said dryly.

"Him, too."

"Too bad you had to waste him," Remo said slowly. "Now he can't tell us who put him up to it."

"We could not risk a stray bullet harming Cheeta."

"Fickle as she is, right?"

"Perhaps something may be learned from that body," Chiun said pointedly.

"Just what I was thinking. You know, it would be a good idea if one of us were to spirit the body away before that hairy barracuda wakes up and starts asking questions."

"*I* do not dispose of bodies," Chiun said icily.

"That means you want the Cheeta detail, huh?"

Chiun considered. "She is fickle, but it may be she will come to see my good qualities."

Remo grinned. "You forget. I have a boon coming to me."

Remo had known the Master of Sinanju a long time. He had seen him angry, greedy, elated, and sad, and every mood in between. But he had never seen the old Korean do a slow burn before.

Chiun first went pale. Then a flush crept up from his neck, which had turned very, very red. The flush suffused his wrinkled visage, until his bald head came to resemble a Christmas bulb with almond eyes.

"Of course," Remo said quickly, not sure that a volcano wasn't about to blow, "for the right word, I might be willing to fetch the body."

The Master of Sinanju's voice was thin. "What word?"

"The P word will do."

"Pale piece of . . ."

"Not what I had in mind. How about 'please'?"

Chiun hesitated. He cleared his throat. Remo waited.

"Aren't you going to say it?" Remo asked.

"I did."

"Huh?"

Chiun cleared his throat again. More clearly, he said, "Is that not sufficient?"

"No. I want to hear the vowels caress my ears."

Chiun parted his dry lips. A word emerged—long, drawn-out, a sibilant hiss.

It sounded like "please." Although it might have been "sneeze" or "bees" or "freeze."

"Close enough for government work," Remo said lightly. "I got the body."

"Then begone, callow one."

On his way to the elevator, Remo called back, "Whatever you do, don't let Esperanza out of your sight!"

"He is safe, never fear."

Remo grinned. "What, me worry?"

Remo took the elevator to the lobby. When the doors opened, he was immediately confronted by a trio of LAPD cops and a flock of press. Since this was the private penthouse elevator, there was no disguising where Remo had come from.

"I don't remember letting you pass," the head cop said.

"Funny, I don't remember passing you," Remo said, offering an ID that identified him as Remo Custer of the Secret Service.

The cop lost his attitude. "Everything all right up there?"

"Shouldn't it be?"

"Guess so."

From that, Remo figured the gunshots hadn't been heard down here. He moved toward the door. The waiting media, smelling a quote, tried to follow him through the lobby.

"Have you any statement?" he was asked.

"Get a life."

Remo foiled them at the revolving door. As soon as he was out on the sidewalk, he gave the door a reverse shove. The door was not meant to go in reverse and it jammed, trapping three reporters in the glass pie-slice sections, and the remainder in the building itself.

Remo slipped across the street and into the office building on the other side. He grabbed the elevator and pressed the highest number, hoping the cage would take him to the top without his having to transfer.

It got as far as the sixth floor. The door opened, and a long-necked mailroom clerk rolled a dirty, canvas-sided mail hamper into the cage, practically squeezing Remo into a corner.

"This going down?" the mail room clerk asked, as the cage resumed its climb.

"This feel like down to you?"

"It feels like up."

"Must be that we're going up."

The mail clerk frowned. "I want down."

"You got up. Tough."

The boy shut his mouth, and started stabbing buttons at random, trying to get the car to stop.

It finally stopped at fifteen. The clerk got out and reached in to pull the hamper out of the cage. The hamper refused to budge.

"I haven't got all day," Remo pointed out.

"It's stuck!"

"This is what happens when you get on the wrong elevator."

"I can't leave it," the clerk said frantically.

"Tell you what," Remo said, "you get off, catch the next elevator to the first floor, and when I get to my floor I'll send this thing down. You can reclaim it in the lobby. How's that?"

"I can't leave this. It's full of important mail."

"I never heard of mail that *wasn't* important," Remo pointed out, "but you can't tie up this elevator until you grow muscles."

The mail clerk was reluctant. Finally he said, "I guess it'll be all right. Promise to send it right down?"

"Scout's honor," said Remo, lifting four fingers ceilingward.

The mail room clerk got off. The doors closed, and Remo removed an inhibiting toe from the metal frame that held the wheels to the hamper.

The rest of the ride was pleasantly uneventful.

On the top floor, Remo pushed the hamper off the elevator, pushed it into a gloomy corner, and went in search of a way to the roof.

It was a drop-down ladder. Remo pulled it down and popped the hatch.

The body of the sniper had almost finished twitching when Remo reached it.

"Chiun musta been nervous," he muttered, gathering up the body. "They almost never twitch this long."

The head wobbled as Remo carted it back to the ladder. That was because the sniper scope, rifle still attached to it, kept swinging with each step.

Down on the top floor, Remo scooped out a bed for the corpse and laid it in the hamper. He covered it with assorted envelopes and packages. The rifle stuck up, so Remo simply snapped it off the scope mount and tossed it away, along with a long mailing tube that kept getting in the way.

That solved the problem.

Whistling, Remo rode the elevator down to the lobby.

The long-necked mailroom clerk was, as Remo had expected, waiting for him impatiently. His eyes were coals of fear. The worried look on his moist, twitchy face turned to one of relief when Remo stepped off, pushing the squeaky-wheeled hamper.

"What took you so long?" the clerk demanded.

Remo pulled his wallet from his chinos and displayed an official-looking ID card.

It read: REMO DRAKE, POSTAL INSPECTOR.

"I'm confiscating this mail hamper," Remo said crisply.

"Why?"

"Random inspection. Washington is looking for reused stamps."

"Reused?"

"Don't play coy with me!" Remo growled. "You know, when they don't get canceled and people peel them off and reuse them."

"I'm sure nobody in this building would—"

"We have machines that can detect postage that has gone through the system once," Remo said solemnly.

"But . . . what about the legal pieces?"

"Don't sweat it. Every piece that passes through the Elmer's sniffer machine without tripping a red light will reach its destination."

"Truth?"

Remo placed his hand over his heart and said, "Son, if I'm lying, may God cancel my soul."

The clerk's eyes widened. "I believe you," he gulped.

"Good for you," Remo said, pushing the hamper out to the sidewalk.

Remo pushed the hamper across the street to the hotel and registered under the name "Remo Ward."

A bellboy came up to him and said, "Luggage, sir?"

Remo pointed out the hamper.

The bellboy went over, peered inside, and said, "This is a mail cart."

"And five bucks says it's my luggage," Remo retorted.

Five bucks was five bucks, so the bellhop obligingly pushed it to one of the regular guest elevators. The police guard and the media got out of his way.

Once they were in the room, Remo paid the bellboy the five dollars and, after he had gone, got on the phone.

"Smitty?" he said. "I have in my possession the sniper who took a shot at Esperanza yesterday."

"Who is he?"

"Good question. There's no ID on him."

"Make him talk. Find out all you can."

"That would be a trick. He's dead."

Smith sighed. "What does he look like, then?"

"Oh, about five-foot-seven, brown complexion, black eyes, and hair you could use for a dry mop."

Remo heard the clicking of rapid keystrokes coming over the phone.

"Distinguishing features?"

"He's got a sniper scope sticking out of his right eye socket."

The keying stopped. The pause on the line was long.

"What about the other one?" Smith asked, his voice like lemonade.

"What other one?" Remo countered.

"Yesterday's attack was the work of two assailants. You say you have only one."

"Good point," Remo said. "I found only one. Maybe he had an accomplice waiting in a getaway car."

"Please investigate further. We need answers."

"Right away," Remo said.

Down on the boulevard Remo circled the neighborhood, checking out parked cars for suspicious people. The only cars parked near the office tower were empty.

Remo pushed into the office building through a revolving door. The minute he started through, he picked up the faint smell of burned gunpowder. Remo kept pushing, following the scent and ending up back in the street.

It was identical to the aroma that still clung to the

sniper rifle Remo had left on the top floor of the building.

Out in the open smells were almost indistinguishable, given the metallic residues in the smog-ridden air. But now that he knew what to smell for, Remo picked up the scent.

He did not sniff. That would have abraded his sensitive olfactory nerves. He simply walked in a careful circle, drawing in a long inhalation through his nose.

The odor seemed to be trailing west, so Remo went west. It grew more bitter. Remo's lungs, taking in the acrid smog, began to burn. He hoped the second killer hadn't gotten far. This was murder on his system.

Around the corner came the sound of a car engine starting. Remo picked up the pace, following the cordite stink around the corner.

He was in time to spot the brown-skinned man pulling away from the curb. In the backseat of his red convertible, a thick mailing tube shifted. It looked like the same one Remo had removed from the mail cart. It was big enough to contain the pieces of the rifle, if it had been disassembled first.

Remo took off after the red convertible, pacing it from the sidewalk. It was easier that way. Less traffic on the sidewalk. Although the roller-blade artists were a problem. Remo sent one into a traffic light and another whipping around a corner, and out of his way.

The typical L.A. traffic helped to slow the red car. Remo came abreast of it before it had cleared the block.

"Pull over!" Remo called, flashing an ID badge. It didn't matter which. The guy wouldn't be able to read it from this distance anyway.

The driver refused to stop. He floored the pedal, and shot out in front of a cab as it came around the corner. The cab driver hit the brakes, spun out of control, and bounced up on the sidewalk.

Remo got out of his way just in time. The driver banged his face on the inside of his windshield. When he took his face out of his hands, Remo saw it was as red as a candied apple.

Angrily, the driver threw the cab into reverse, spun around, and raced off after the red convertible. Remo raced after the taxi. He drew up behind it, his feet seeming to float along the street. When he was in perfect sync with the cab, Remo gave a graceful leap.

The leap looked weak. To a bystander, the cab should have outdistanced Remo easily. Instead, Remo's right foot touched the cab's trunk. His left kept going and found the roof. The other joined it.

Arms wide, bending at the waist like a surfer, Remo kept his balance as the taxi accelerated. He called down, "Don't lose him!"

"Who the fuck are you?" the cabby yelled up.

"A creative passenger," Remo shot back.

"What's your beef with that guy?"

"Tell you when we catch up."

"Well, I want that guy's ass!"

"I won't need that part," Remo said. "It's yours."

The red convertible screeched through an intersection. The cab driver took the right-hand turn before it. Remo leaned into the turn, keeping his balance.

The cabby called up. "You still there, buddy?"

"So far."

The taxi driver knew his streets. He ran the cab up a side street and across, getting in front of the convertible. He slammed on the brakes so hard Remo's body was thrown forward. But his feet stuck to the taxi roof as if Krazy-glued.

There was almost a collision. The red convertible J-turned, burned rubber backing up, and sped back the way it had come. In reverse.

The cabby screeched after him.

"This is a one-way street," Remo warned.

"Tell that to the other guy," the cabby snarled.

"You pull this off, and there's twenty bucks in it."

"Don't worry. The meter's running."

Squinting into the airstream, Remo saw the convertible closing in on the oncoming traffic. It would have to slow down soon, or dart up a side street. If the driver could stop in time, which Remo doubted. The maniac was doing sixty, the wrong way on a busy downtown street.

Whether the convertible would have braked in time to cut down a side street will never be known. As it passed one intersection, it ran a red light.

Coming in from the north was a Backgammon Pizza delivery truck, running a yellow.

The person who had ordered the pizza collected a free Pepperoni Supreme later that day. The next of kin of the deliveryman received a sixty-thousand-dollar death benefit, and collected one-point-three million in a wrongful-death suit from the company.

The driver of the red convertible got a pauper's grave, because he was mangled beyond recognition at the moment of impact, then incinerated to a blackened twist of meat when his gas tank ignited.

The smell of burning pizza and human flesh was not long in coming.

The taxi slowed to a stop and Remo hopped off the cab roof. The cabby came out from behind the wheel, his mouth slack in horror and his eyes sick.

Remo reached the twisted, burning mass of metal, and saw the flames shrivel and blacken the driver of the red convertible. When the flames reached the backseat, and the mailing tube, it began jumping and making popcorn sounds. A bullet whined up through the bubbling paint of the roof and knocked out an overhead streetlight.

Remo pulled the cab driver back. "Bullets," he warned.

"You a cop?" the shaken driver croaked.

Remo ignored the question. "So, what's the fare?" he asked.

"How can you think of money at a time like this?"

"Good point," Remo said cheerfully. "Can I keep the tip, too?"

The cabby picked that moment to vomit up his lunch. While he was filling the gutter, Remo slipped away.

He was not having a good day. But there's one consolation, he thought to himself. If there were only two people out to snuff Enrique Espiritu Esperanza, both are now out of the picture.

Even Harold Smith couldn't find fault with that.

11

When Remo reached him by phone, Harold W. Smith's reaction was typically Smith.

"You say the second gunman was burned to death?"

"To a crisp," Remo said sourly. "If you're going to quote me, do it right."

"Remo, this is serious."

"The way I see it, Smitty," Remo said absently, lifting the covers of his bed to check on the first gunman, "this is a happy ending. We have our killers."

"But we do not know who hired them," Smith pointed out.

"No, but we can put on our little thinking caps and guess. General Nogeira. Since he's dead and they're dead, Chiun and I should be outta here by sundown. And not a moment too soon."

"I would rather you remained in Los Angeles, Remo."

"Sure you don't want what's behind Door Number Two?" Remo asked airily.

"Er, what do you mean?"

"I mean even as we speak, several floors over my head, Chiun is mooning over a certain hatchet-faced Korean anchorwitch."

Harold Smith sucked in a dry breath that seemed forceful enough to dislodge Remo's right eardrum. "Not Cheeta Ching?"

"Funny," Remo said dryly, "that was my exact thought when I first spotted her."

"Ah, do you think this represents a security threat?"

"If by 'threat,' you mean do I think Chiun is on the verge of making a major conquest, no."

"Good."

"On the other hand," Remo added, "she has the hots for me."

"Cheeta *Ching*?"

"Wants me to be her partner in procreation," Remo said lightly.

"Remo, under no circumstance are you to appear on camera with Cheeta Ching," Harold Smith said tightly.

"Smitty, where Cheeta Ching is concerned, I'm strictly behind the camera. I was running her minicam when her interview was interrupted by the sniper."

"Is there a chance your camera picked up anything important?"

"Search me. I dropped it when the ruckus started. It could have picked up anything, from the sniper to Chiun."

"Remo," Smith said, urgency coming into the lemon-flavored voice, "obtain that tape. I do not care how you do it."

Remo sighed resignedly. So much for heading east. "Anything else?"

"Yes. I would like a photograph of the dead man. He is still with you?"

"Decomposing peacefully," Remo said lightly, dropping the bedding on the dead sniper's waxy gray face. "What do I do with the body afterward?"

"I do not care. But before you dispose of it, I would like fingerprint samples as well."

"Anything else? Blood type? Nose hair clippings? Ear-wax samples?"

"Remo, this is serious."

"Tell you what, Smitty. Looks like I'm going to have a busy day. Why don't I just ship the guy to Folcroft?"

"Absolutely not!"

"Oh, don't thank me," Remo said sweetly. "I'll even include return correct postage."

"Remo!"

Laughing, Remo hung up. Things were getting better. He had Smith's goat, and Chiun owed him peace of mind for an unspecified period of time and a boon to be named at a later date. No sense squandering that one too soon.

As he took the stairs to the penthouse, Remo thought that he might hold that boon over Chiun's head for a good long time.

* * *

When Remo came over the parapet—the only way to the penthouse that didn't involve returning to the lobby and catching the penthouse elevator—Cheeta Ching was interviewing herself.

She stood in a corner of the living room, the minicam in her hands. She was pointing it at her own face and speaking into the directional mike. Her thumb was holding down the trigger.

"For the first time in the history of television, an attempt has been made on the life of a network anchor," she said shrilly. "Only moments ago, in this very room, this reporter narrowly escaped a sniper's bullet. Obviously, the killer had been aiming at my head, and—"

Remo sidled up to the Master of Sinanju, who stood off to one side with Enrique Espiritu Esperanza and Harmon Cashman, watching the spectacle with varying degrees of disbelief written on their faces.

"How long has this been going on?" Remo asked.

"Since you left," Harmon Cashman murmured. "She actually believes she was the target."

"Maybe that's good. You don't want this kind of bad publicity for the campaign."

"Of course we do," Cashman said instantly.

Remo blinked. "You do?"

"This is better than an endorsement from the President."

Remo looked at Harmon Cashman. Then at Chiun. Chiun shrugged as if to say, "All whites are mad. Did you not know?"

Enrique Espiritu Esperanza introduced a note of sanity.

"It would be better for all concerned if this embarrassing spectacle did not go out over the air," he said quietly.

"I like your thinking," Remo said. "How about I steal it?"

"I do not like that word. I am a moral man."

"Borrow it, then?" Remo suggested.

"Borrow is good," Harmon Cashman said quickly.

"The trick," Remo said, looking at the white-knuckled way Cheeta Ching was holding the minicam up to her flat face, "will be prying those bony talons from the camera grip."

They decided to wait until Cheeta ran out of tape. The

way she was going, only that would bring the self-interview to a bloodless conclusion.

Meanwhile, Remo filled them in on his attempt to locate the killers.

"They are dead?" asked Enrique Espiritu Esperanza, his cherubic face sad. It was clear that the deaths saddened him. Even the deaths of murderers.

"We do not fail," Chiun said sternly, his wistful eyes on Cheeta's flat profile, as if beholding true beauty.

"What do you see in her?" Remo whispered.

"Grace," said the Master of Sinanju.

Remo thought she looked like Medusa staring down the minicam.

"Unless there are more of these guys in the woodwork, this should be the end of it," he added.

"Have you no idea as to their identity, these two men?" asked Esperanza.

Remo shook his head. "No ID on them. But they looked Hispanic."

"Hispanic?" Harmon Cashman mumbled. "They're our core support. Why would Hispanics want to kill Ricky?"

Remo shrugged. He decided not to mention the Nogeira connection. It would only complicate things. "Maybe they were just crazies," he suggested.

Enrique Esperanza nodded. "Ah, *loco*. That I understand."

Over in the corner the minicam clicked, and the faint whir of the videotape cartridge came to a stop.

"Oh, damn!" Cheeta Ching swore.

Chiun gasped, as if a priest had loudly passed gas.

"Let me get that," Remo said helpfully, seeing his opportunity.

Cheeta turned. Her eyes took in Remo. They lost their dagger's edge, softened to melting hot-tar blobs.

"Demo!" she squeaked.

"Remo."

"Romeo!"

"Demo is fine. Call me Demo."

"Oh, Demo, would you be a darling and get me a fresh tape from that arthritic cameraman of mine? He's down in the lobby—probably updating his resumé."

"Sure," Remo said. "In fact, why don't I get fresh batteries for this thing while I'm at it?"

"That," Cheeta Ching said breathily, "is the most brilliant suggestion I ever heard. Anyone ever tell you you're a natural-born cameraman?"

"Not this week," Remo said brightly, taking the minicam from Cheeta's slow-to-unclench hands. He noted that the pistol grip was slippery with sweat when he took hold of it.

"I won't be a moment," Remo said. He winked. Cheeta beamed. In the corner, Chiun glowered.

Remo felt Cheeta Ching's eyes follow him as he floated to the elevator. On his way out, he bared his teeth. It made him look like he was smiling. No point in blowing this when it was going to be so easy.

Remo had barely reached the elevator when he heard a squeaky voice say, "I know something you do not."

"Oh, no," Remo said under his breath. "Chiun. Don't do this to me."

"What's that?" Cheeta asked suspiciously.

"Chiun . . ." Remo groaned.

"You have surrendered your precious tape to a notorious kleptomaniac," Chiun warned.

"What!"

"It is true," Chiun said loftily. "He is tricky-fingered. Notoriously tricky-fingered."

"He's just jealous!" Remo called back. He made his lips grin. By grinding his teeth, he seemed to smile wider. He hoped his eyes smiled with them. He doubted it very much.

The doors opened just in time. Giving Cheeta a limp little wave, Remo stepped back.

Cheeta, her eyes stricken, torn between hope and fear, waved back. Her wave was even more feeble than Remo's.

The doors snicked shut.

Remo breathed a sigh of relief as he rode the elevator down.

In the lobby, he called out, "Where's Cheeta Ching's cameraman?"

"Out committing suicide," someone said in a bored voice.

"Why?"

"He was too slow. He knows he's dead. He just doesn't want to die the Shark's way."

"Cheeta the Shark?" Remo asked.

"They call her the Korean Shark."

"They," Remo said, "have a higher opinion of her than I do."

Remo got a ripple of nervous laughter that broke the ice enough for him to ask, "I need two fresh videocassettes, and I'll pay well for them."

"How well?" a voice asked.

"A hundred each."

Minicams popped their ports and began disgorging black, plastic boxes. No two looked alike.

"I need ones that will fit this baby," Remo said, hefting his minicam. Half the tapes were withdrawn.

Remo exchanged two hundred-dollar bills for two cassettes. He went off into corner to change tapes.

A minute later he called out, "A fifty to the guy who shows me how to open this thing."

Remo hurried back to his hotel room, took the original tape, and shoved it down the front of the dead man's shirt. Then he tucked him back into bed, making sure his head was covered. He was beginning to smell, Remo found. He would deal with that later. Before he shipped the stiff back east to Folcroft.

Then he took the lobby route back to the penthouse. The sooner I get this over with the better, he told himself.

Cheeta Ching's stiff mask of a face almost cracked with joy when Remo sauntered into the penthouse, brandishing the two tapes. In fact, makeup flecks from the anchorwoman's chin rained onto the carpet like pink dandruff.

"Ta-dah!" he crowed.

"Excellent!" Cheeta said, grabbing the minicam. She popped a cassette in and handed the rig back to Remo.

"Now interview me," she ordered. "All of us. Ask me any question that comes to mind. Just leave my fallopian tubes out of it, okay?"

"What about Ricky's interview?" asked Harmon Cashman.

Cheeta looked blank. "Ricky?"

"The guy you came to talk to in the first place," Harmon pointed out. "You know, the candidate."

Cheeta's face fell. "Oh. That's right. I guess I should

do that, too, shouldn't I?" She looked to Remo. Remo said, "I can get you all the videotape you could ever want. Or I can send my little friend, Chiun, to fetch it. He owes me a favor. A big one."

The Master of Sinanju drank in this spectacle with widening eyes. His face was ashen, the wrinkles flattening in shock.

"Augh!" he said, storming from the room.

That left the coast clear for the interview. Remo got the minicam going, and Enrique Espiritu Esperanza took a seat opposite Cheeta Ching.

The interview began. Cheeta was obviously distracted. At one point she noticed the blood on her thumb, and began sucking on it. Remo made sure he captured the precious sight on tape.

When it was over, Remo realized he had learned almost nothing about Enrique Esperanza that he hadn't already known. And he knew almost nothing about the man.

"Got enough?" Remo said doubtfully.

"Plenty. This will be a sidebar to the main story," she said, snatching the minicam from Remo's hand and the other blank from the coffee table and starting for the elevator.

"I have to rush this to editing in time for the five-o'clock feed. Coming?"

"I'm not hungry," Remo said, straight-faced.

"I'll be in touch, Nemo."

"Demo."

"Get your resumé together."

"Count on it," Remo said, waving Cheeta off.

After she had gone, the Master of Sinanju reentered the penthouse.

"Never have I been so humiliated in all my life," he huffed.

"Wait'll I call in my marker," Remo said dryly.

"Augh!" said Chiun, storming out into the smog-laden air once more.

Remo started for the elevator. "Chiun will keep an eye on you," he told Enrique and Harmon Cashman.

"Where are going?" Cashman asked.

"I got a package to mail to the folks back home, and I want to hit the post office before it closes."

12

That evening, the second attempt to assassinate gubernatorial candidate Enrique Espiritu Esperanza led the BCN *Evening News with Don Cooder*.

There was no tape shown. Instead, after an opening background piece, they went to a satellite hook-up interview between Don Cooder and Cheeta Ching. Millions of viewers nationwide were treated to a rare view of the back of the anchor's thick helmet of black hair and the sight of Cheeta Ching, teeth on edge, answering harsh questions.

"Cheeta. About this alleged second attempt . . ."

Cheeta glowered. "It was *not* alleged. I was there!"

"True. But I was not. So let's say 'alleged.' The sniper, he was shooting at random, was he?"

"No! He was shooting at me! He grazed my thumb."

Cheeta Ching held up her heavily bandaged thumb for ninety million Americans to behold.

Don Cooder pressed on. "What about the candidate? Was he frightened? Obviously cowed? Did he wet his pants?"

"I didn't notice," Cheeta admitted glumly. "I was too busy protecting my reproductive system with my body. I lose that, and there will be no future Cheeta Chings to carry on the superanchorwoman tradition I single-handedly pioneered."

Don Cooder swung around in his seat, gave the camera a steely look, and said, "Obviously, Cheeta has yet to recover from her remarkable brush with death. Speaking for her colleagues here at BCN, I wish her godspeed and good news on the fertility front. More news, after this."

"They didn't even show the interview!" Harmon Cashman complained, jumping up from his seat.

Enrique Esperanza patted the air with his hands. "Harmon, sit down please. It is of no moment. There will be other interviews."

"I'll bet that damn Cooder killed the piece. You could just see the jealousy crackle between those two."

Harmon Cashman resumed his seat in the living room of the penthouse suite overlooking Los Angeles, now a forest of fiery towers in the setting sun. Absently, he took an Oreo cookie off a silver tray and gave it a hard squeeze. Creme filling oozed out, and he began licking it. His eyes went to the tiny wisp of a Korean, who stood out on the parapet, taking in the blazing sunset.

"I don't get it. Why bring that little guy into the campaign organization?" he asked.

"He is Korean. We must reach out to all people, all colors, if we are to win."

"You know, Ricky, no matter what you do, you're still a long shot."

Enrique Espiritu Esperanza laughed good-naturedly. "I do not mind being a long shot. Just so long as I am not shot before election day."

Harmon Cashman stopped licking. "Who the hell could be trying to kill you? It doesn't make sense."

"Perhaps someone who sees that I am a threat to the established order. You know, Harmon, that this state simmers with racial tension."

"Yeah, white people are petrified at the numbers of illegals coming across the border, and jealous of the Asians coming in from Hong Kong. The black people see their piece of the pie being gobbled up by everyone else. One day, it may just explode."

"Not if all these people come together."

"Never happen."

"What if they are *brought* together?" asked Enrique Esperanza, taking his empty brown fists and bringing them together, with a sound like tupperware containers bumping.

"By you?"

Enrique Espiritu Esperanza nodded. "By me."

"Look," Harmon said, "you got the Hispanic vote sewed up, if you stick with that. The white liberals will help. Yeah. Might even bring us in second. But you go after the black and Asian vote, and you're wasting your time. Hell, most of the blacks don't even vote. And the Asians are too busy holding down two-three jobs to have the time."

"Harmon, do you know why I chose Los Angeles County to launch my campaign?"

"Sure. Because it's got a humungous Hispanic population. No mystery there."

"No. Because L.A. County is the blueprint for the future of this country. The black, Asian, and Hispanic populations are mushrooming. The white people are in decline. In twenty, thirty, perhaps fifty years, all of America will be like this."

Harmon Cashman paused in the act of separating an Oreo sandwich in halves, exposing the white creme filling. "It will?"

"These are the trends. I have studied them. Carefully."

Harmon Cashman put down his Oreo. He was from the South, had grown up in Virginia. He remembered the Old South. How intolerant it had been. He also remembered how much safer it had been.

Enrique Espiritu Esperanza went on. "White people, whom I call *blancos*, are growing nervous. They see their cultural dominance in decline. They fear for their future, and the future of their children and grandchildren. But there is nothing they can do. Immigration is immigration. New children are born every day, in all colors. Their skin colors happen not to be white."

"My God!"

"But there is a way to allay these fears," Enrique Esperanza added quickly.

"What? Tell me!"

"A new idea. One that is taking root all over. One that will erase these fears, all barriers."

"What? What is it?"

"Multiculturalism."

"Huh?"

"It is a brave new philosophy," Esperanza said. "I am not the candidate of color, but of hope. I represent the man who will lift up people of color, while at the same time protecting the *blancos* from the erosion of their estate in life."

Harmon Cashman frowned. "Sounds like Rainbow Coalition stuff. You sure you're not talking Rainbow Coalition? You know that won't fly with the electorate.
Especially down in Orange County."

"No, it will not fly," Enrique Esperanza admitted.
"But multiculturalism will."

Harmon Cashman's eyes went to the tiny wisp of a
Korean then.

"Tell you what—you bring that little fellow in here
and tell him that. Let's see if it goes over with him."

"Agreed," said Enrique Espiritu Esperanza.

The Master of Sinanju stared into the setting sun. It
burned his tender features, wise with age. Never had he
felt such pain. Never before had he been so wounded.

The mellow sound of Enrique Espiritu Esperanza's
voice dispelled his pain like a soothing pool of light.

Turning, the Master of Sinanju padded into the room
where the man called Esperanza waited with his white
lackey.

"I am at your service," said Chiun, using polite words
he did not feel.

"I am glad to hear this, because I have a favor to ask
of you," said Enrique Espiritu Esperanza.

"Speak."

"I will be governor of this state in less than a month's
time."

"If the people are with you," Chiun added pointedly.

"They are with me. With your help."

"As long as the Master of Sinanju stands at your side,
you need not fear for your safety."

"And I do not. But I need more than that."

Chiun wrinkled his button nose. "I am no soldier, who
volunteers to perform lesser tasks. You know what I
am?"

"I do. And it is with that in mind that I make the
following offer to you."

"Continue."

"I have yet to select my cabinet."

Hearing this, Harmon Cashman gulped. "Ricky . . .
Think about this," he said hotly.

"I will soon be governor of the state with the largest
economy in this country. An economy that is ranked as

the seventh largest on the face of this earth. I need someone to attend to the financial concerns of this economy.
Someone to handle the money."

Between anguished fingers, Harmon Cashman ground
his bifurcated Oreo into crumbly bits.

"How much money?" asked the Master of Sinanju
coolly.

"Billions," replied Enrique Esperanza.

"Continue," Chiun invited.

"The person who performs this task is called a
'treasurer.' "

"An honored post, since before Egyptian times."

"I would be honored if you would consent to be my
treasurer," said Enrique Espiritu Esperanza.

The Master of Sinanju took in the words of the man
called Esperanza. He saw a man of vision, of unsurpassed
brilliance, one who knew the value of the House of Sinanju without being told. One who recognized greatness
when he came upon it.

In this bitter hour, it was more than enough.

"I accept," said the Master of Sinanju, bowing deeply.

"I am honored," returned Enrique Esperanza, matching the bow.

Off to one side, Harmon Cashman groaned as if he'd
been impaled by a Zulu spear.

"Now let me tell you how I plan to achieve this goal
and bring us both to power. . . ." Enrique Espiritu
Esperanza continued smoothly.

"It is called cultimulcherism," Chiun said into the
telephone.

"Good for it," Remo said. "I've booked a room in the
hotel. Forty-four D. Any time you feel like coming
down, feel free."

"It will not be necessary."

"Okay, I guess we take turns guarding Esperanza then.
When do you want to be relieved?"

"Your services will no longer be required."

"Cut it out, Chiun. For crying out loud. You don't
speak for the organization. And until Smitty pulls us both
off this one, I'm as stuck as you are."

"I am not speaking for Smith or for the organization,"

said Chiun testily. "I am speaking for Esperanza. I have joined his crusade in cultimulcherism."

"Never heard of it."

"In return, he has promised me the exalted position of Lord Treasurer of California."

"He what!"

"Where I shall rule in splendor, issuing wise decrees, and being appreciated by all."

"And skimming any small change that passes through your hands," Remo suggested darkly.

"Of course there is a magnificent salary attendant to this position," Chiun said loftily. "As befits one of my grace."

"Smitty won't like this, Chiun."

"I will leave it to you to convey my regret to Emperor Smith that our current contract negotiations have borne no fruit."

Remo said, "You're not quitting, are you?"

Silence.

"Chiun?"

"This is a decision I will make at a later date," Chiun said at last.

"How much later?"

"Possibly after the glorious day of election."

"Somehow I knew you were going to say that. But I gotta tell Smitty what you're up to anyway."

"I am certain he will understand. I can better serve him here in the outlying provinces of his empire, if I am in a position of responsibility."

"Don't bet on it," Remo said, hanging up.

Harold W. Smith should have reached for the Maalox when he received the news from Remo Williams. But his stomach did not flare with acid. He should have grabbed the aspirin and wolfed down two or three chewable orange tablets, but strangely, his head felt fine.

"Could you repeat that, Remo?" he said into the receiver. His knuckles tightened imperceptibly. The other hovered over the drawer where he kept his array of medicines.

"Chiun's joining the Esperanza campaign," Remo said wearily. "Says Esperanza has offered him the post of treasurer if he's elected."

"According to the most recent polls, there is a very slim chance of that," Smith pointed out dryly.

"That's a relief. But where does that leave me? I've been laid off from the campaign."

Smith's hand came away from the drawer. He definitely did not feel like a Tums or a chewable aspirin. It was a liberating feeling.

"Simply await developments," he told Remo.

"Did I mention that Esperanza knows about Sinanju?"

"He does?"

"At least, he claims to."

"Sinanju is not a secret," Smith said calmly. "CURE is. It is entirely possible that Esperanza is familiar with the legends of the House of Sinanju. He might accept Chiun as the inheritor of a long-dead tradition. Certainly, no more than that."

"I didn't know, Smitty. Once he understood we were on the job, he acted as if he was immune from harm."

"Hmmm. Curious."

"You okay, Smitty?"

"Why do you ask?"

"Oh, nothing. It's just that you usually don't take bad news this well."

"I do not see a great problem here. Chiun will continue to protect Esperanza, and you will remain in the area in case you are needed. And there is no chance of Chiun's assuming a cabinet post. When he realizes this, I will be in a better bargaining position when we start serious contract negotiations."

"Makes sense. But you're not acting like yourself."

"There is still the matter of the dead assassin's photograph and fingerprints," Smith reminded.

"Not to mention the Cheeta Ching tape."

"Yes, that too."

"All are winging their merry way to Folcroft. I just hope the tape doesn't smell too bad by the time it gets there."

"Why would it be?" Smith asked, his voice puzzled.

"You'll find out," Remo said, hanging up quickly.

At the other end of the nation, Harold W. Smith replaced the receiver. His necktie felt too tight, and he loosened the precise Windsor knot.

Remo, he was confident, was only bluffing. There was no way on earth he had expressed a corpse to Folcroft. It was preposterous.

But to be on the safe side, Harold Smith stopped to speak with the lobby guard on his way out of the building. He gave explicit instructions that any unusually large crates or boxes that arrived at the front desk were to be placed, unopened, in a storage room and the arrival brought to his attention. Immediately.

Then he went home, feeling liberated. He was especially glad to be free of his daily antacid pills. He had read that they contained aluminum, which had a tendency to build up deposits in the brain. Aluminum was suspected of contributing to Alzheimer's disease, a fate Harold W. Smith wished very much to avoid. Otherwise, how could he remember to take his poison pill if the need ever arose?

13

The overnight polls changed the public perception of the California governor's race.

Before, only two candidates had placed in the running. Barry Black, Junior and Rona Ripper. They had been virtually neck-and-neck in the eyes of an electorate which had come to despise the previous governor and was apathetic about electing his replacement.

The previous poll had showed Black and Ripper tied, with less than twenty percent of the respondents expressing a preference. Two percent had endorsed Esperanza. Less than one percent wanted the interim governor— the previous California Secretary of State—to continue in office. The remaining seventy-seven percent had declared themselves undecided.

The new poll put it at a three-way tie between Black, Ripper, and Enrique Espiritu Esperanza.

When Harmon Cashman read the poll results in the morning edition of *The Los Angeles Times*, over coffee and Oreos, he leaped from his seat and said, "I'm jazzed! I'm really jazzed!"

Enrique Espiritu Esperanza came out of the shower, wrapping a terry-cloth robe about his sturdy body and saying, "Good news?"

Cashman started to dance about the room. "It's a dead heat! Look at these polls! We have a chance! We have a chance!"

From the living room, a squeaky querulous voice came.

"Silence! An artist is at work!"

Harmon Cashman subsided. "Artist?"

"My very good friend Chiun is preparing new campaign posters," Enrique Esperanza said.

"What's wrong with the old?"

"They were in English and Spanish. These are in Korean, Chinese, and Japanese."

"This, I gotta see," said Harmon Cashman, snatching up a fresh cookie.

In the next room, the little Asian sat on a reed mat. Offset posters featuring the wide, benevolent face of Enrique Espiritu Esperanza were scattered about the rug. The old Korean was dipping a goose quill in a flat shallow stone that was dark with ink.

Holding the quill over a poster with a seemingly awkward grip, the old Korean stared at the blank space under the image of Esperanza.

Then he began painting broad strokes, which he bisected by thinner, more ornate ones. When he was through he lifted the quill, laid the poster aside, and exposed another one in its place.

The quill went to work again.

Harmon Cashman turned to his candidate. "Chinese?"

"I am not sure. I just know what he is writing."

"If you don't know the language, how can you tell what it says?"

Enrique Espiritu Esperanza smiled. "The word 'hope' is a universal one, my friend."

The posters began appearing in Chinatown, Little Tokyo, and Koreatown by ten o'clock.

The Master of Sinanju stood on a street in Koreatown, before a mural depicting Shin Saim-Dong, a mother figure from Korean folklore, surveying his handiwork.

On buildings and light poles all around, portraits of Enrique Esperanza stared out. Passersby paused to look, and read, then walked on.

The Master of Sinanju allowed himself a tight smile. It was working. Who could *not* vote for the man called "Esperanza," with the endorsement of the Master of Sinanju?

As he paused to drink in his triumph, a pair of young Koreans dressed in ridiculous jeans and Western shirts walked past.

"Who the heck is the Master of Sinanju?" one asked the other.

"Search me."

Chiun's eyes went wide. Were these Koreans, or Japanese wearing Korean faces?

An old woman strolled by, laden with bundles. Her back was bent with a lifetime of cares, and her hair was the color of steel wool. She stopped before a light pole and blinked owlishly at the poster there.

Chiun approached. He cleared his throat respectfully.

"This says that the candidate Esperanza is endorsed by no less than the Master of Sinanju," he said politely. "How could one not vote for such a man?"

The old woman spat. "It is a trick. The Masters of Sinanju are long dead. Besides, of what value is the recommendation of a pack of killers and thieves?"

"We were never thieves!" Chiun howled.

"Do not shout at me, old man."

"I am not shouting, you bony cow! I am spreading enlightenment. You must be from the lazy south."

"And you from the cold and bitter north."

"Southern farmer's wife!" Chiun fumed.

"Northern fishmonger!" snapped the old woman, storming off.

Face tight, the Master of Sinanju retreated to the mural of Shin Saim-Dong. He looked up at the benevolent features, her hair tied up in the traditional *ch'ok*, delicate hands properly resting in the lap of her kimono.

It was a good face, he saw. A country face. Solid and of the earth. At least some traditions were honored, in this degenerate colony of his countrymen.

Perhaps, Chiun thought, when the election was done with, he would take up residence here. It would be fitting. His former home had been confiscated by his emperor, due to yet another transgression on Remo's part. He would need a new home. Perhaps here. Once the people were reeducated, they would make good subjects. Of course, the Japanese and Chinese would have to be moved. It would not be seemly for a Master of Sinanju to dwell in too close proximity to such as they.

He was certain there would be a cultimulcheral way to accomplish this.

As the Master of Sinanju considered these weighty matters, he heard a tearing sound. He spun.

A man—a white, beefy of face—was removing one of

the posters the Master of Sinanju had carefully affixed to a wall.

Chiun flew to this man, demanding, "Why do you do this, white?"

"They gotta come down," the white grunted, ripping down the poster in stubborn strips.

"Explain!"

"No union bug."

"Bug?"

He pointed to a black spot on the poster, where the Master of Sinanju had obscured some white graffiti.

"Orders from my union chief. Posters without the bug come down."

With a flourish, the white stripped the wall bare of all remnants of the poster.

"There are many similar posters," Chiun pointed out, his voice steely. "You cannot remove them all."

"Wanna bet?"

"They will be restored."

"All my shop will be out tomorrow to tear 'em down all over again," the white said, in the stubborn fashion of his kind.

"Not if they are dissuaded from this."

"What's gonna dissuade them? We're union. You can't buck a union."

"I understand that the Master of Sinanju himself has endorsed this man Esperanza," Chiun said, hoping to appeal to the white's innate sense of respect for his betters.

"Fuck the Master of Sinanju," said the beefy white, spitting on the artfully calligraphed poster that lay on the sidewalk.

Fred Huntoon weighed nearly two hundred and fifteen pounds. He was a pressman. Rotary presses. The muscles he had developed in the course of pursuing his trade had not grown soft in the years since he had become a union steward. If anything, he had become more formidable. Rotary presses do not punch back.

As he turned to deal with the offending campaign posters plastered all over Koreatown, Fred Huntoon felt every muscle in his thick body spasm and twitch.

"It will stop when the poster is restored to the wall," a squeaky voice said through the ringing in his ears.

"I want it to stop now!" Fred Huntoon howled, feeling his out-of-control feet dance in pain. Even his earlobes hurt. How could that be?

"It will stop," the squeaky voice repeated, "when the poster is restored."

"It . . . it's torn!"

"So too will you be," promised the squeaky voice.

The voice was no more threatening than Pee-Wee Herman's, but what was happening to Fred Huntoon's big body was real. And he wanted it to stop. Lord, how he wanted it to stop.

Through eyes that were blurred by hot tears of pain, Fred Huntoon knelt to the sidewalk and gathered up the poster fragments.

He arranged them in order, and using his tongue, licked the blank sides like a gargantuan stamp.

They would not stick. The poster pieces peeled back, as if treated with wall-repellent.

"It don't stick!" he bleated.

"Lick the wall, too."

It was an excellent suggestion. Fred Huntoon had a tongue as big as his desire to please the owner of the squeaky voice. He lathered saliva onto the gritty brick wall and freshened the application on the back side of the poster. He tried again.

"It sticks! It's sticking! It's stuck!" he said gratefully.

"For now. It might fall."

"I'll stand here and hold it up if I have to," he offered.

"You have to," said the squeaky voice.

Then, and only then, the pain went away. Just like that. Fred Huntoon, when he had blinked the last bitter tear from his face, turned around to look.

He saw the little Asian guy strolling off, casually as can be. He disappeared around a corner. The danger seemed to have passed.

Still, Fred Huntoon decided that he should keep his hands on the poster, at least until sundown.

As people passed him by, Fred Huntoon, to cover his embarrassment, offered a piece of friendly advice.

"Vote for Esperanza! The union guy's friend!"

Gregory Sagadelli was President and treasurer of the California Pressman's Union. It was a strong union. It was strong because the men who comprised the membership roll were strong. Weak men did not run presses. And weak men did not lead pressmen.

So when the first reports of campaign posters appearing in the Asian part of town without the union bug—*his* union bug—reached his ears, Gregory Sagadelli ordered the membership out into the streets to take corrective action.

"No wonder someone's trying to whack out that Esperanza guy. He's nuts!" he joked, as he ordered his men to tear down every offending poster in Koreatown.

They started coming back in ones and twos. Some limped. A few had broken fingers. Some did not return at all. They were discovered in the hospital, invoking their union insurance benefits.

"This is fuckin' war!" Gregory Sagadelli screamed, when he had heard the same story for the fifth time. A little gook had done this. A little gook working for the Esperanza campaign.

He was on his way out of the union meeting hall when the little gook came in, escorted by two of his stewards.

"This him?" Gregory Sagadelli demanded.

"This is him," one of the pair said, in a dispirited voice.

Gregory Sagadelli gave his trousers a belligerent hitch. "You did right to bring him here," he grunted, jabbing a thick finger into the little gook's stern face. "You, chum, are going to pay for this."

"I am called Chiun, not Chum."

"After today, your name will be mud."

"After today," said the little gook named Chiun, "you will be proud to say that you stand with Esperanza the Cultimulcheral."

"I what?"

"After you have atoned for your transgressions against him, of course."

"Say . . . that . . . again," Gregory Sagadelli said through clenched teeth.

The little gook snapped his long-nailed fingers. Instantly, the flanking union men produced stacks of Esperanza campaign posters.

"You will have your minions and lackeys place these where they will do the most good," said the little gook named Chiun.

Gregory Sagadelli grunted. "You got balls."

"He's also got hands like you've never seen," said one of the flanking men.

"Huh?"

"Mr. Sagadelli," said the other, "if you don't do exactly like he says, we're all headed for traction."

That was enough for Gregory Sagadelli. He was a street fighter, with a street fighter's instincts. Old or not, he took a poke at the frail little gook.

The fist traveled less than a foot. The little gook brought his open hands up to intercept the fist, like a catcher without a mitt.

Gregory Sagadelli felt the impact. He was sure he felt the impact. Swore to it, for many years after.

When they had finished pouring cold water on his face, and after he had batted the smelling salts away with his sprained fist, the membership put it another way.

"You hit yourself in the jaw."

"I hit the gook," Gregory Sagadelli insisted.

"There's a bruise on your jaw, and those knuckles are sprained," a delegate pointed out.

"I felt a fuckin' impact."

"In your jaw. The membership wants to know if we can start putting up the Esperanza posters now."

"The hell with the posters."

"We'd like you to reconsider."

"Why?"

"Because if you don't, we gotta run your dumb ass through a rotary press to protect our own dumb asses. Sorry."

It was then that Gregory Sagadelli noticed the little gook standing off to one side, looking stern and confident. It was as if he were looking at the tiny fellow for the first time. There was something cold and deadly in those eyes. They were like steel ball bearings.

Gregory Sagadelli allowed himself to be helped to his feet. "Put up the damn posters," he snarled.

He strode over to the tiny Oriental. He looked down. The Oriental looked up.

"Anything else you want?" Gregory Sagadelli asked.

"Yes. Your endorsement of my candidate."

"Bull! We can't endorse someone who doesn't buy union. What'll we tell the press?"

A low voice whispered in his ear. "Maybe this is the exception that proves the rule."

That afternoon, with the entire ambulatory membership of the California Pressmen's Union Local 334 out affixing Esperanza posters to walls all over L.A. County, Gregory Sagadelli called a press conference and announced that the entire union was coming out for Enrique Espiritu Esperanza.

There were only three reporters present. Such was the state of union activity in the nineties. One said, "We understand they don't use union printed placards."

"This is the exception that proves the rule," said Gregory Sagadelli with a straight face. Or as straight as it could be, with his jaw permanently skewed to the left.

"We just picked up our first union endorsement!" Harmon Cashman screamed. "I'm hyped! I'm really, really hyped!"

"Calm yourself," said Enrique Esperanza, hitting the TV remote control. "It is a small victory. We will need much, much more in the weeks that remain."

"But this is the first union endorsement of the campaign! Sometimes that's all you need to get the ball rolling!"

"The ball, as you say, is already rolling."

"What I don't figure is, how did it happen?"

"It is simple. Chiun."

Harmon Cashman dug into his pockets and pulled out a minipack of Oreo cookies. "The little guy? How'd he pull it off?"

"Because there is nothing he cannot do. You must understand, Harmon. He is Sinanju."

"What's that?"

"Sinanju is a house of assassins."

At the sound of the word assassin, Harmon Cashman spit out the half-chewed sticky pulp of an Oreo sandwich cookie. He stared at the dark blob on the rug, as if he were contemplating gobbling it back up. His eyes, sick with fear, went to the bland face of Enrique Esperanza. "Ricky . . ."

"Yes. I did say 'assassin,'" Enrique Esperanza said calmly. "For many, many years the assassins of Sinanju worked for governments all over the Old World, protecting thrones and preventing wars."

"You're joking!"

"Have you ever known me to joke?"

"Never. But I had to check. Okay, let's say this is true. What's this Chiun doing here?"

"Obviously he was sent here."

"To kill you?"

"Hardly. To protect me."

"I don't get it."

Enrique Esperanza fixed Harmon Cashman with his soft, dark eyes. "It is very clear, Harmon. The Master of Sinanju has been sent here by his employer to protect my life and see that the election turns out a certain way."

"Who would that be?"

"I am not sure, but everything in my being tells me it is the President of the United States."

"Oh, him," said Harmon Cashman. "The thank-you-note king."

"Do not hold grudges. Because if what I believe is true, then our campaign has the blessing of the President, which virtually assures us of success."

"Okay," Harmon said, digging out another chocolate cookie. "I'll buy it. But an assassin?"

"Think of him as a protector."

"And the Italian guy?" Harmon snapped his fingers. "What's his name . . . ? Remo?"

"No doubt CIA. Probably a control agent. He is of no importance. What is of significance is the fact that the President of the United States employs an assassin."

"I guess," Harmon Cashman said vaguely.

"In spite of the congressional prohibition against assassination as a tool of Executive Branch policy."

Harmon Cashman stopped in mid-bite. He looked up.

"Are you saying we have some political dirt on the President?"

"Such an unsavory way of putting it. Let us say that the President inadvertently has betrayed to us probably his greatest secret."

"How's that gonna help the campaign?"

"Harmon, my friend. Sometimes it is enough to know a secret, without turning it to one's advantage," said Enrique Espiritu Esperanza quietly.

14

The next day a gleaming, white-chocolate Mercedes tooled through Chinatown.

It drew up before an ornate temple, and Enrique Espiritu Esperanza, resplendent in white, emerged. Harmon Cashman followed.

The Master of Sinanju was there to greet him. He bowed once. Enrique Esperanza bowed in return.

Esperanza looked around. His own image stared back from every wall and lamp post, and although he could not read the calligraphy under the multitude of identical faces, the sight of his repeated image gave him a warm feeling of hope.

"You have done well," he said.

"I have only begun," Chiun replied. And, raising his voice, the Master of Sinanju began to chant in a singsong voice.

The words were unintelligible. But the reaction was immediate.

From out of shops and tenements came curious Chinese.

They gathered around as Chiun lifted his arms and began to speak. He gestured broadly, as if scolding the crowd.

"Sounds like a harangue," whispered Harmon Cashman, in a worried voice. "Maybe I'd better break out some Oreos."

"They will not be necessary."

The harangue—or whatever it was—continued.

At the end of it, a sea of blank, bland faces stared back.

"They don't look very impressed," Cashman muttered uneasily.

"How can one tell?" answered Enrique Esperanza, not a care evident in his voice or on his face.

Then, while they were considering edging back to the car, the Chinese began to lift their voices.

"Syiwang! Syiwang! Syiwang!"

"What the heck are they saying?" muttered Harmon Cashman.

"They are saying," said Enrique Esperanza proudly, " 'Hope.' "

In Little Tokyo, it was the same.

Only the word was *Kibo*.

In Koreatown, it was *Somang*. To the Vietnamese of Little Saigon, it was *Hyvong*. Whatever the tongue, it was music to the ears of Harmon Cashman.

"This is incredible!" he breathed. "You can hardly get the Chinese and Japanese to pay attention to local politics. And look at this! If that little guy can do this all over the state," he said enthusiastically, "we got the Asian vote sewed up slicker than a sackful of stray kittens."

"He can."

And once again, Enrique Espiritu Esperanza stepped forward to address the crowd. He spoke in English. The Master of Sinanju translated. The crowd applauded whenever the old Korean lifted his thin hands, as if responding to an applause sign.

Harmon Cashman could only marvel at the sight.

"If we could only move the white people this way," he said wistfully, as they walked back to the waiting Mercedes.

"We will," promised Enrique Esperanza.

"How? There aren't enough Oreos on the planet to hand out to everybody. If there were, our campaign war chest could go broke trying."

"Harmon," said Enrique Espiritu Esperanza, "I wish you to alert the press that I will give an important speech at four o'clock this afternoon."

"Done. Where?"

"In South Central."

"The barrio!"

"South Central, yes."

"But that's the Hispanic and black district!" Harmon

protested. "You got the Hispanic vote in your hip pocket."

"I am not going to South Central to sway the Hispanic vote," said Enrique Espiritu Esperanza smoothly. "I am going there to court the white vote."

"Ricky," Harmon Cashman said in a firm voice, "I think you've been out in the sun too long. Not only are there practically no whites to speak of down there, but it's downright dangerous. It's gang heaven. They have to send in the National Guard just to collect the garbage."

"I have no fear."

"I know you don't. But in everything you've done so far, you've showed good sense. People have already taken shots at you. Brown people. Your people. Why don't we move on to San Francisco? I know they'll love you up there."

"Because I have not yet taken L.A. County," said Enrique Esperanza, gesturing to the Master of Sinanju, who was regaling the scattering crowd in their own tongue.

Out of the corner of his eye, the Master of Sinanju caught the beckoning gesture of his candidate. He finished his remarks to the gathering crowd.

"Remember. If you all vote intelligently, a person of correct color and properly shaped eyes will soon occupy a position of great importance in this province. This is all to your benefit. This is cultimulcherism at work. Vote early and often," he added, parroting a phrase he had heard spoken between whites in the campaign organization of Enrique Espiritu Esperanza.

Then, with a flourish of skirts, he returned to his candidate's side.

"They are with you, gracious one," said Chiun.

"That is good. This afternoon, I go to speak before the brown-skinned peoples."

Chiun nodded. "As the prophet of cultimulcherism, it is proper that you do so."

"But it is very dangerous down there," Enrique Esperanza continued. "There are young men with no futures, who carry guns and kill one another."

"Their fates are sealed," Chiun promised.

"No, no. I do not wish to vanquish them. That is not my way. It is my hope that they will join my cause. I know that they will be receptive to the message of Esperanza, if only they can be made to listen."

"Their ears shall be your playthings," vowed the Master of Sinanju.

"These young men go by certain names—the Crips and the Blood. The Crips wear blue bandannas. The Bloods wear red. Both groups carry weapons."

"They will carry their fingers loosely at their sides when you enter their domain in triumph," vowed the Master of Sinanju.

"A driver will take you to this place," said Enrique Espiritu Esperanza, bowing.

Jambo Jambone X—formerly Melvin Dicer—was all of fifteen, and had killed three men. The term "men" was open to debate, because none of the three members of the blue-jacketed Crips had lived long enough to graduate from high school before he had capped them.

Jambo Jambone X—someone had told him it was a name with true African roots, and so he adopted it as a gesture of black pride and further insurance against paternity suits—considered himself a man. A man killed. Therefore he was a man. Anybody who said different had better watch where he trooped.

Today, Jambo Jambone X was out to prove his manhood. He was going to pull out on someone. It didn't matter who. A cop was as good as a Crip. He might shoot a cop. It was good for a man's reputation to do that sometimes. As he aged, he noticed that younger members eyed him with increasing envy. They called him an "Original Gangster." Jambo Jambone X liked that.

As he trooped along Century Boulevard, Jambo Jambone X noticed the white dude. Not many white dudes rolled through Century Boulevard. Not in broad daylight.

There was something about this white guy, Jambo Jambone X thought. The way the dude walked, cool and casual like he owned Watts. He also had the thickest wrists Jambo had ever seen. They looked like transplants from a different guy entirely.

Jambo stopped on a corner to light up a cigarette. Really a *frio*—a menthol cigarette dipped in PCP. It helped to steady his gun hand.

The white guy was looking around as he was walking

along. He had deep eyes. Deep and cold. Cop eyes. Jambo Jambone X knew cop eyes on sight. This guy had cop eyes, no doubt about it.

He wore tan chinos, and a white T-shirt that still had that crisp look that meant it had never seen the inside of washer. Brand-new. His arms were bare. No tattoos. No nothing. His clothes were too tight for him to be packing heavy. Maybe a .38 in an ankle holster, at most.

Jambo Jambone X packed a Glock 9. Fifteen-round clip. A man's tool. You just point and pull. Didn't hardly have to aim.

Because he was dead-certain that the skinny guy with the wrists like two-by-fours was an undercover Gang Unit detective, Jambo Jambone X decided that he would put the muzzle of his Glock to the guy's white face and pull the trigger way down.

And because he made that fateful decision, Jambo Jambone X was destined to undergo a unique life-affirming experience.

The white guy walked over to a pay phone. He dropped a quarter in the slot and leaned on the one button with his thumb. Jambo noticed that especially. It was not something people normally did.

He decided it was further confirmation that the guy was a cop. Probably it was some secret cop number he was dialing.

Jambo reached into the inner pocket of his camo varsity jacket and felt the warm plastic handle of his Glock. He slipped up behind the guy on his quiet pump sneakers while he was speaking into the phone.

"That's right, Smitty. No sign of Chiun. If Esperanza is going to make an appearance down here, I'd better get to work. Otherwise we'll have a bloodbath. This place is practically a war zone."

"You got that right, jack," said Jambo Jambone X, whipping out his high-impact plastic pistol and putting it to the back of the white cop's head. "And you be the next statistic." His brown finger caressed the trigger. Caressing the trigger was a trick an older Blood had taught him. He had bubbled out the secret as he lay dying, saying it was his wish to pass on the one great truth he had learned in life before he died, the sum total of eighteen rich years on the street.

"You don't jerk the trigger. You kinda squeeze it. Keeps the sight on the guy you wanna do."

"Squeeze?" Jambo had asked.

"Yeah. Uhhhh." A fountain of blood erupted from the Blood's mouth. Jambo thanked the man as he stripped the corpse of valuables, including the Glock 9 he first used to practice the secret art of squeezing the trigger. He quickly discovered that it worked. After that, he hardly ever popped preschoolers when he was aiming at their older relatives.

So, with the white dude's head before his muzzle, Jambo Jambone X began to squeeze the trigger, not yank it back hard.

He was eternally grateful he remembered to do this. He even said a prayer for the repose of the soul of his dead brother, whose name he no longer remembered.

"Jesus Lord, you watch out for his black ass," murmured Jambo Jambone X, as the cold sweat oozed down his forehead and washed his dark face.

The prayer made him feel much, much better—although it did nothing to clarify the situation confronting him. This was new. He would have to think this through. What does a Blood do when he finds himself with his finger on his own trigger and his Glock tucked up under his chin?

This was definitely new. It would take extra thought. The first thing Jambo Jambone X thought to do was figure out what had happened.

He had been about to smoke the white cop when the dude, casual as can be, had turned around and taken hold of Jambo's steady wrists with the fingers of one cool hand.

The Glock was under his own chin directly after that. Couldn't have taken the blink of a rat's eye.

In this unique circumstance, Jambo Jambone X felt moved to compliment the white dude. "You cool, jack. You the downest."

"Keep it down," said the cool cop in an equally cool voice. "I'll finish with you when I'm through with my conversation."

"Take your time," said Jambo Jambone X respectfully.

The cool cop continued doing his thing.

"Yeah. Right. I'll be in touch, Smitty."

The cool cop hung up the phone. Jambo Jambone X heard the phone mechanism click the quarter into the change-return slot. The dude was so cool he didn't even check the slot. That was way cool.

Still holding on to Jambo's wrist with a grip that felt like a redwood tree had grown up and around it, the cool cop started talking.

"I'm looking for a friend," he said.

"You got one. I am your friend for life, which I hope extends beyond the millennium what is comin'."

"Glad to hear it. But I already got a friend. He's about five feet tall, old as your mother's reputation, and he wears a Korean kimono."

"I know what a Korean is, but the kimono part's got me stumped."

"It's like a robe."

"Ain't seen no robe Korean," Jambo said.

"Tell you what, you help me look for him and I'll give you a quarter."

"A whole quarter?" asked Jambo Jambone X, who just last week had cleared three grand selling crack back of the high school. He wouldn't pick a quarter off the soles of his pumps, ordinarily. But the quarter the dude now offered meant his Glock wouldn't go off with his chin under it.

"No teeth marks, either. How about it?"

"Deal. Do I get my wrist back?"

"Sure."

The cool dude's fingers came away, leaving white marks and a spreading numbness. The numbness made Jambo drop his Glock.

The cool dude caught it up in one hand. His hand was like a blur. The other hand joined it, and they started squeezing the Glock like it was dirty tinfoil.

"Only it didn't make a tinfoil kinda sound," said Jambo Jambone X, a few minutes later at a crack house on Manchester Street.

"Yeah?" said Jambo's right arm, Dexter Dogget. "What did it sound like?"

"Like . . . like . . . like the guy was mushing up Silly Putty."

"What's Silly Putty?" asked a thirteen-year-old, wiping oil off the breech of his Mac-11.

"They used to have it when I was a kid, back before kids had guns," Jambo explained. "They played with this stuff. It's kinda like chewing gum, only you don't chew it."

"How high it get you?"

Jambo had to think about that one.

"Pretty damn buzzed, but not the way you know," he said truthfully.

"You been doing PCP again, Jambo?"

"Yeah, as a matter of fact."

"Better take a hit of this stuff. Clear your head."

Jambo swiped the tinfoil crack pipe away.

"Don't need that!" he snapped. "This is serious. We gotta help the cool dude find his friend."

"Why?"

"Because I got a feelin' bad things gonna happen to us if we don't," Jambo said truthfully.

"What makes you say that?"

"This white guy, he could rule the 'hood if he had a mind. I seen it in the way he carried himself. No lie."

The other Bloods conferred among themselves. The discussion was brief. There were only two options raised. Smoke Jambo to shut up his stupid face, or go along.

"I say we go along," said Dexter. "Man who smokes the white guy and shows up Jambo rules the Blood. Any dissent?"

There was none. Smiling faces came out of the huddle.

"Lead the way and we'll take the day," said Dexter.

"What's that supposed to mean?" asked Jambo, as they strolled out.

"Who cares?" he was told. "It rhyme, don't it?"

Jambo frowned. Things are deteriorating. In the old days, about three-four months ago, everybody could lay down a cool rap. Now they'd become a bunch of mushmouths. What the hell was going on? They were doing only premium blow.

They found the old Korean on Compton Street, putting a poster on a peeling stucco wall that was covered with competing gangs' graffiti, until it was like a dead computer screen covered with the fading ghosts of its memory banks.

"Hey, you—old guy!" Jambo called.

The old Korean declined to turn around. Deep in thought, he positioned and repositioned the poster several times.

"We lookin' for you."

"Yeah," added Dexter. "Wanna word with you. You coverin' up our spray."

"I'll take this," said Jambo Jambone X, striding up to the guy.

"You deaf, coot?"

The old Korean looked up, as if noticing Jambo Jambone X for the first time.

Jambo Jambone X received two simultaneous impressions of the old Korean.

One, that his face was a network of wrinkles.

Two, that his eyes somehow reminded him of the cool white dude's eyes. There was the same scary confidence in them.

This second impression made more of an impression.

Jambo Jambone X had just started to backpedal to safety when a bony yellow claw took hold of his throat and squeezed. Jambo started choking. His tongue came out of his mouth.

And without any seeming effort, the old Korean used his head like a brush, washing the back of the poster and the face of the stucco wall with Jambo's long tongue.

Jambo was released only when he had no more moisture to give. He fell on his rump. The poster was smacked on the wall.

Jambo Jambone X pulled himself to his feet, trembling. He swallowed unidentifiable grit, which scraped his throat raw.

"Dude wants to see you," he croaked.

Behind him, the Blood were all laughing. He heard the click of safety latches.

"What's the matter, Jambo?" Dexter taunted. "You lost yourself?"

More laughter. They didn't know. What did they know? They were kids. Kids with just a few Glocks between them facing . . . Jambo Jambone X didn't know *what* they were facing, but he instinctually understood that it was better than a Glock. Better than any weapon.

"You jerks don't know!" he shouted. "This guy's a

friend of the cool white guy! You better not disrespect
him none!"

The laughter rang out in raucous peals.

"I am the Master of Sinanju," said the old Korean.

"You tell 'em, Master."

"I am with Esperanza, who would be governor."

"You hear that?" Jambo said. "This man with the governor! He be important. You listen up, you punks."

"When the one called Esperanza comes to this place
of despair," the old Korean went on, "he will be treated
with proper respect."

"Say it again!" Jambo exclaimed.

"There will be no shooting. No violence. You will listen quietly, and you will vote as I say you will vote."

"Hey! You can't say that!" Dexter protested.

"I am saying it."

"It's un-American. Besides, we can't vote. We're too
young."

"I say we shoot the un-American gook," a youth announced, waving his pistol.

"I second that."

"Yeah," Dexter growled. "This we can vote on. All
those in favor of smoking the uppity gook, vote with
your pieces."

A fan of pistol muzzles arrayed themselves in the precise direction of the old Korean, whose eyes narrowed
before the menace. Cold fingers touched colder triggers.

Jambo Jambone X realized that when those triggers were
jerked back—jerked, not squeezed—the old guy who was
a friend of the cool white guy was probably going to get
dead. If he got dead, then Jambo Jambone X was going
to have to tell the cool white guy with the thick wrists and
very fast hands that his own brothers had done this.

Jambo Jambone X then made one of the most intelli-
gent decisions in his short life. He stepped between the
fan of pistols and the old Korean.

It was not bravery. It was not self-sacrifice. It was a
simple subtraction. Take away the old Korean, and the
white guy was going to take away Jambo Jambone X.
One from one equals zero. Even a Blood could do that
kind of subtraction.

"You sayin' don't shoot?" asked Dexter Dogget of
Jambo Jambone X.

"I ain't sayin'."

"You sayin' shoot, then?"

"I ain't sayin' that, either."

"Then what *are* you sayin', man?"

"I'm sayin' you shoot him, you might as well shoot me."

"Okay," said Dexter Dogget, the second oldest and next in line to lead the Blood. The trigger fingers began turning white at the knuckle joints.

Jambo Jambone X closed his eyes. He said another prayer. It rhymed perfectly. "Lord, save my ass, or my ass is grass."

Then a frantic voice rang out. "Nobody better shoot that gook!"

"Anyone who shoots the gook gets capped!" a second voice warned.

Jambo Jambone X opened his eyes. They kept opening until they were very wide.

Coming up Compton was a wedge of blue varsity jackets. It was the Crips. And they were rolling.

One of the Blood called out, "What's this gook to you?"

"Cool guy made me promise to find him."

Jambo Jambone X blinked.

"Cool guy with thick wrists and fast hands?" he asked.

"No. Cool guy with thick wrists and fast feet. Our man Rollo jump him from behind. Rollo too slow. White guy gave out a Kung Fu kinda kick. Rollo, he roll one way and Rollo's head roll another."

Jambo Jambone X made the sign of the Cross, even though technically he considered himself a Black Muslim. But for the whispered words of a dying Blood, it might have been his own head rolling every which way.

"You listen to that dude," Jambo cautioned his fellow gang members. "He know what he be talkin' about."

Dexter scoffed. "You shermed, Jambo. Them's Crips. Big and blue as life."

"Don't say I didn't warn you," Jambo warned.

The old Korean, who up to this point had remained silent but unconcerned, stepped around Jambo Jambone X. He shook his wide emerald sleeves back from his skinny little arms. Jambo could tell he meant business.

Jambo whispered, "The one with the gold earring, he be my brother. Don't hurt him too much."

"That is up to him," the old Korean said in a cold tone.

"If you gotta kill him, I try to understand," said Jambo.

"You will lay down your weapons," said the old Korean.

"Crips'll smoke us," Dexter pointed out.

"They will not."

"Good," said Dexter, grinning thinly. "Because we gonna smoke them."

The fan of muzzles turned, as if mounted on the rail of a circling battleship.

The Crips froze. They were not carrying their weapons in their hands.

And a moment later, neither were the Blood.

They went, "Ouch! Ow! Yeow! Yikes!" as a flurry of campaign posters zipped by their gun hands, inflicting wicked and painful paper cuts and forcing them to drop their weapons to the dirty pavement.

The blizzard of posters fell at their feet. Some fell face-up. Some facedown. The upward-facing posters caught the attention of the Blood, now well named because of the conditions of their gun hands. Looking up at them were the liquid eyes of Enrique Espiritu Esperanza.

"He the guy you want us to vote for?" Dexter gulped.

"He is," intoned the wise old Korean—the wisest, kindest Korean ever to roll through the South Central District.

"He got my vote," Dexter promised.

"Mine, too."

"First, he must know that you are loyal," Chiun suggested.

"What we gotta do?"

"These posters must be placed in appropriate places in this neighborhood," said the wise old Korean.

"You got it!"

"And we get the old guy," said the approaching Crips.

"Who you calling 'old'?" protested Jambo Jambone X. "This here's my man. Yo, Master. Tell these cheese-eaters."

"Begone, eaters of cheese," intoned the Master of Sinanju sternly. "I will have nothing to do with you."

"White guy wants you," said the spokesman for the Crips, pulling out a .357 Magnum. "So you come."

Other Crip armaments came into view then. The

Blood, their weapons on the ground and their hands dripping red, gave a collective, "Oh, shit."

The Blood dived for their guns. The Crips picked their targets. Jambo Jambone X threw himself in front of the old Korean. A bloodbath impended.

Remo Williams picked that moment to saunter around the corner.

"Nobody do anything stupider than being born," he said.

Nobody did. The sound of his easy, no-nonsense voice caused faces on both sides of the imminent bloodbath to freeze. Eyes went round. A few crotches darkened from the contents of fear-struck bladders.

"In fact, everybody better lay down their guns," he added.

This instruction was obeyed with military precision. Pistols of all types clicked as they were carefully laid on the sidewalk.

"Look what I found for you," Jambo Jambone X said, pointing to the Master of Sinanju.

"He lie," said the Crip spokesman. "We found him. You owe us quarters."

"No. I get the quarter."

"I'll give you *all* a quarter, if you shut up," said Remo.

"I want *the* quarter," Jambo insisted. "It gonna be my lucky piece."

"Or I can juggle a few heads for the entertainment of the survivors," Remo added.

"You the man," Jambo said instantly. "Whatever you say."

Remo strode up to Chiun, whose hands found themselves in the sleeves of his kimono.

"I have nothing to say to you, white."

"Yeee!" said Jambo. "Don't call him no names!"

The old Korean sniffed disdainfully. "He is white. He will always be white. I will call him what I choose."

The eyes of the assembled Crips and Bloods went from the face of the old Oriental to that of the white dude, their pupils reflecting various degrees of fear, horror, and consternation.

"What you sayin'?" Jambo hissed. "You can't talk to the dude that way. He take your head off."

"He is a pale piece of pig's ear," intoned the old Oriental.

"Yiii!" hissed the assembled Crips and Bloods. They backed away. They had no desire to see their jackets soiled when the old Oriental's neck stump began to pump blood all over the place, because his head wasn't there to receive it.

"You gonna take that?" asked a Crip.

"Little Father," the white dude said simply. "I have just one thing to tell you."

"I am not interested, stealer of sweethearts."

The Crips and Bloods shrank further. They were fighting over a chick. Somebody was bound to die.

"Cheeta Ching is going to cover Esperanza's speech."

"Quick!" Chiun shrieked, pointing to the paper snowfall of campaign posters at their feet. "The posters! They must be in their proper places! The streets must be cleaned! I do not want to see a speck of dust when the beauteous Cheeta comes!"

The Crips and Bloods frowned, like a bas-relief of basalt idols.

"He crazy?" Dexter demanded of the white dude.

"Better do what he says," Remo put in. "When he gets excited like that, even *I* get nervous."

The faces of the assembled Crips and Bloods went from the cold mask of the white dude they all feared to the frowning face of the wispy Oriental, with stupefaction growing in their eyes.

"You, afraid? Of *him*?" asked one.

Remo nodded. "He taught me everything I know. *Everything*."

That was all the Crips and the Bloods needed to hear. Madly, they scooped up Esperanza campaign posters. They stole push brooms and barrels from hardware store displays. They got to work on Compton Street, determined to make it presentable for the old Korean who had taught the downest white men in the world everything he knew.

15

Cheeta Ching had not slept in two days. There were hollows under her sharp, predatory eyes. Her brain felt like it had been dipped in Alka-Seltzer fizz.

A face haunted her. A strong, white face with prominent, almost Korean cheekbones and deep-set hollow eyes. Those eyes had pierced her ambitious soul. His name was burned into her soul.

"Nero." She spoke the name aloud, tasting its un-Korean vowels. "Nero."

She had never met anyone like him. Well, maybe once before. Years ago.

She had almost forgotten the experience. A strange man had broke into her apartment and tied her to a chair. After he had perversely dressed her in a flowing Korean native dress.

Cheeta had thought she was going to be raped. So she had resorted to the formidable weapon that had brought her to national prominence: her razor-sharp tongue. Cheeta heaped abuse on the man. Threatened him. Taunted him. Nothing seemed to work. It was a first. No man—from network presidents to her husband—had ever failed to wither under a Cheeta Ching tongue-lashing.

She had steeled herself for the worst.

Instead of raping or kidnapping her, the attacker simply shot a roll of thirty-five-millimeter film of Cheeta, tied to the chair, dressed in Lyi dynasty *han-bok* dress, and sputtering scorn.

Then he had left, much to Cheeta's relief.

After she had struggled free of her bonds, Cheeta

Ching had contacted Don Cooder, her arch-rival, and accused him of staging the attack. Cooder had denied it.

"You're not even in my class," Cooder had snarled.

Cheeta then hung up and hired thugs to beat him up, shouting "What's the frequency, Kenneth?"

Satisfied, Cheeta then waited for the photos to appear in some tabloid. They never had. Nor had they been used to blackmail her.

It was a mystery, and eventually Cheeta Ching had put it out of her mind. But she had never been able to put her strange assailant out of her mind. There was something about his cruel forcefulness that lingered, and sometimes made her fantasize about his return—even though the memory of that ugly incident still made her shiver.

The man who had attacked her reminded her of Nero. A little. The face was different. The eyes were alike. But it was not the same man, she was sure of that. The other had been a pig.

But Nero was different from other men. He was . . .

Words failed Cheeta Ching. No surprise. Most of her on-air material was written for her. Still, there was something about him, something that had made her shiver at the first glimpse of his lean, strong body. Shiver in the same way she had just shivered at the memory of the strange, picture-taking intruder. He was . . .

"A dreamboat," she decided finally, dipping into her half-forgotten teenage vocabulary. "That's what he is. A dreamboat."

Cheeta was hunched in a cubbyhole of the local network affiliate, eating spicy *jungol* casserole soup. It was in her contract that she be catered in Korean ethnic foods, and God help the idiot who served her Moo Goo Gai Pan. She was trying to figure out what had happened to the tape of her self-interview.

Nero couldn't have stolen it, she told herself. Never.

Yet the tape he had given her proved to be blank. And the network had refused to run her interview with Enrique Espiritu Esperanza, calling it "Soft and unprofessional."

Cheeta had instantly blamed this on her cameraman. But the missing tape still bothered her.

There is only one way to solve this mystery, she decided, as she stirred her *jungol* and let the scrumptious turnip-and-cabbage odor soothe her flaring nostrils.

She picked up the phone and called personnel.

"Did anyone named Nero drop off a resumé today?" she asked the personnel manager.

"No. Nor Demo. Nor Nemo, or any of the other names you keep mentioning."

"Well, if anyone with any of those names drops off a resumé, I am to be notified instantly or it's your job."

"You don't hire and fire at this station," the personnel manager had said.

"Fine," Cheeta Ching replied tartly. "I won't fire you. What I'll do is rip your Adam's apple out of your gullet with my naked teeth."

There was a pregnant pause while the threat sank in.

"The very minute anyone with those vowels in his name drops off a resumé, you'll be the first to know, Miss Ching," the personnel manager said, helpfully.

"Thank you," Cheeta said sweetly. "I'm glad we understand each other."

Cheeta hung up the phone. It rang a second later. It was the station news director.

"We just received word that Esperanza is giving a speech down in the South Central district. I can get you a cameraman, if you want to cover it."

"I want to cover it," Cheeta said quickly, bolting from her chair. Here was her chance to redeem herself. And maybe run into Nero the Divine, too.

The thought of coming into contact with the dark-eyed Nero made more delicious shivers course up and down her spine. She wondered if it would stimulate ovulation. She had tried just about everything else.

The station microwave van came off the freeway and into the worst section of South Central Los Angeles.

The driver looked startled. He pulled over to the side of the road, his face wearing a confused expression.

From the back of the van, Cheeta poked her sticky-haired head forward.

"What's wrong?" she demanded, shrill-voiced.

"I think I took a wrong turn," he said, pulling a folding map from the glove compartment.

"Don't you know your own city, you nitwit?"

"I thought I did. But this can't be South Central."

Cheeta peered through the windshield. She saw a neat downtown area. No litter clogged its gutters. The sides of buildings were wet from recent scrubbing. Even the sidewalks looked freshly washed.

More incredibly, there were no loitering gang members, no back-alley drug dealing, no hookers in tight clothes leaning against building facades.

"Why not?" she asked, her too-smooth face puckering in perplexity.

"Look at this place," said the driver. "It's neat as a pin. South Central is a dump."

"Maybe the city cleaned it in preparation for Esperanza's speech," Cheeta suggested.

"Lady, you don't know this city. Or South Central. The cops are petrified to come here after dark."

The driver returned to the map.

"Says here we should be on Compton Street," he said doubtfully.

"The sign *says* Compton," Cheeta pointed out.

"I know," the driver said bleakly. "I feel like I'm in The Twilight Zone."

"If we miss this speech," Cheeta warned, "I promise to cable you to a fire plug and leave you there after sundown."

The driver pulled out into traffic. "We're on the right street. We gotta be."

As he tooled his van further down the street, the driver began feeling light-headed. Gone were the graffiti. The gutters were immaculate. Even the air smelled good. He noticed air-wick dispensers located at strategic points, on window sills and storm drains.

And surreally, he saw two black teenagers scrubbing spray-painted profanity off the side of a church. One wore a blue Crips bandanna on his head, and the other had a bloodred Bloods bandanna stuffed into the back pocket of his jeans.

"I *am* in The Twilight Zone," he muttered.

The media had already set up cameras and microwave stations in front of the Ebeneezer Tabernacle Church, where Enrique Espiritu Esperanza was scheduled to make a speech. Rival anchors milled about. They were merely local anchors, but to Cheeta Ching all anchors were potential rivals. They were either clawing their way up to her slot, or they were sniping at her as their careers crashed and burned.

Cheeta saw that two of the female reporters were of Asian descent, and her eyes became catlike slits.

"Look at that," she hissed to her trembling cameraman. "Those sluts. Trying to steal my thunder. Why can't they be teachers, or work in restaurants, like the rest of their kind?"

The cameraman said a discreet nothing. He lugged his minicam out of the back of the van, saying, "Looks like we got here too late for a choice position."

"I'll fix that," Cheeta hissed, storming ahead.

Her red nails flashing in the California sun, Cheeta Ching waded into the crowd. She yanked cords from belt battery packs and hit fast-forward buttons where she could.

Instantly, cameramen began to curse and check their equipment for malfunctions.

Cheeta turned and waved to her cameraman to follow. The man dashed through the path Cheeta's sabotage had opened up. He made excellent time. He had been told his predecessor had been demoted to the mail room for being too slow.

By the time they reached the front of the pack, Cheeta had staked out a prominent position. From her handbag, she pulled out a tiny can of hair varnish and began applying it liberally to her crowning glory, turning so that stray bursts got into the eyes of selected rivals. That cleared even more space.

Her timing was perfect. The white Mercedes came around a corner while rival newscasters were still dabbing water into their smarting eyes.

It came slowly. Ahead, behind, and on either side of it was a mass of strutting teenagers. They wore the blue bandannas of the Crips and the red of the Blood, plus the caps of the Chicano gang known as Los Aranas Espana.

Gasps came from the reporters.

"What? What is it?" Cheeta demanded, craning her long neck to see over their heads.

The cameraman was just tall enough to manage this feat.

"It's Esperanza's car," he reported. "And it's surrounded by gang-bangers."

"They've captured him!"

"Looks like they're *escorting* him, if you want my opinion."

"I don't. Turn that camera on me."

The cameraman obeyed.

Picking up a mike, Cheeta screamed, "I'm broadcasting live from South Central L.A., one of the most crimeridden areas of the city, where vicious teenage gangsters have surrounded the Hispanic candidate for governor, Enrique Espiritu Esperanza!"

Just then, voices rose: *"Esperanza! Esperanza! Esperanza!"*

"They're calling for his death!" Cheeta cried.

"I don't think so," the cameraman put in.

"Stay out of this!" Cheeta flared. "Cameramen shouldn't be seen or heard!"

"Esperanza! Esperanza!"

"What are they doing now?"

The cameraman said, "Looks to me like they're sticking their hands into the car windows."

"They're trying to drag him out!" she said, licking her lips. "A political assassination, and we're covering it live!"

"No," the cameraman corrected, "they're accepting cookies."

Cheeta Ching's pencil-thin eyebrows went for each other like vicious vipers. "Cookies?"

"They look like Oreos."

"Let me see," Cheeta said, jumping up and down. "How?"

"On your knees, buster."

The cameraman obliged. He got down on all fours and grunted manfully as Cheeta Ching impaled his broad back with stiletto heels, designed to make her stand taller than any interviewee under six feet.

Over the bobbing heads of the crowd, Cheeta beheld a remarkable sight.

The white Mercedes coasted up to the church steps. Gang members were walking along either side. Out of a rear window, a brown hand was passing out dark Oreo cookies.

The smiling gang members accepted these eagerly and passed them around. A few shot clenched fists into the air.

"Esperanza's our main man! Esperanza's our main man!"

Presently, the Mercedes rolled to a halt. The gang members lined up in two protective rows between the rear door and the podium that had been erected for the speech.

Enrique Espiritu Esperanza emerged, smiling. He walked down the path made for him, as the media surged toward the spectacle.

Cheeta leaped off the cameraman's back, crying, "Get off your knees, you idiot! We're mssing the shot of our careers!"

By the time they reached the car, Enrique Esperanza had made it to the podium. He wore white.

He began speaking.

"I have come here to make a speech," Enrique Esperanza began.

A hush fell over the crowd.

"But I will not make a speech," Esperanza said.

A murmur went through the crowd.

"Instead, I will have the fine young men of South Central speak for me."

Enrique Esperanza waved to his honor guard. A black youth in Blood colors took the podium.

"My name is Jambo Jambone X, and until this morning I never heard of Mr. Esperanza. But now that I have met the dude, I see that I got hope. No more gang-banging for me. No more crack. From now on I eat Oreo cookies and go to school. Oreos taste better than crack, anyway."

Nervous applause rippled through the crowd.

The next to take the microphone was the leader of the Crips. He took credit for cleaning up South Central. And quickly added that his brothers from the Blood and Los Aranas had pitched in.

"Mr. Esperanza showed me my pride. I say down with crimes. Anybody doing crimes in my neighborhood had better watch out. I see any more crimes going down, and I drop a dime on his crown."

The leader of Los Aranas Espana came next. His speech was shorter and more to the point.

"I say, 'Esperanza *mucho hombre*.' "

Wild applause greeted this. The Aranas leader rejoined the honor guard behind the podium.

Then a smiling Enrique Espiritu Esperanza returned to the mike.

"I thank my black and brown friends for their kind words in my behalf," he said magnanimously. "They have seen their future. The multicultural future that is uniquely Californian. When I am elected, all Californians, regardless of skin color or ethnic background, will be able to coexist as friends. No more fear. No more hate. No more trouble. This, Enrique Espiritu Esperanza promises you."

From a dozen places in the crowd, placards rose. They read ESPERANZA MEANS HOPE in three languages.

The cameraman, his minicam capturing the most sensational sight in South Central since the last monthly riot, said, "Isn't this something?"

As the crowd roared its approval, Cheeta Ching looked around distractedly.

"See anything of a dreamboat named Ramiro?" she asked hopefully.

Remo Williams was in hiding.

He lay on his stomach, peering over the crumbling edge of an apartment house roof, his eyes guarded.

"Is she still there?" he asked.

"She is looking about with her magnificent feline eyes," replied the Master of Sinanju in a chill voice.

Remo scuttled away. "Get back. We don't want her to spot us."

"Speak for yourself, white," sniffed Chiun. "I only stand on this dirty roof because I know it would anger Emperor Smith were I to appear on the television."

"I'm glad you're being sensible."

"I am willing to wait until I am Exalted Treasurer of California before stepping into the lemonlight," he said.

"That's limelight, and if you get the urge to step into it, remember what happened to me the last time I got *my* face on TV."

Chiun retreated with alacrity, saying, "Emperor Smith

would not dare to require that a Master of Sinanju submit to surgeons of plastic, as you have."

"My face still hurts from that last facelift."

Chiun stepped back even further. His nose wrinkled.

"All glory comes to him who is patient," he said quietly.

"What do you see in that witch, anyway?" asked Remo, climbing to his feet.

The Master of Sinanju turned his face toward the snowy peaks of the San Gabriel Mountains to the east. His long nails touched one another, his bony fingers splayed.

"Once," he intoned, "I was a young man."

"You and about half the human race," Remo returned.

A hand lifted. "Hush!" Chiun said sharply. "You have asked a question, and now you will hear the answer."

"I guess I asked for it. . . ."

"I was young, and the world was wide," Chiun murmured. "It was in the days when I was still a Master-in-training. Now a Master-in-training must perform many feats. Endure many hardships. Suffer much pain. One day, my father, the Master who began my training, called me into his presence and said unto me, 'My son, you must now face your severest test.'

"I trembled, for before this I had endured much. I could not imagine what my father had in store for me. And he said, 'You must go to the city of which you have heard, many leagues from this fishing village of ours, and dwell there for one month.' "

Remo grunted. "Horrors."

"My father said that many young men before me had gone to the city and never come back," Chiun continued in an arid voice. "I asked him what dangers awaited me, and he said, 'You will not know their face until they have inflicted grievous wounds upon your soul.' And hearing these portentous words I trembled anew, for I did not comprehend this riddle.

"And so I walked to the city of Pyongyang, which is now in North Korea, but in those days was merely a city in the north of an undivided land. I went on foot, with a few coins in my pocket and only the kimono on my back."

The Master of Sinanju lifted his tiny chin, his hazel eyes going opaque with memories.

"The way was long, and my heart was tight with many emotions," he said. "Would I return alive? Would I be swallowed by the harlot guile of the city-dwellers, tales of which I had heard since childhood?

"After two days, I came to the outskirts of Pyongyang. It was much bigger than I had ever dreamed. Its towers rose to the very sky. Its people were more numerous than I had imagined. There were sights undreamed of. Foods whose names I did not know. There were also people of foreign birth: Japanese, Chinese, and even big-nosed whites. But the astounding thing was the Koreans I encountered. At first, I did not understand that they were Koreans. For their faces were quite different from those of the village of Sinanju. And they had taken Japanese names."

"Really?" Remo asked.

"Yes. It is unbelievable, but true. For these were the days when Korea was a vassal of Japan." Chiun frowned at the memory. "As I walked among these Koreans-who-were-not, I marveled at the women I encountered along the way. They, too, looked unlike Sinanju women. For they wore fine clothes and painted their faces and lips in most unusual and artful ways. I had not gone very far when it came to me that this Pyongyang would be a pleasant place to spend my days." Chiun bowed his bald head sadly.

"No!" Remo said, voice mock-serious.

"Yes," Chiun admitted.

Remo grinned. "Well, you know what they say: 'Can't keep 'em down on the farm once they've seen gay Pyongyang.' "

Chiun's stern face wrinkled. "I do not understand."

"Never mind. What happened next?"

"I came upon a painted-faced maiden who caught my fancy."

"This isn't going to be one of those unrequited love things, is it?" Remo asked. "Because if it is, I'd just as soon throw myself into the arms of Cheeta Ching and end the misery right now."

"It is nothing of the kind," Chiun sniffed. "Of course, it was love at first sight."

Remo suppressed a smile. "Of course."

"The maiden, beholding my manly splendor, was instantly smitten with Chiun the Younger, which is what I was called in those long-ago days."

"Chiun the Younger?"

"Not that I am now old," Chiun said hastily.

"Course not."

"As I was saying, this maiden, whose name was Ch'amnari, was smitten with the young man that I was. She employed all manner of enticements and other blandishments to lure me into her womanly snares, but I kept the warning of my father, Chiun the Elder, in mind, and passed her by."

"Junks in the night," Remo said with a sober face.

"That night, this maiden haunted my sleep. Her painted face swam before my dream-eye, and troubled my slumber deeply. Remo, it was true love."

"Sounds like hormones to me."

"Philistine!"

"Okay, okay, it was love. Let's cut to the chase. Did you bed her, or what?"

The Master of Sinanju's tiny face stiffened. His hands, nails touching, separated and found concealment in the closing sleeves of his elaborate kimono.

"I refuse to say."

"You didn't."

"I did!" Chiun snapped.

"Okay, you did. You obviously practiced safe sex, too. So what happened then?"

Chiun looked off toward the mountains. "When I awoke, Remo, she was gone."

"So much for true love."

"And with her had gone my meager allotment of gold coins, which I had carried in a purse at my waist."

"Ah-ha, I'll bet you jingled when you walked, and it was your jingle, not your jangle, that gave her the hots for you."

"It was my splendid strong body!" Chiun flared.

"Keep it down," Remo cautioned, looking over his shoulder. "We don't want Cheeta climbing the building with a mike clenched in her teeth."

"Speak for yourself," Chiun sniffed. Then, his voice

going low, he added, "For you see, Cheeta is the image of the maiden I have told you about, Remo."

"You fell for her? Ch'amnari, I mean."

Chiun nodded. "Even though she was a thief. For you see, she had what was called in the village a 'city face'— fine-featured and delicate. The women of Sinanju are country-faced. The woman I later married was country-faced. Yet I never forgot the city-faced Ch'amnari, and our rapturous night together."

"That good, huh?"

"She was lavish in her compliments," Chiun added crisply.

"Ever get your money back?"

"Yes. With interest."

"Interest?"

"I searched Pyongyang for this Ch'amnari, eventually finding her in the company of a Japanese colonel. Ito. An oppressor."

"Uh-oh . . ."

"He sneered at me. Called me a barbarian. And when I demanded justice, he told me to be gone."

"So you wasted him?" Remo said.

"I laid his yapping head at the feet of Ch'amnari, who with trembling hands surrendered my purse of gold coins, and others beside. Then I gave her the coldness of my retreating back and never saw her again. Although I have carried her beauteous image within me down to this very day. I returned to my village a sadder man, Remo. When my father saw the expression on my face, he said nothing. But I could see in his eyes that he knew I had learned the hard lesson he had hoped I would come to understand."

"You're serious about this? You really want that barracu— Cheeta?"

Chiun shrugged carelessly. "Her beauty pleases me. She is worthy to bear the child my country-faced wife never bestowed upon me—and the male heir you have yet to produce."

"Ah-ha!" Remo said, holding his arms stubbornly. "Now the real stuff comes out. Correct me if I'm wrong, Little Father, but quite a few years ago you got zapped by microwaves. You said you'd been sterilized."

"That was, as you say, years ago," Chiun said, with a

dismissive flap of a kimono sleeve. "It may be that my inner essence has come to life again."

"You saying you're horny?" Remo demanded.

Chiun whirled, his eyes cold fire. "Pale piece of pig's ear! I am speaking of possibilities. Cheeta and Chiun. Chiun and Cheeta. And the offspring that may blossom from our perfect union."

Remo shook his head slowly. "I don't know, Little Father. I just can't see it."

Chiun snorted. "You have the imagination of a flea."

"Okay, never mind that. What do you propose doing about this Cheeta problem?"

"She likes you."

"That depends. If she figured out I palmed her tape, she may want to strangle me with piano wire."

"I wish you to arrange a tryst for Cheeta. A romantic encounter. She will heed your request. But I will go in your stead."

"Sorry, John Alden."

"Why not?"

"One, you'll be made a fool of. Her name may be Cheeta, but it might as well be Ch'amnari."

"Please."

Remo frowned. Behind him, the crowd roared the name "Esperanza." The speech was ending.

"I'll think about it," he said. "First, I want you to drop this 'treasurer' crap."

Chiun stiffened. "Is this the boon you wish to invoke?"

Remo thought about that. "No. At least not yet. Smitty wants you to watch over Esperanza. But that's as far as it goes."

"Then you will not speak to Cheeta on my behalf?" Chiun inquired.

"Little Father," Remo said wearily, "I sincerely hope to avoid Cheeta Ching for the rest of my natural life."

"That is your final word?"

"No. Let me think about it. Okay?"

"I will accept that. But not for long."

"We friends again?"

"For now."

Remo smiled. Chiun's face remained set. "I must return to the side of my patron, Esperanza," he said.

"You know, he might be another Ch'amnari, too."

"What makes you say that?" Chiun said thinly.

"He offered you the treasurer's post. Just like that. Sounds too good to be true."

"I have delivered to him Koreatown, and all the votes that come with it," Chiun said loftily. "This is how empires are built."

"Just watch your step."

"That lesson," Chiun said loftily, "I learned long ago in old Pyongyang." The Master of Sinanju turned and padded toward the roof trap, disappearing down and out of sight.

Remo Williams watched his Master go.

"Great," he muttered. "I'm stuck in the middle of a love triangle between the Wicked Witch of the East and the only person I care about."

And down below the roaring crowd cried, *"Esperanza!"*

16

By the next morning, the name Enrique Espiritu Esperanza was on the lips of every man, woman, and child in California. And beyond.

"We're hot! Oh, we're so hot!" Harmon Cashman said enthusiastically. He had arrayed three rows of Oreo cookies on the breakfast nook table, and was separating them with a butter knife so that the creme centers were exposed, like cataracted whale eyes. "The numbers are starting to move our way! I am so amped!"

"It is time to widen our campaign," Enrique Esperanza decided.

Harmon Cashman began scraping the dry creme filling onto a bread dish, making a gooey little pile.

"We got L.A. County practically sewed up," he agreed. "The white—I mean *blanco*—campaign offices are reporting a flood of new volunteers and contributions. You got the white people thinking you're California's savior."

"I think we should next take the battle to San Francisco."

"Yeah. Barry Black's home turf. That ought to spook that Frisco flake good."

When he had every Oreo scraped clean, and a nice sweet pile of white creme filling, Harmon Cashman lifted the plate to his mouth and began licking.

He paused only once. To spoon a dab into his black coffee.

When he had licked the plate clean, he drank the coffee in one gulp.

"I hear the stores are having a run on these cookies wherever we're passed them out," Harman said, smack-

ing his lips with relish. "Maybe we can get an endorsement out of the company. We must be buying them by
the freight-train load, and I've never seen an invoice."

"They are donations," Esperanza said flatly.

"No kidding? That's better than an endorsement."

"I think so," said Enrique Esperanza, looking out at
the San Gabriel Mountains, his voice as far away as their
hazy peaks.

Barry Black, Junior had grown up in the California
governor's mansion. He had first sat in the corner office,
not behind the desk but bouncing on his father's knee.

Barry Black, Senior had been the first Democratic governor of California since the Great Depression. That had
been in the 1950s.

It had taken until the 1970s for another California
Democrat to occupy the corner office. That had been
Barry Black, Junior.

The two terms Barry Black, Junior had served had
almost ensured that California would not elect another
Democrat to the governorship until the next Great Depression. If even then.

After a string of debacles, ranging from his attempts
to protect the Medfly from an eradication program designed to save the state citrus crop to his proposal to put
a Californian on Mars by the year 2,000 the man the
press had dubbed "Governor Glowworm" had been
turned out of office quicker than a shoplifter from a Wal-
Mart.

On his last day in office, Barry Black announced that
he was going to the mysterious East to study in India
and help Mother Teresa.

"You won't have Barry Black to ridicule anymore,"
he announced, plagiarizing the words of a famous
predecessor.

In fact, he hoped to acquire the power to cloud men's
minds in India. He knew his only ticket back to the governor's office would be to hypnotize the electorate into
forgetting his disastrous terms.

Barry Black, Junior never did pick up that unique skill.
Instead, he meditated. A decade of meditating on his
future brought only flashbacks on his past.

Deciding that his future lay in his past, and after shaving his thick ascetic beard—his only accomplishment during his decade spent seeking wisdom—Barry Black, Junior returned to sunny California.

The return of Barry Black delighted California Republicans. It petrified the Democrats, who made Barry Black an irresistible offer almost before he had stepped off the jumbo jet.

"We want you to head up the party," a nervous delegation told him. "Please."

"I want to serve my party," Barry Black said, "but I also want to serve the people. Mother Teresa taught me that."

"The party needs you. We need you."

"I don't know. . . ."

"Mother Teresa said it would be okay," a scared delegate said in desperation.

"She did?"

"Her exact words were, 'Barry should go where he'll do the most good.' "

And so Barry Black, Junior became the Democratic Party Chairman of the state of California and hustled a small fortune in campaign contributions. Inside of six months, he was on his way to becoming the most successful fund-raiser the party had ever seen.

"I'm really good at this," he said when the coffers had topped three million dollars. "Mother Teresa was right."

Barry Black, Junior raised so much money he succumbed to a distinctly Democratic impulse. He squandered every cent. On an excessive and unnecessary staff.

His grassroots political efforts collapsed for lack of funds and he was canned, forcing Barry Black to run for senator. He garnered an unimpressive three percent of the popular vote, and narrowly escaped being hanged from a eucalyptus tree. By his own party machinery.

The experience created in Barry Black, Junior a sense of moral outrage, a new sense of moral outrage unlike any sense of moral outrage that had ever possessed him.

"I raised millions for those bastards," he howled from the safety of Oregon.

"And you blew it in two years flat," his most trusted advisor pointed out bitterly. "While you were building a useless political machine, the Republicans were out-registering us four-to-one."

"You know, the problem with this country is incumbency," said Barry Black, stumbling on a new campaign theme.

"You were an incumbent once."

"And if I were back in office, you can be damn sure this country wouldn't be in the mess it's in."

"Barry," said the advisor, his voice cracking like that of a bullfrog. "You're not thinking of doing *it* again. Are you?"

"What's wrong with . . . *it*?"

The other began ticking off reasons on fingers. "You washed out in 1980. You washed in 1984. California doesn't want you. What makes you think the rest of the country wants you?"

Barry Black squared his well-tailored shoulders. "They don't want me. That's the message. They need me. Washington is full of fat cats wasting the tax dollars. I only waste campaign contributions. It's an entirely different thing."

"Please, please, don't run for President again. I'm *begging* you."

But Barry Black was not to be swayed. His chipmunk eyes were already aglow with pure populist ambition.

"It's the White House or nothing," he vowed.

"It's nothing," the other man sobbed. "It's nothing."

Barry Black, Junior didn't even bother with an exploratory committee. He just got out in front of the cameras one day, his thinning hair now graying at the temples, and announced that he was a candidate for President of the United States.

"Again?" asked a reporter.

"This is what—the third time?" another wanted to know.

Barry Black became indignant.

"No, not *again*. That was a different Barry Black. I'm the new Barry Black, out to unseat the incumbents. I'm determined to reclaim the country, and reinvent the system. And the first thing I'm doing is to absolutely refuse any campaign contribution larger than a hundred dollars."

Coming from a man who had raised millions as California's Democratic Party Chairman, this was akin to Donald Trump offering to spend a night in a holding cell rather than squander a cent bailing himself out of jail.

The Barry Black for President campaign was mercifully short. After six months of stumping and speech-giving, and railing against everything from incumbency to what he called the "medical-industrial complex," he had raised a grand total of three thousand, two hundred and twelve dollars and six cents. One of which was Canadian.

"Not even enough to cover our phone bills," sobbed his most trusted advisor, now campaign manager.

"The trouble with you is you have no vision," Barry Black accused.

"The trouble with you is you have no brains. I quit!" said the campaign manager, slamming the door behind him.

That slamming door also closed out his ill-fated campaign. Without a campaign manager, Barry Black, Junior was reduced to doing his own laundry. The burden proved too much.

He was forced to pull out of the Presidential campaign early in the primaries. Back in his Pacific Park home overlooking San Francisco Bay, he once again took stock of his political future.

"Ommmmm. Ommmmm," he moaned, attempting to meditate.

It was in the middle of his mantra that the bulletin broke over the New Age mandolin music wafting from a table radio:

"The Governor's office has just announced that the governor and his lieutenant governor have both perished in an airliner crash. Further details when they become available."

Barry Black, Junior snapped his beady eyes open.

"It was a dream. I dreamed that, didn't I?" he asked the emptiness.

Flinging himself to the radio, he roved all over the dial until he had heard three variations of the same bulletin.

Barry Black, Junior took the next shuttle to Sacramento, to put in a surprise appearance at the double state funeral.

At the grave site, as the first clods of dirt clumped onto the side-by-side coffins, Barry Black, Junior worked the bereaved with an appropriately solemn expression on his chipmunk face.

"I share your loss," he told the first weeping widow

quietly. "I hope you'll vote for me in the special election. I share your loss," he told the second weeping widow. "I hope you'll consider me worthy of your vote in your time of grief."

The funeral had been a model of decorum until then. After Barry Black, Junior had finished offering his condolences to the immediate families, sobbing broke out.

Word rippled through the crowd. The press, catching word, descended upon Barry Black, Junior, quickly surrounding him.

"This is unseemly!" Barry Black said indignantly. "This is a state funeral, a morose occasion!"

"What's this we hear about you declaring your intention to run in the special election?" he was asked.

"Special election? You mean they're planning a special election?" Barry Black said blankly. "It's true I have been considering a reentry into local affairs, but I have made no determinations at this time."

"Do you think California is ready for Barry Black in the corner office again?"

"The old Barry Black, no."

"Which old Barry Black is that? The old Barry Black who was party chairman, or the old, old Barry Black who was governor?"

"I am neither of those Barry Blacks," Barry Black said firmly. "I am a whole new Barry Black. Think of it as a political reincarnation."

A cynical voice spoke up.

"How do you define the new improved Barry Black?"

"I define him," Barry Black, Junior said, to the jaw-dropping astonishment of the assembled press, "as a dyed-in-the-wool Republican."

Upon hearing the announcement, the California Republican Party chairman said, "We disown the flake."

The President's spokesman in Washington was moved to declare, "He can call himself whatever he wants, that doesn't make it so."

The *Sacramento Bee*, reviving the old political nickname, headlined it, GOVERNOR GLOWWORM TURNS.

Unfortunately for the California Republican party, they felt obliged to run the secretary of state and interim governor. He had two strikes against him: He had zero name recognition, and he was seen as the political creation of the hated but now lamented governor. Not a dark horse, but a dead one.

In protest, campaign contributions poured into Barry Black, Junior's war chest. No one believed he would win, anyway. He represented the protest-vote candidate. Everybody knew that.

Everybody except Barry Black, Junior.

"I love being a Republican!" he crowed, "It's so darn easy!"

"Don't get your hopes up," cautioned his new campaign manager.

"Why not? My only competition is Rambette the Ripper. Ever since she quite smoking, she's been hot to outlaw cigarettes."

"Barry, there's an old political saying, 'Dance with the one what brung ya.' "

Barry blinked beady, uncomprehending eyes.

"I don't know that one. It doesn't sound chantable."

"It means you came into politics a Democrat, and people won't respect you for switching horses in midstream. Just because you call yourself a Republican, doesn't mean the voters will buy it come election day."

"Tell that to David Duke," returned Barry Black, Junior.

"You wanna be the next David Duke, pull a sheet over your head and move to Louisiana."

With virtually no competition, Barry Black, Junior became an unstoppable juggernaut. In the polls.

Then came the first reports of the attempt on the life of dark-horse candidate Enrique Espiritu Esperanza.

"Who is Enrique Espiritu Esperanza?" Barry Black had asked when word reached him.

He had to have it explained to him twice.

When Enrique Esperanza began climbing up the polls, the question became, "Who the heck is Enrique Espiritu Esperanza?"

It was explained to him again. This time with newspaper clippings.

"No problem," he said. "He's nobody."

When the first footage of the South Central district of Los Angeles rally showed Enrique Esperanza lording it over the gangs like a modern-day Caesar, Barry Black was moved to shout, "Who the fucking hell is this Esperanza?"

"I don't know, but according to the political calendar, he's coming to town today."

"Let's get our troops mustered," said Barry Black.

Barry Black fumed as he was driven to his campaign headquarters on Nob Hill in a stretch limousine, a legacy from his party chairman days. He had purchased it from petty cash.

"I gotta do something about this guy," he muttered.

"Like what?"

"I'm a Republican now. I should do something appropriately Republican. Establish my new credentials."

"Good idea."

Barry Black's brow furrowed. "What would a Republican do in a situation like this?"

"I thought you *were* a Republican."

"I mean hypothetically."

"Maybe you should play the race card. Isn't that what they do?"

"Great thinking. I'll make a speech. Call him a low-down wetback greaser."

"Uh, Barry, I don't think that would be the way to go."

"Why not? It's the Republican way, isn't it?"

"No. It's what the Democrats call the Republican way."

"Darn. You're right. I'm still thinking like a Democrat. I gotta cure these tendencies." Barry Black closed his eyes. "Ommmmm. Ommmmm."

"You okay, Barry?"

"I'm meditating on Republicanism."

"Let me know if you see Lincoln," sighed his campaign manager.

Barry Black still hadn't arrived at a response to the Esperanza challenge when his limo pulled up before the storefront campaign headquarters.

He got out of the car, adjusting his Republican tie. He straightened his Republican coat and, his Republican shoes clicking on the sidewalk confidently, strode to the door.

Came a screeching of tires around a corner. Barry

Black turned instinctively. He saw an unusual sight, even for San Francisco.

A wide red convertible screeched around the corner. There was a brown-skinned man behind the wheel.

Squatting in the open backseat, like a machine-gunner in the rear of a jeep, was another brown-skinned man hanging off a fifty-caliber machine gun, which swayed on a pedestal mount.

The convertible straightened. The man at the machine gun got the perforated barrel pointed where he wanted it to point.

He wanted it to point in the general direction of Barry Black, Junior. Then he wanted it to open fire on Barry Black, Junior, because with a percussive stutter, it did.

Fifty-caliber bullets recognize few obstacles. These chopped through the campaign car, chewed up a fire plug, and reduced the Barry Black for Governor campaign headquarters to a ruin of chipped brick, broken glass, and shattered, bleeding bodies.

The convertible zoomed past, leaving Barry Black, Junior spread-eagled on the sidewalk.

The candidate for governor lay face-up, eyes staring skyward, in a welter of plate glass.

After the sound of the convertible's roar had died away in the distance, Barry Black's lips quirked. His eyes seemed to acquire focus.

Then a low, mournful sound escaped his lips.

"Ommm! Ommm! Ommm!"

17

Cheeta Ching was the first news person to arrive on the scene of what the next day's *San Francisco Examiner* would call "The Nob Hill Massacre."

The police had cordoned off the block. They no sooner had their yellow-plastic guard tape up than the FBI counter-terrorist team descended on the scene and tore it all down. They made the police stand off to one side, handling reduced to crowd control.

They were putting up their own guard tape when Cheeta Ching swooped in, like a harpy on wheels.

"I'm Cheeta Ching!" she called, dragging her cameraman by his collar.

She was pointedly ignored.

"I said, I'm Cheeta Ching, you racists!"

"Stay behind the lines, ma'am," an FBI agent cautioned.

"Where's the candidate? I demand to see the candidate."

A hand was raised. It was attached to a long, lean body that lay just outside the guard tape. Cheeta rushed up to the man.

"You have a statement?"

The hand formed a finger. It wobbled unsteadily.

A low moan escaped his lips.

"He's trying to communicate!" Cheeta said breathlessly. "He's trying to point out the candidate for us. Keep trying, you brave person."

"Cheeta . . ." the cameraman said.

"Quiet! I can't hear his moans!"

"Cheeta . . ."

"What!"

"I think that *is* the candidate."

"Oh my God!" Cheeta said, dropping to her knees.

156

"Are you hurt? Where are you hurt? America wants to see your wounds!"

"Not . . . hurt . . ." moaned Barry Black, Junior.

Cheeta leaped to her feet. "Then you can wait. I need some wet footage. Somebody find me a bleeding casualty."

They were still carrying out bodies from the demolished campaign headquarters.

Cheeta turned on her cameraman. "You get in there and get some 'If it bleeds, it leads' footage."

"Anyone stepping over the guard tape," a cold voice called, "will be arrested!"

The cameraman looked from the FBI agent to the cold face of Cheeta Ching. Calmly, he stepped over the guard tape, laid down his minicam, and lifted his hands in surrender.

An FBI agent stormed up. "What did I tell you?"

"I work with Cheeta Ching. What's the worst you're going to do to me?"

"I see your point," the agent said. He waved for a cop, saying, "Place this man in protective custody. For his own good."

As he was being led away in handcuffs, the cameraman said sheepishly to Cheeta Ching in passing, "I tried."

"You did not!" Cheeta flared. And while the cameraman, his head hanging low, was hustled into a police van, she recovered the minicam, saying, "Who needs cameramen, anyway?"

Hefting the minicam onto her padded shoulders, Cheeta returned to the prone form of Barry Black.

"Let's do a two-shot, okay?"

"Ommm," moaned Barry Black.

"Do you suspect that the assailants whose attempt on your life here today failed so miserably were the same who attempted to kill me?"

"Ommmm."

"Is that a yes or a no?"

"Ommm."

"Obviously in shock," Cheeta said, dropping the camera from her shoulders.

While she was trying to figure out her next move, a glossy-white Mercedes rolled to a halt a block away.

Out stepped Enrique Espiritu Esperanza, Harmon

Cashman, and a tiny old Korean man Cheeta Ching recognized at a glance.

"You!" she shrieked. Lugging the minicam, she jumped for the approaching trio. "I need to talk with you."

Enrique Esperanza said, "I will be happy to continue our interview."

"Not you," spat Cheeta Ching, pointing to the tiny wisp of a Korean. "I mean him."

The Master of Sinanju beheld the vision that swept toward him. His heart leaped high in his throat. His almond eyes widened, and for a moment he was a young man back in Pyongyang, beholding the beauteous Ch'amnari.

"I've been dying to talk to you!" Cheeta said urgently.

"I understand your desire," said Chiun, bowing, his voice tense, his heart a balloon of joy. Remo had granted his deepest wish.

"Great. Where can I find Rambo?"

Chiun straightened. "Rambo?"

"Yeah. Your dreamy friend. The one with the wrists."

"You mean Remo?"

"Is that what he's calling himself now? Where can I locate him? It's urgent!"

"No doubt he is sleeping under a rock, overcome with slothfulness and ingratitude," Chiun huffed. He turned and stalked off.

Cheeta Ching watched him go, her face blank. "What's got into him?"

"We do not know," said Enrique Esperanza. "We have come here to offer condolences to the Black campaign. This is a tragic thing."

"Great quote," said Cheeta Ching. "Mind repeating it for the camera?"

"Why don't you follow us?" Esperanza suggested. "We wish to speak with candidate Black personally."

"Okay, but talk slowly. I'm not used to being my own cameraman."

Barry Black, Junior was still lying on the sidewalk when they reached him.

"I am Esperanza," said Enrique Esperanza in a formal voice.

"Ohhmmm," said Barry Black.

"He keeps saying that," Cheeta pointed out. "I think he's in shock."

"I have just the thing," Esperanza said, kneeling beside the stricken candidate. He took a minipack of Oreo cookies from inside his white coat, undid the top, and placed one in Barry Black's open mouth.

"Chew slowly. Chocolate is a stimulant. The Aztecs knew this."

Somewhere deep in Barry Black's shattered mind, a synapse fired. He began chewing.

A moment later he sat up, saying, "My karma must have gotten mixed up with Yassar Arafat's."

"Do you have any idea who would do this thing?"

"Hey!" inserted Cheeta. "Asking questions is my job. You don't see *me* running for governor! Not that I couldn't do a better job than any of you men."

"Have you any enemies who would do this?" Esperanza asked in a soothing voice.

"The Democrats. The Republicans. Any Californian who remembers my last term in office. Maybe it's a conspiracy."

"I do not think so," said Enrique Esperanza, helping the man to his feet. "I am Enrique Esperanza," he added, shaking the man's hand.

"Got any more of those nifty cookies?" Barry Black asked.

Enrique Esperanza smiled. He offered the rest of the minipack.

As Barry Black munched away, he said, "Great! What are these things, anyway?"

"Oreos," Harmon Cashman explained. "You don't know Oreo cookies when you taste them? Where have you been?"

"India. Tibet. Nifty places like that. I accomplished a lot. I even grew a beard, but I shaved it. Beards are seventies."

While the minicam recorded every syllable, Enrique Esperanza said, "We must not allow terror and violence to determine the outcome of this important election."

"You got my vote," Barry Black said enthusiastically, saluting his rival with a half-chewed sandwich cookie.

"I do?"

"If you vote for me, too. Sort of a karmic exchange."

Enrique Esperanza laughed heartily. He agreed to vote for the former governor of California in return for his vote.

"This way we cancel each other out," said Barry Black Junior.

Harmon Cashman shoved an Oreo into his own mouth to suppress a grin of pleasure. He knew how this would play on the evening newscast. Gubernatorial candidate Enrique Espiritu Esperanza comforts rival and receives endorsement in return. It couldn't have played any better if he had set the whole thing up himself.

The attack on Black campaign headquarters led the evening local broadcast throughout California, and topped the national news on all three networks and CNN.

It was deplored from the White House on down to the San Francisco mayor's office. The President, en route to oversee renovations to his Maine home, paused under the whirling blades of Marine One to denounce the situation in the Golden State.

"We're not gonna let the California governor's race degenerate into the kind of thing we're seeing here," he promised. "I've asked the FBI and Secret Service to look into this. Mark my words, we're gonna nail the dastards behind this outrage. Our best people are on top of it."

Watching the news break from his Folcroft office, Harold W. Smith understood that the last remark referred to his organization. He had had a brittle conversation with the President only minutes before he'd left the White House.

"What's going on out there?" the President had asked testily.

"I do not know," Smith had admitted. "The last report from our special person was that two assassins had been terminated."

"I never heard that."

"We like to handle these matters quietly," Smith said. "At the moment I am awaiting a positive identification on one of the deceased terrorists."

"Are you sure it's terrorists?"

"My information is sketchy," Smith admitted. "We

have reason to believe the men behind this wave of political arson are Hispanic. Possibly foreign nationals."

"What nation?"

"Unknown. I am merely speculating in the absence of hard information."

"Well, dammit, get some facts. We need to know if this is connected with the double assassination of the two governors out there."

"I hope to have some concrete intelligence within a day or two," Smith assured the President. "In the meantime, I will move our special person into the Black campaign as a precaution."

"Won't that leave that Esperanza guy unprotected?"

"Our other special person has that aspect well in hand."

"I hope so, Smith. We can't tolerate this kind of stuff within our borders. This is America. Not some banana republic."

"Yes, Mr. President," said Harold W. Smith, replacing the red telephone receiver.

He looked at his watch. He hoped Remo would check in soon. His last report was that he was on his way to San Francisco, because that was where the Esperanza entourage—and therefore, Chiun—was relocating.

Smith returned to his computer. He accessed crime-statistics computers throughout the Golden State. They told him nothing. The only anomaly was an uptick of activity in the area of the Border Patrol. They were being stretched to the limit. Not from the surge of illegals coming across the U.S.–Mexican border, but illegals coming from other states to take advantage of the amnesty program. A number of them were being picked up before they could apply for citizenship.

The intercom buzzed while Smith was digesting this phenomenon.

"Yes, Mrs. Milkulka?"

"The lobby guard says there's a package for you, Dr. Smith."

"Have him bring it up," Smith said absently.

"I'm afraid it's too large for the elevator."

Smith's prim mouth puckered. "Tell him I'll be right down. And not to open that package."

Harold Smith reached the lobby in fifteen seconds flat.

The lobby guard said, "There it is."

His pointing finger indicated a long wooden crate, whose dimensions roughly matched those of a standard-sized coffin.

"Have it taken to the basement," Smith directed.

"Yes, sir."

In the dank basement, Harold Smith dismissed the pair of burly orderlies who had lugged the coffin-shaped box down there. They had placed it in a dim corner, beside the false wall that concealed the Folcroft mainframes that fed Smith's desktop terminal.

Taking a pry bar, Smith attacked the wooden slat cover. He cracked one of the slats free.

The smell made him recoil.

"Damn!" he choked, gasping for breath. He continued breaking slats until he had the upper torso of the dead man uncovered.

Smith reached in and felt about, distaste on his prim face. He finally found the videotape tucked into the corpse's shirt. It smelled of decay, as he brought it into the light of a naked twenty-five-watt bulb.

It was a struggle to get fingerprint samples. Rigor mortis had set in. But he managed the chore of inking the greenish fingers and impressing the prints onto a sheet of paper.

The face meant nothing to Smith. He committed it to memory, then hammered the slats back into place.

He returned to his office feeling very much in need of a shower.

Smith faxed the prints to the FBI, who thought they were receiving a routine CIA inter-agency information request.

While he was waiting for a reply, the blue contact phone rang. Smith picked it up.

"Remo?"

"Just checked into my hotel. What's up?"

"There has been an attempt on the life of Barry Black, Junior."

"No kidding."

"I never kid. And I do not appreciate the manner in which you responded to my request for the dead man's fingerprints."

"Find the tape?" Remo asked lightly.

"Yes."

"Anything on it?"

"I have not yet looked. I am awaiting the fingerprint report."

The computer beeped, and Smith said, "One moment, please." His adjusted his rimless eyeglasses and peered at the terminal screen. His eyes went wide. He returned to the phone.

"Remo. We have a break."

"Yeah?"

"According to the FBI, the dead man you—er—shipped to me is Queque Baez, an enforcer for the Medellin Cartel."

"Why would they want to hit Esperanza—or Black, for that matter?"

"Unknown. But we cannot take chances. I want you to join the Black campaign."

"Do I have to?" Remo asked glumly.

"You have to."

"Could be worse," Remo said resignedly. "You could be sending me into the Rona Ripper organization."

"Let us hope it does not come to that."

"Maybe she's behind this."

"Unlikely."

"Don't forget she helped General Nogeira get sprung for the baptism."

"I had not thought of that," Smith said slowly.

"I'll be in touch, Smitty."

Harold Smith replaced the blue receiver. A worried frown caused his lemony face to twitch. He looked to his closed medicine drawer. Despite the escalating situation, he felt no desire to reach for any of the remedies that in the past had gotten him through situations more dire than this one.

Although none of those situations, he recalled, had included having to dispose of a body in the basement of Folcroft.

18

Barry Black, Junior felt safe. In fact, he felt almost as safe in the attic of his Pacific Park home as he had been in India, doing the good work of Mother Teresa. Mainly her laundry.

After all, they didn't have personal pyramids in India. Pyramids were Egyptian. Pyramids, Barry Black, Junior knew, were also the ultimate in personal protection. They were impervious to uncool vibrations, bad karma, and cosmic rays. They also filtered out the more harmful effects of direct sunlight, which is why Barry had had his installed in the attic. The roof was skylight city.

Unfortunately, his imported-from-Ceylon formstone pyramid didn't repel sound waves.

"Barry, you gotta come out," pleaded the voice of his campaign manager.

Barry Black put aside a half-eaten Oreo cookie. "Where is it engraved in granite that Barry Black, Junior, Mr. Outsider, persecuted by the system, has to come out of his personal pyramid and be a target for every anti-reform whacko in the state?" he demanded.

"Because you can't campaign for governor inside a formstone pyramid in an attic."

"Where is that written? I'm a declared candidate. I can campaign any way I want. This is America."

"No, this is California. Not the same thing. And you've got to press the flesh if you wanna win."

"Let the voters come to me," Barry retorted firmly, "One at a time. After being frisked. Have those magnetometers and X-ray screens I ordered arrived yet?"

"Barry, this is going to get out. The press has been clamoring for a statement all afternoon."

"Write this down. I, Barry Black, Junior, the next governor of the fantabulous state of California, solemnly vow to cast his sacred vote on election day, and urge all citizens to do the same. Type that up and distribute copies to all interested parties."

"That's all you're gonna do?"

"What do you want? The ozone layer is breaking down. Melanomia is practically epidemic. I can't govern with black, hairy, precancerous moles on my face."

"Barry, please. Make a public appearance. Show the electorate you're not afraid."

"I'm not. I'm perfectly safe as long as I'm in my pyramid."

"If word gets out you're holed up in an obelisk," the campaign manager said sternly, "the campaign is over."

"If I come out and get my head shot off, the campaign is *really* over," Barry Black, Junior countered.

"You know, a true Republican wouldn't be caught dead in a pyramid."

The pyramid was silent. Except for a single dry crunch.

"I *am* a Republican," Barry Black said huffily. "Color me business-friendly."

"Prove it. Get out of that thing."

"No. I can prove it another way."

"I'm listening, Barry."

"I have a secret plan. Just like the great Republican, Richard M. Nixon."

"Richard M. Nixon's so-called 'secret plan' was to end the Vietnam War, and it turned out to be just smoke and mirrors—a scam to get him elected."

"Exactly. I have a secret scam-plan which will get me elected governor, and then and only then will I announce it."

"You're going to *announce* this scam *after* you're elected?" the campaign manager blurted out.

"Well, I can't very well announce it beforehand. It wouldn't work."

"If you announce it afterward, you might get lynched."

"Never happen. My secret scam-plan is so brilliant, people will applaud my genius."

"Er, is this scam—I mean *plan*—a secret from your campaign manager?"

"Yes. Wild horses couldn't drag it out of me."

"What," the campaign manager wondered, "would be big enough to drag you out of that thing?"

"I'll come out once I'm elected," Barry Black, Junior answered. "On inauguration day. We'll airlift me to the capitol and I'll emerge in triumph and fanfare, like a born Republican."

"Somehow I have trouble envisioning that."

"Try meditation. After I've meditated two-three hours, I see the most unbelievable colors."

"I'll bet you do. But you gotta do more than sit on your behind if you're going to beat Esperanza. He's moving major numbers in the polls."

In the New Age security of his pyramid, Barry Black, Junior put his agile mind to the task of winning over the voters of California. He closed his eyes and watched the colors his retina picked up. He got purple. Just purple. One color. No matter how much he squinched his eyes tight, no patterns or symbols emerged. Barry Black knew it had to mean something. But what?

"Enrique Esperanza is a one-note candidate," he said at last. "He's Mr. Multiculturalism. Multiculturalism is good, but it won't solve the problems of this great state. The recession. Taxes. The drought. The poinsettia whitefly. These are the issues that must be addressed with Republican forthrightness."

"You should be saying these things before the camera," his campaign manager pointed out, "not inside a formstone teepee."

"Teepee!" Barry Black cried. "That's it! We'll break the drought!"

"We will?"

"Not *we*, directly. I want *you* to scour the Indian Reservations. Find me a medicine man. A photogenic one, with lots of seams in his face and sad but wise-looking eyes."

"Sad but wise?"

"One who knows how to perform the sacred rain dance."

"Rain dance . . . ?"

"Go for a Chippewa. They have the best karma. Have him perform the dance in my name. Pick someplace splashy, like the La Brea Tar Pits. When the rain pours down, hand out umbrellas that say 'Vote For Black.'"

"We can't afford preprinted umbrellas, Barry."

"Use the tiny paper ones you get in Mai Tais."

"Barry," the campaign manager protested in exasperation, "if it works, the voters will be drenched. If it doesn't, we'll look like fools. We can't win."

"We can't fail. And voters will be soaked by election day. And a soaked voter is a Black voter. I want bumper stickers that say that."

"If you go through with this, they'll go back to calling you Governor Glowworm."

"As long as I'm governor again, who cares what they call me?" Barry Black retorted firmly.

The Black for Governor campaign manager let out a leaky sigh.

"Barry," he said wearily, "I'm going downstairs and renew my acquaintance with Valium. When I feel up to it, I'll come back and we'll have this conversation again. Okay?"

"Remember. Chippewas are best. A Hopi might do in a pinch. But no Sioux. They were scalpers. The bad karma will rebound on us. And bad karma doesn't wash off. I learned that in India."

In the dark confines of his personal pyramid, Barry Black, Junior listened as his campaign manager descended the attic stairs. It was going to work out. It would all work out, if everyone found their centers and held on for dear life.

And as long as Barry Black, Junior remained in his pyramid, safe from assassins.

19

Remo Williams had tried every Barry Black for Governor campaign office in San Francisco.

All were under police guard, and all were deserted.

At the third deserted storefront, Remo presented a UPI press pass in the name of "Remo Cannon" to an SFPD sergeant and asked, "Did Black pull out of the race?"

"Not that I heard," the sergeant said.

"So where are his campaign people?"

"Hunkered down in bomb shelters, from what I hear."

"I thought the attempt was on Black's life?"

"That's what everyone says, but the only ones who died were campaign staff. Now the bomb threats are pouring in."

"Bomb threats?"

"Every campaign office received one. When the staffers heard that, they went home. A lot of them quit outright. Guess they decided it was too much trouble to give the Glowworm a third shot at Sacramento."

"Thanks," Remo said, returning to his rented car.

At a phone booth, Remo called Folcroft.

"Smitty, I can't join the Black campaign."

"Why not?"

"Because there is no campaign."

"He pulled out?"

"No, his organization did. They all got bomb threats and decided to call it a day."

"Peculiar," said Smith.

Ignoring an intermittent whistling in the background, Remo said, "I think it's interesting that Black's people got hurt, but he wasn't."

"You do not think Barry Black has engineered this entire charade?" Smith said, his voice rising.

"Why not? He was taking a beating in the polls. Esperanza was pulling ahead of him. This was his way of recapturing sympathy."

"A little while ago," Smith pointed out, "you suggested that Rona Ripper might have engineered the attempts on Esperanza's life."

The whistle came again. It sounded different. But when Remo turned around, he saw only passersby minding their own business.

"I haven't ruled her out yet," he said. "For all we know, she was on Nogeira's payroll."

"Speaking of Nogeira, I am receiving ongoing reports of undocumented aliens pouring into California from other states, with the purpose of applying for amnesty and citizenship."

The whistling continued. Remo changed ears. "So?"

"They are registering to vote in record numbers."

"What's that got to do with Nogeira?"

"Before he was deposed, Remo, General Nogeira was heavily involved in smuggling illegals into this country, primarily from El Salvador and other Central American republics."

"You saying this could be part of Nogeira's master plan, if there was one?"

"Esperanza's call for undocumented aliens to come forward and take advantage of these programs has been picked up only by the California media. I cannot imagine how the word is spreading, unless the ball had been started even before the campaign began."

"By Nogeira?"

"By Nogeira."

"Well," Remo said, switching ears again, "I'm going to take Barry Black by the scruff of the neck and shake him a little."

Smith's voice became chilly. "Remo, that man is a registered gubernatorial candidate. You are not to molest or intimidate him in any way."

"What if he's guilty of subverting the process?"

The line hummed. Remo stuck his finger in his free ear to keep out the annoying whistles. It was a moment before Harold W. Smith spoke again.

"We are in the business of upholding the Constitution whenever we can," he said firmly. "Political assassination is a line CURE has yet to cross in any meaningful way."

"There's always a first time," Remo said flatly.

"My instructions stand."

"How about I just *talk* to Black?"

"I will accept that."

"Good, because I hope you have his home address. He's not in the book."

"According to the latest reports, Black has gone into seclusion. But he is believed to be in his Pacific Park home. At least, the local media believe that. They are virtually laying siege to the house."

Remo groaned. "Oh, no."

"What is it?" Smith asked.

"That means Cheeta Ching is sure to be there, yapping at the head of the pack," Remo said unhappily.

"I am sure you will find a way to avoid her," Smith said dryly.

"Count on it," Remo said, hanging up.

On his way to the car, Remo was accosted by a thin-voiced young man, with a kerchief hanging out his back pocket and another one loose about his throat.

"Hello, sailor," he said, smiling. "Going my way?"

"If your way is what I think it is, not in your lifetime."

"How about a detour?"

"How about you suck your thumb?"

"Not what I had in mind."

Remo tapped the man's right elbow, forcing him to grab his funny bone, but the words sputtering out of his mouth weren't funny.

Remo quieted the man by inserting one of his own thumbs into his mouth and freezing his jaw muscles closed with a paralyzing tap.

"You don't know 'til you try it," he said.

Remo left him sucking on his thumb while walking in circles, trying to shake the pins and needles from his arm.

He still wondered what that whistling was.

The Pacific Park home of Barry Black, Junior could be seen clearly from the foot of the hill where Remo had parked his car.

It was a sprawling Victorian that was equal parts Bohemia and Addams Family. The house was painted a pumpkin-orange, with jet-black shutters. There was a Pennsylvania Dutch hex sign over the front door. The weathervane sticking up from the chimney pot was in the shape of a yin-yang sign, and seemed to have rusted one day when there was a brisk east wind blowing.

The house must have been a hundred years old, but the peaked roof was a modern mosaic of solar panels, space-age satellite dishes, and ordinary Plexiglas skylights.

The steep street leading up to the house was lined with microwave satellite vans. Most were empty. Remo could see the front walk of the orange-and-black monstrosity. That was where the local press had camped out. A few were skulking through the hedges, which had been sculpted, apparently, in the shapes of endangered species. At least Remo thought he recognized a dodo.

Remo also recognized Cheeta Ching. The Korean anchor was at the cellar door, trying to detach the padlock with her teeth.

Spying the van belonging to the local affiliate of the network that employed her, Remo slipped up to it. He was in luck. There was a driver sitting behind the wheel, looking bored.

Remo tapped on the glass. It was rolled down.

"Yeah?" asked the driver.

Remo smiled. "I'm with the medical lab," he said brightly.

"What medical lab?"

"The one Cheeta Ching uses. I got good news for her. The rabbit died."

The driver's bored eyes got unbored. "That *is* good news! In fact, it's great news! She'll probably be on the first jet back to New York after she hears this."

"You wanna deliver the message?" Remo asked.

"A pleasure," the driver said, bolting from the van.

Grinning, Remo retreated to the backyard of an adjacent house to await developments.

"This ought to be great," he said to himself.

To his surprise, the driver didn't even try to look for Cheeta. Instead, he jumped into the milling mass of media representatives and began spreading the joyous news.

"Cheeta's gonna drop one!" he howled.

The pack broke in all directions.

"Everyone loves good news," Remo chortled.

And as he watched, Cheeta Ching was pounced upon. The questions flew fast and furious.

"Miss Ching, is it true?"

"Is what true?"

"That you're with child."

"Who said that? My husband?"

"The lab said the rabbit died."

Cheeta turned predatory. "It did? What's your source for that? Did the rabbit have a name? Did he suffer?"

"Your driver told us. He just heard the word."

"I'm preggers!" Cheeta shrieked, throwing up her hands.

Then a strange look came over her flat face. Like an Asian Gorgon, Cheeta Ching lowered her sticky-haired head until she was looking up from under her perfect viper eyebrows into a ring of minicam lenses.

"Everybody better not be filming this," she hissed.

"Why not? It's news."

"It's *my* news. It's my body. It's my story, and I intend to be the first to break it!"

"Too late," a chipper voice called out. "You gave us the quote. Remember the First Amendment."

"Remember that if any of you have careers after today, you'll have to deal with me. Somewhere. In some city. In some station."

"Are you planning on taking maternity leave, Miss Ching?" a reporter asked pleasantly.

"Cut it out!" Cheeta howled.

"Do you have any ovulation tips for aging baby-boomers who want to be mothers?" another wanted to know.

"Do you have a favorite position for procreating, Miss Ching?" demanded a third.

"The first person to break this story," Cheeta Ching said in a venomous voice, "I will publicly name as the father."

"Then I guess the story's mine," said a bright female voice.

"Who said that?" Cheeta shrieked.

Out from the pack of reporters bolted Jade Ling, a local San Francisco anchorwoman of Asian descent. She made for her van.

Cheeta gave chase, crying, "You Jap tart! Come back with that footage!"

The cameras followed them down the steep street on Pacific Park, filming every shriek and threat Cheeta Ching vomited from her leathery lungs.

While they were sorting out broadcast rights, Remo circled around to the blind side of the house and mounted the gingerbread and nameless wooden decorations to the roof. Amid a forest of satellite dishes, he found an unobstructed skylight and peered down.

He saw a bare attic, with Navajo blankets hanging from the rafters. In one corner there was a squat, featureless pyramid, which looked like it had been formed of concrete.

Remo looked around for a catch or fastener and, finding none, simply popped the Plexiglas from the skylight mounting. He simply pressed down on the bulbous top, until the caulking surrendered and the Plexiglas jumped up into his hands.

Remo set it in a handy satellite dish and dropped down.

As soon as his feet hit the bare flooring, he froze.

His Sinanju-trained senses instantly detected a heartbeat, and the slow, shallow inhale-exhale of human lungs.

There was no one in the attic. In fact, there was no thing in the attic. Except the pyramid.

Remo slipped up to this. The sound of respiration grew louder. There was someone inside the thing.

Remo looked for an opening. There was none. He decided to knock anyway.

"Anyone home in there?" he called.

"Who are you?" a suspicious voice demanded.

"Secret Service. You Barry Black, by any wild chance?"

"Chance," said Barry Black, "has nothing to do with how I got to be Barry Black."

"I'll buy that," Remo said quickly. "I have a few questions for you."

"I am not answering questions today," said Barry Black.

"You have to."

"As long as I'm in my personal pyramid, I don't have to do anything I don't want to."

"Okay," Remo said lightly, reaching down and grasping the base of the formstone. He straightened.

The pyramid was lifted off the squatting form of Barry Black, like a witch's hat coming off her head. Remo kept it high.

Barry Black, Junior sat in a lotus position on a tatami mat, his hands loose on his knees and his eyes closed. His brow was furrowed in concentration.

"Come out, come out," Remo called.

Barry Black opened his eyes. He seemed surprised to see Remo.

"You don't look like a Secret Service agent," he said meekly.

"I'm in disguise," Remo told him.

"Show me some ID."

"My hands are full right now," Remo pointed out, indicating with a tilt of his chin the pyramid suspended over Barry Black's graying head by Remo's bare, ramrod-straight arms.

Barry Black looked up. His chipmunk face grew worried. "Don't drop that. It's imported from Ceylon."

"Says 'Made in Mexico' on the base here," Remo said.

"Oh my God!" Barry Black squealed in horror. "I've been hiding in a counterfeit pyramid! I could have been killed!"

Remo set the pyramid down. It cracked in three places, and the apex fell in like the crown of a broken tooth.

"Now that we know the awful truth," Remo said lightly, "it's time to come clean."

"It is?"

"I know all about it."

"What 'it'?"

"Every it," Remo said. "You don't think you can hide this kinda stuff from the Secret Service, do you?"

"Just because I'm bucking the establishment doesn't give you Washington insiders the right to harass me," Barry Black said in an indignant tone.

"Who's harassing? I'm just saying that the jig is up."

Barry Black, Junior folded his arms. "Then it's up. So what? You can't prove anything."

"Wanna bet?"

"Until I announce, you can't prove anything."

"Announce what?"

Barry Black, Junior compressed his lips and said, "For all I know you're wired for sound. I will not incriminate myself."

"Okay," Remo told him. "Then by the powers vested in me by the President of the United States, your Secret Service protection is hereby revoked."

Barry Black looked stricken. "It is?"

Remo nodded firmly. "I quit."

And to make sure the point was driven home, Remo gave the formstone pyramid a careless kick. It collapsed in a clatter of rubble.

Barry Black, Junior, seeing this, lost his composure.

"I'll do anything!" he said. "I don't care anymore! The voter anger out there is more than I can stand!"

"The truth," Remo prompted.

"It's true. Just as you suspected. I have a secret scam— I mean, plan. Once I'm elected, I'm switching back."

Remo blinked. "Switching what back?"

"Is that a trick question?" asked Barry Black, Junior.

"Yes, and you'd better answer it truthfully."

"Switching back to the Democrats. I knew I couldn't get elected as a Democrat, so I switched to the Republican party, even though they wouldn't have me on a popsicle stick. Once I'm elected, I'll just switch back."

"That's crazy," Remo said.

"It worked for Buddy Roemer in Louisiana."

"Buddy Roemer had his head handed to him," Remo pointed out. "He got trounced in the primaries."

"That was Louisiana. This is California. People understand creative politics out here."

"And that's it? You're running as a Republican, but you're not?"

"Brilliant, isn't it?"

"In a goofball kind of way, I suppose. What about the attempts on your life? Who's behind that?"

"I have no idea. Probably the Republicans."

"I doubt it," Remo said dryly.

"Then the Democrats. They probably see me as a traitor."

"I think they're probably happy to be rid of you."

"Then I don't know who's trying to get me," Barry Black snapped.

"Then neither do I," Remo said glumly.

At that moment, feet came pounding up the stairs.

"They're coming for me!" Barry Black said, jumping to his slippered feet. He got behind Remo, who wondered aloud, "What's this?"

"You're Secret Service, right?"

"Right."

"It's your job to take the bullet meant for the candidates, right?"

"Normally, yeah," Remo admitted.

"They're yours. Every bullet. With my best wishes for a happy next incarnation."

Frowning, Remo made for the door and threw it open, one second before the man on the other side could take hold of the cut-glass knob. Losing his balance, the other man fell forward. Remo caught him and pulled him into the room.

"Who are you?" he demanded.

"Who the hell are *you*?" the other shot back.

"Remo Drake. Secret Service."

"Where's your ID?"

"I answered that one already," Remo said.

"It's true," Barry Black said helpfully. "He answered that question. Remo's okay. Except that he knows about my secret plan to get elected."

"Well, then he's one up on me, and I'm in charge of this campaign," said the campaign manager.

"Trust me. You're better off not knowing," Remo said.

The Black campaign manager turned to his candidate and said, "Barry, they're reporting that Rona Ripper was just shot."

"Is that good or bad?" Barry Black asked, face warping as the brain behind it attempted to assimilate this bizarre turn of the Karmic wheel.

"She's alive."

"Where is she?" Remo demanded.

"They rushed her to St. John's in Santa Monica."

Remo started for the door.

Barry Black, Junior started after him, his voice anguished. "Wait, where are you going? You promised to protect me."

"Consider yourself protected," Remo growled, slipping down the stairs. "Reality won't ever touch you."

20

When he reached him by phone, Remo Williams was surprised at the lack of concern in Harold W. Smith's lemony voice.

"Yes, I know about the Ripper shooting," he said crisply. "Regrettable."

"The third candidate shot in almost as many days, and that's all you can say?"

"You obviously did not catch the follow-up reports," Smith said dryly.

"I didn't catch any reports," Remo retorted. "I was in The Twilight Zone with Barry Black when his campaign manager came charging in with the news."

"Remo, Rona Ripper suffered a bullet wound at the hands of one of her personal security guards."

"Huh?"

"When the Black campaign was hit," Smith explained, "Miss Ripper ordered members of her entourage to arm themselves. One was cleaning his weapon in her presence, and it discharged. Rona Ripper suffered a flesh wound."

"So it wasn't an assassination attempt?"

"The weapon was a .22-caliber, and the projectile lodged in Miss Ripper's . . . ah . . . posterior."

"Rona Ripper was shot in the butt?" Remo said in disbelief.

"The security guard has apologized. Miss Ripper is suing him in return."

"Why doesn't that surprise me?" Remo growled, clapping a hand over his free ear to keep out that damn whistling. He couldn't understand it. He was at a phone booth in a completely different part of San Francisco, yet he was hearing it again.

"I do not know. What did you learn from Barry Black?"

"He's got a secret plan to win the election."

"Is it legal?"

"Oh, I don't know," Remo said. "Is impersonating a Republican against any law that you know of?"

"Impersonating . . . ?"

"Barry Black is a donkey in elephant's clothing," Remo said flatly. "He figures he can get elected as a Republican and then revert to being what he is—a horse's ass."

"This is unsettling," Smith said glumly.

"No argument there. It's so screwy that it means Black's not behind these political hits."

"Are you certain of that, Remo?"

"Barry Black is so flaky he belongs in dandruff commercials," Remo said flatly.

"I wonder . . ." Smith mused.

"Wonder what?"

"This Ripper shooting. Perhaps it is a charade."

"Could be. I've seen Rona Ripper in the flesh. You could shoot her in the butt all day long and not hit bone."

"Remo, why don't you look into the Ripper campaign?"

"Not me. I draw the line there. She's almost as bad as Cheeta Ching."

"Speaking of Miss Ching, your problems with her may be over."

Remo brightened. "How so?"

"It was just announced that she is expecting a child."

Remo's unhappy expression returned. "I guess that Japanese newscaster outran her."

"What did you say?"

"Never mind, Smitty. I wouldn't believe anything Cheeta Ching says, okay? As for Rona the Ripper, count me out."

"Could you pursuade Chiun to handle that end?" Smith asked.

"I doubt it."

"Then you have no choice," Smith said crisply. "Join the Ripper campaign, and learn all you can."

"With my luck," Remo growled, "I'll end up with Cheeta on one side and Rona on the other."

"In the meantime, we will just have to hope that Barry Black's personal security is enough."

"No sweat. He's in his attic and refuses to come down. You know, Esperanza is starting to look better every day."

"We are not taking sides in this," Smith said sternly.

"Maybe not. But that doesn't mean we can't back the horse we want."

"Let me know if anything breaks," Smith said, hanging up.

Remo left the phone booth and almost made it to his rented car unaccosted.

He ignored a wolf whistle, thinking it was directed at a busty blonde on the other side of the street.

A second wolf whistle was followed by the comment, "Where'd you get those wrists, tall, dark, and limber?"

Remo had never heard the word "limber" used to describe a member of the opposite sex, and looked up. There was a construction worker in a hard hat and with a beer belly, three stories up in an under-construction high-rise.

When he caught Remo's eye, he blew him a kiss.

Remo gave him half the peace sign in return, and continued on to his car, muttering, "It'll be great to get out of this city. Santa Monica has to be a thousand times better than this."

Santa Monica, when Remo reached it after a six-hour drive, looked as though a neutron bomb had detonated in the middle of Main Street.

Main Street was the main drag, just up from the beach. The ocean tang, flavored by salt-water taffy, refreshed the air, and the store windows on either side displayed surfboards and bathing suits.

So did the undulating bodies strolling up and down the walks.

But it was the bodies lying in the streets and bright-painted alleys that caught Remo's attention.

They were everywhere. As Remo drove past Palisades Park, he saw that almost every square inch of greenery was occupied by disheveled, unwashed, and unshaven people of both sexes. There were Hispanics drinking out of paper bag-covered bottles. Asians lying in sleeping bags like caterpillars, and others playing cards. Most of them were asleep under the summer sunshine, however. The snoring was enough to keep the trees free of birds.

Under a eucalyptus tree, a man was roasting a squirrel.

A neat hand-carved sign at the park entrance read: HOMELESS SHELTER. TAXPAYERS KEEP OFF THE GRASS.

Remo spotted a cop guarding the entrance and pulled over. He leaned out the window.

"Where can I find St. John's?"

The cop gave precise directions, then Remo asked, "How long has it been like this?"

"Since the city council voted to make Santa Monica a nuclear-free town."

"That doesn't explain all these homeless people," Remo pointed out.

"They added a rider that hung a Welcome to the Homeless sign at the town limits, and a statute against arresting them for anything less than a capital crime," explained the cop. "Word got out, and now we're the homeless capital of California."

"What about the taxpapers?" Remo asked.

"If they don't like it, they can move. It's a free country."

"Unless you pay taxes," Remo muttered, sliding back into traffic.

At the next light, Remo's car was surrounded by three beggars who refused to let him pass unless he paid the toll.

"What's the toll?" Remo asked.

"Five bucks. For each of us."

"I think I'll take the detour, thanks," Remo said.

"You go down that street and the toll's twenty. Get a better deal from us."

Remo gunned the motor, saying, "I bet I'd be doing the squirrel population a big favor if I just floored the pedal."

"You do that and the man will arrest you."

"I hear bail's pretty cheap out here," Remo countered.

The man shrugged. "Don't know. Never been in no jail. You gonna pay, or what?"

"Or what," Remo said instantly, spinning his rear wheels until they sent up clouds of lung-stinging rubber smoke. He reached for the parking brake.

The intersection suddenly cleared. The light changed and Remo zoomed through.

There were homeless sleeping on the grounds of St. John's Hospital and Health Center. They had taken every free patch of lawn and were making inroads into the parking lot.

Remo found a space in the handicapped zone. No sooner had he slid in than a disreputable man called up from a sterno fire in another space.

"Hey, you! You can't park in no handicapped zone!"

"Why not?"

"That's for Charlie One-leg. He sleep there."

"Tell Charlie I'm only here for an hour."

"Squatter!" the man yelled. "I'm gonna call a cop on you!"

"Scare me some more," Remo growled. He collected abuse all the way to the hospital entrance, where he stepped over a snoring Mexican and entered.

He walked up to the admissions desk, noticing that every waiting room chair was filled.

"I'm looking for—"

"Hush," the admissions nurse hissed. "Do you want to get us closed down?"

"Huh?"

The admissions nurse pointed to the patients slumped in chairs. Remo noticed that most were asleep, their mouths hanging open. One slid off his seat and slipped to the floor, where he continued to snore enthusiastically.

"It's against the law to wake them during the Nap Hour."

"Nap Hour?"

"Sir," the admissions nurse said sternly, "I will be forced to have you ejected if you persist in flaunting Santa Monica Public Ordinance 55-Z."

Remo sighed and attempted to communicate his needs. First, he showed his Secret Service ID card. The admissions nurse nodded her understanding. Then he took her over to a California map and pointed to the town of Ramona.

The admissions nurse nodded.

Finally, Remo tore a sheet of paper in two while pointing at the map.

"Ramona Tear?" she mouthed.

"Rip," Remo mouthed back.

"Rip Ramona?" the admissions nurse mouthed, her face blank.

"Rona Ripper," Remo snapped in exasperation.

In a corner a sleeping man made a snuffling sound, and the admissions nurse's eyes went wide in horror.

"Tell me which room she's in, or I'll wake them all," Remo threatened.

"Four seventy-eight! Third floor!" the admissions nurse bleated.

Remo wasted a minute waiting for an elevator. When it arrived, it was occupied by a trio of Chileans playing three-card monte.

"Do you mind?" one asked.

"I'm beginning to," Remo grumbled. He took the stairs.

On the third floor, he passed the same game in progress in the same elevator.

"Cause of you I'm losing!" one of the players shouted at him. "Broke my concentration!"

"Sue me," Remo shot back, working his way to Room 478. He was beginning to look forward to meeting Rona Ripper—if only because she probably bathed more than once a month.

Rona Ripper lay on her stomach like a beached whale, her chin on a fluffy pillow, her intensely black eyes on the TV screen set on a high wall shelf opposite her hospital bed. She looked like the Goodyear version of Elvira.

The room smelled hospital-clean. But it was not clean enough for Rona Ripper. The window fan was busy sucking out the offending odor of disinfectants. She had ordered the keyhole of the door sealed with wax, so that no disagreeable smell of sickness or blood or pus could find its way into the pristine environment of her room.

After the physician had changed the dressing on her wound, she had ordered him banished.

"You can't banish me," the doctor had complained.

"You're a smoker. I can tell."

"That's none of your business. Besides, I'm not smoking now."

"Your clothing reeks of tobacco. You get out, or I'll sue you for every penny."

"On what grounds?" the doctor asked.

"Spreading second-hand smoke."

"Miss Ripper, at best there are trace elements on my smock."

"Carcinogens are insidious. The smaller they are, the more damage they do. Out!"

The doctor had withdrawn in a huff. Another sign of a chronic tobacco fiend. They were ill tempered. When Rona Ripper became governor of California, she vowed, no one would smoke. All billboards would be replaced with giant No Smoking signs. Tobacco products would be outlawed. Smoking fines would run to five figures. Per violation.

"It will be," Rona Ripper had said, when she'd announced her candidacy before a packed meeting of the Southern California branch of the American Civil Rights Collective, "a paradise on earth."

The ACRC had applauded wildly. They already thought California was a paradise on earth. But they knew it was not a perfect paradise. For one thing, there were too many Republicans.

"I intend," Rona had shouted, "to run on a strict no-smoking platform. Smoking is at the root of all our troubles in this wonderful progressive state of ours."

More applause. The fact that Rona Ripper was Executive Director of the Southern California branch of the ACRC had nothing to do with their enthusiasm. They always applauded sentences containing the word "progressive," whether spoken or not. If Rona Ripper had announced that she had contracted progressive throat cancer, they would have begun applauding before she got out the word, "throat."

"If we stamp out cigarettes, cigars, and pipes, our studies show," Rona added, "the smog levels will drop accordingly."

That had brought them to their feet. No one thought
to ask what "accordingly" meant in terms of cubic vol-
ume. Had they learned that tobacco smoke was a negligi-
ble contributor to the California pollution problem, they
would have denounced the results as a cover-up perpe-
trated by big business and the tobacco lobby.

When Rona Ripper added her personal belief that
smoking had contributed in not-yet-understood ways to
the six-year drought, they carried her through the streets
on their shoulders.

That night, the Southern California ACRC came out
in total support of Rona Ripper for Governor. The fact
that she had no economic recovery plan, no strategy to
deal with the drought, and no interest in the illegal alien
crunch other than to note that California had belonged
to Mexico before it belonged to the fascist United States,
meant nothing. She was against smokers' rights. In a
state where local laws already had sent tobacco users
slinking and skulking, to exercise their right to smoke
freely in woods and back alleys and under freeways, that
was enough to mobilize a political organization and get
Rona Ripper on the ballot.

The early weeks of the campaign had been promising.
She had been polling even with the traitor, Barry Black,
Junior.

Then Enrique Espiritu Esperanza, having narrowly escaped assassination, had begun moving up.

It had presented Rona Ripper with an incredible
dilemma.

Esperanza was a Hispanic, and therefore above criti-
cism. There was no way the Executive Director of the
ACRC could publicly criticize an Hispanic candidate.
They belonged to the underprivileged underclass. To criticize one of them would have been tantamount to heresy.

"We have to get something on this guy," Rona had
complained to her inner circle. "Something that will
knock him out of the race, and keep our hands clean."

"He's a straight arrow. Son of an immigrant. Built a
vineyard in the Napa Valley and made good. He's
clean."

Rona Ripper's black eyes narrowed. She frowned like
a thundercloud.

"Has he ever . . . smoked?"

"Not that we can prove."

"But it's possible," Rona pressed.

"Doubtful."

"Maybe we can doctor up a photo showing him with a Camel in his mouth. I hear they can do that with computer-enhancement now."

The campaign director of the Ripper for Governor organization shook his head. "Too risky. Could backfire."

Rona's frown deepened. "You're right. We can't take the chance. If I lose, this state is doomed."

Around the conference table, heads nodded in solemn agreement. There was no question: Without Rona Ripper of the ACRC to guide the Golden State, it might as well fall into the Pacific.

"Then we have no choice," Rona had decided. "We'll have to run on the issue."

"Issues, you mean."

"There is only one issue," Rona Ripper said tartly. "Making California's air breathable again. And the only obstacle is the evil weed called tobacco."

When it was reported that Barry Black, Junior had escaped an assassination attempt, Rona Ripper had greeted the news with wide eyes and a shift in strategy.

"It's a two-issue race now," she decreed. "Tobacco, and the right to campaign in safety. I want round-the-clock protection."

"I'll put in a request with the authorities."

"Are you insane? The way we've been suing them for years? Those Neanderthals are probably *behind* this campaign violence. I want everybody armed and ready to lay down their lives in the name of Governor Ripper."

This presented the Ripper for Governor campaign with a new crisis. They were against private ownership of firearms.

"If we arm now," Rona was told, "the National Rifle Association will throw it back in our faces into the next century."

Rona stood firm. "My election is more important than mere principle. I want one sacrificial lamb to buy a gun and stand by my side, ready to kill or be killed."

In the end, they drew straws. One of the press liaisons drew the short straw. He bought a .22 Ruger and showed it to Rona Ripper the same day.

"Is it loaded?" Rona asked, curious.

"Good question," said the press liaison. He lifted the shiny weapon to his face and looked down the barrel. He squinted.

"Well?" Rona demanded.

"I don't see any bullets."

Someone suggested that he pull the trigger. The press liaison did just that, neglecting to remove his face from the line of fire.

Fortunately, the campaign manager for the Ripper campaign understood that pistols sometimes go off even when pointed at unintended targets. He lunged for the press liaison's gun hand and attempted to wrestle it free.

He was both just in time and too late, simultaneously.

He was just in time to keep the press liaison from blowing his head off, and too late to prevent the bullet from snarling out of the barrel.

It burned past the liaison's head, ricocheted off an overhead pipe, and imbedded itself in the most generous target in the room.

Rona Ripper suddenly found herself seated in the middle of the floor, with a surprised look on her face and a dull pain in her ample behind.

"What happened?" she gasped. "Is it an earthquake?"

No one wanted to tell the probable future governor of California that she had been shot in the ass. They weren't sure, but somehow her rights probably had been violated. And there was an excellent chance she would sue them all into bankruptcy. She had done it to major corporations all over the state after a lot less provocation.

Rona Ripper had solved the problem for them. She tried to stand up. Her body refused to work. She looked around her and saw the blood.

Then, with a soft but vicious "I'll sue" issuing from her lips, she fainted.

Rona Ripper had awoken on her stomach, with her backside swathed in bandages, repeating that same mantra over and over.

The doctor on staff immediately put her under with an injection, then transferred to another hospital. He knew Rona Ripper had single-handedly raised malpractice insurance rates all over California.

So it was that, when Rona Ripper finally regained consciousness, she was reduced to describing her symptoms to an anonymous doctor on the other side of the closed hospital room door.

"How do you think I feel? I have a bullet in my butt!"

"Is there anything else we can do for you?" the doctor said, smiling inanely, as if at a homicidal maniac.

Rona Ripper dictated a thirty-seven-item list of demands, and the anonymous doctor went away.

She knew she was going to get what she wanted when demand number twelve, the sealing of the keyhole against intrusive odors, was carried out. Total obedience. That's the way it always should be, she thought smugly.

"When I'm in charge of this state," she muttered to herself, "people are going to jump when I bark."

"Woof-woof," a voice said, as the door opened.

"Hold it right there," Rona commanded.

Remo Williams paused on the threshold.

"Before you enter, do you, or have you ever, smoked in your life?" demanded Rona Ripper.

"Not in years," Remo said.

"Then you can't come in."

"Too late. I'm in," Remo said, flashing his Secret Service ID. He looked around the room and noticed it was empty.

"No press?" he asked.

"They know I'd sue them if they so much as pointed a camera in my face," sniffed Rona Ripper.

"I don't think your face is where they'd be pointing their cameras," Remo said dryly. "No offense," he added quickly, as he saw Rona Ripper's bloated face turn purple.

"You get out of here right now!" she screamed.

"Now now, you'll wake the homeless," Remo chided.

"Too late," came a growling voice from under the bed. "I'm already awake, man."

Remo looked under the bed, where he discovered a man in a dirty green nylon sleeping bag. The man said, "City Ordinance 42-D. We get the beds if they're empty, and the space under them if they ain't."

"I would like to have a private conversation with this woman," Remo said wearily.

"He stays," said Rona Ripper. "He's part of my natural constituency."

"No, I ain't. I'm voting for Esperanza. He gives me hope."

"Get that bum out of here!" Rona screamed.

"A pleasure," said Remo, reaching down and pulling the sleeping bag into the light. The man was struggling to get out. Remo zipped the sleeping bag as far as it would zip, entangling the slide in the man's blond beard.

Remo then dragged the sleeping bag out into the corridor and into the elevator, where the card game was still in progress. He set down the wriggling, nylon-sheathed form on the pot.

"Going down!" Remo called, hitting the LOBBY button. The steel doors closed as the players scrambled for the pot.

Back in the hospital room, Rona Ripper was in no better mood.

"I don't talk to pigs from Washington," she snarled.

"Then listen. Someone tried to kill Enrique Esperanza. Someone tried to kill Barry Black. You're the only other candidate in the running. The finger of guilt points to you."

"It does not."

To prove his point, Remo took the steel-hard index finger of his right hand and used it to test the thickness of the bandage over Rona Ripper's generous left cheek.

This produced an ear-splitting howl from Rona's other end.

"Answers. Are you behind this or not?"

"No!"

"Then someone in your organization is?"

"No, I swear!"

"There's no third suspect. Do better than that. The finger of guilt is very, very angry."

Remo pressed harder. Tears streamed from Rona Ripper's pain-squinted eyes. Her long black hair threshed about, like a bloated octopus struggling to free itself from a net. She bit her lips to fight back the waves of hot pain.

"I can't tell you what I don't know!" Rona Ripper moaned.

"Okay," Remo said, trying not to sound disappointed.

"You're not behind the shootings. But someone is. Maybe someone who's willing to go pretty far to put you in office. I need entry into your organization."

"Any . . . anything!" Rona gasped. "Just . . . just stop!"

Remo scooped up the telephone and handed the receiver to Rona Ripper. "Set it up. The name's Remo Gerrymander."

"The card said Drake."

"The card lied." Remo folded his arms as Rona Ripper called her campaign headquarters.

"Blaise? Rona. I have a new man for you. What? Of course I sound strange. I'm lying on my belly with a slug in one cheek. How do you think I should sound? Bubbly? Now this guy. His name is Remo. When he shows up, put him to work where he'll do the most good."

Rona Ripper hung up, saying, "It's all set. Go to the Main Street office."

"Remember, mum's the word," said Remo, as he left the room.

After Remo had gone, Rona Ripper scooped up the telephone and stabbed the redial button.

"Blaise. Rona again. That Remo I told you about. He's dangerous. Get rid of him before he learns too much."

21

In the Santa Monica headquarters for the Rona Ripper campaign, Blaise Perrin hung up the telephone with trembling fingers.

Almost immediately the phone rang again. Thinking it was the candidate herself calling a third time, he scooped up the receiver and fumbled it to his pinched face.

"Hello?"

A sharp voice announced, "This is Cheeta Ching, demanding a statement from your candidate."

"Aren't you on maternity leave?" Blaise asked.

"You leave my womb out of this! Do I get to talk to Rona or not?"

"Not," said Blaise Perrin, hanging up. He left the phone off the hook after that. He had enough on his mind. First, Rona had been shot in a freak accident, freaking out the organization. Now there was a problem with someone named "Remo."

Only the day before, Blaise had been presiding over a busy campaign headquarters. But ever since the first report that Rona had been shot—never mind that it had been an accident—the volunteers had begun deserting in droves.

Now, less than six hours later, Blaise Perrin was responsible for every ringing phone in the office. Under a barrage of reporters' phone calls, he had been forced to disconnect all but the unlisted number that existed for the candidate's personal use.

How Cheeta Ching had gotten it was another matter. When Rona Ripper was governor of California, Cheeta Ching would be taken care of too, just like all the rest of them.

And just like this "Remo"—whoever he was.

Blaise Perrin knew exactly how to handle this guy. He'd never know what happened to him. And it would be a hell of a long time before he saw daylight again. He picked up the receiver, and punched out a phone number Blaise Perrin had committed to memory before the start of the Ripper campaign.

"Get ready, commandant," he whispered. "We have another candidate to be stubbed out."

Remo whatever-his-name-was arrived within the hour. He pulled up in a blue sedan and got out.

Blaise Perrin hadn't known what to expect. Rona hadn't said who the guy was. Blaise had assumed he was a reporter. He wouldn't be the first one.

But this guy was dressed like no reporter Blaise Perrin had ever seen. Unless he was from the gay press.

He wore a tight white T-shirt over tan chinos and walked with a casual, almost arrogant grace. He had parked across the street and stood beside his car, looking both ways before crossing.

It was still light, and Main Street was busy. Blaise hastily locked up and met the man on the street, so there would be no witness that he'd actually entered the storefront.

"You Remo?" he asked, giving him a disarming grin.

"I'm Remo," the guy said in a slightly bored voice. Mentally, Blaise Perrin rubbed his hands together. This would be a piece of cake. The guy looked like a pushover.

"Great. This your car? Great. Great. Let's go for a ride."

"Where?"

"Where you can get a position to help Rona into that corner office," Blaise said, grinning like a Rodeo Drive manikin.

"Suits me."

Blaise got into the passenger's side, thinking, This guy's dead meat. I can't believe how lucky I am.

"Take the Pacific Coast Highway north," he told Remo, as Remo started the ignition.

Nodding toward the empty storefront, Remo said, "You shut down this early?"

"I gave the staff the afternoon off. It's such a great day. Don't you think it's a great day, Remo?"

"I've had better," Remo said.

"Hah! I like a pessimist. They work that much harder."

Remo sent the sedan into traffic and up Main.

Coming down Main was a satellite TV van, and beside the driver was the cameo oval of a face that Blaise Perrin recognized at fifty yards.

"Cheeta!" Blaise croaked.

"Oh no," Remo moaned.

"Omar!" Cheeta Ching cried, as the two vehicles passed like high-speed trains on opposite tracks.

Blaise turned to Remo. "What did she say?"

"Sounded like 'Omar,' " Remo said, pressing the accelerator.

"Who's Omar?"

"I don't know, but I'm glad I'm not him."

Craning his head to look back, Blaise Perrin saw the satellite van screaming into an illegal U-turn.

"Damn! She must have recognized me. Floor it, will you?"

"My pleasure," said Remo, sending the car rocketing in the direction of the Pacific Coast Highway.

"Go north," Blaise urged.

"North it is," Remo said grimly.

When they had blended in with the afternoon traffic, Blaise Perrin, his eyes sick, all but turned around in his seat in an effort to locate the pursuing van.

"I think we shook them," he said at last.

"You don't know that Korean barracuda."

"Do you?"

"Only by reputation," Remo said, sending the car weaving in and out of traffic with an easy skill that impressed Blaise Perrin. It was like the guy had personal collision-avoidance radar. The other cars seemed to slide away from him, not vice versa.

Cheeta Ching had one claw on the dashboard, and with the other was digging her bloodred nails into the shoulder of her driver.

"Don't lose them, you Caucasian idiot!"

"I'm trying," the driver snapped. "Just get your nails out of my shoulder. I can't drive with major blood loss."

"Sorry," said Cheeta, noticing that her bloodred nails were still bloodred, but now moist. She licked them experimentally. They tasted salty. Blood. She decided she needed all the iron she could ingest if she was going to give birth in nine months, so she finished the job with relish.

When she was done, the blue sedan had come into view.

"There it is!" she shrieked. "Catch up! Catch up!"

No sooner had the van pulled closer than the blue car pulled away.

"Floor it!" Cheeta howled. "I want this one big story! It'll make up for that Jade creature scooping me!"

"I'll try."

He did. But every time he pulled close, the other driver weaved with incredible skill, dancing in and out of traffic.

As they came to a long stretch of open, undulating coastal road, the speedometer crawled toward ninety, and the van's driver fought to hold the wheels to the road. The rear tires of the other car spat up dust and rocks, and dropped bolts and other car parts that littered the road.

The van's windshield began to collect some of these. Craters and cracks appeared. After five miles, it was impossible to see out the windshield.

Cheeta remedied that by knocking out the safety glass with her forehead. She did it in two tries. The glass cracked loose in brittle cubes, like magnified salt.

"How's my hair?" Cheeta asked, over the howl and rush of wind.

"Not even mussed!" the driver shouted, shielding his eyes against the slipstream.

"I use industrial-strength hair varnish," Cheeta said proudly.

"It shows."

Cheeta Ching took that as a compliment and continued to hector her driver. By sundown, she vowed, she would have a hot story and maybe that dreamy Omar, too.

She wondered what he was doing, involved with the Ripper campaign.

Blaise Perrin was saying, "Can't you shake them?"

"If I could, don't you think I would have by now?" Remo said heatedly.

"Okay, okay. Tell you what. Bring it down to the speed limit, and we'll let them just follow along."

"Nothing doing!" Remo snapped.

"Excuse me, but you work for me, not vice versa. Got that?"

"Got it," Remo said unhappily.

Remo slowed the car. The TV van kept on coming. Remo got out of the way, and the van promptly overshot them.

The razor-sharp voice of Cheeta Ching roared back at them, in a cloud of carbon monoxide fumes, "You idiot! They're behind us now. Slow down!"

The van fell in step, pacing them. Cheeta Ching stuck her predatory face out of the passenger side.

"Yoo-hoo! Omar!"

"My name's not Omar," Remo growled.

"What is this?" Blaise demanded. "She acts like she knows you."

"She acts like a lunatic."

Cheeta tried again. "Nemo? Don't you remember me?"

"I don't know you from Jade Ling!" Remo called out.

Her face stung, Cheeta Ching withdrew her head.

"Whatever you said, looks like it worked," Blaise said admiringly.

"You gotta know how to handle these anchors. Go for the ego."

"All right, Remo. You're doing great so far. Just keep it up. About three miles ahead, take the off-ramp. I'll handle everything from there. Do you understand? It is important that you understand."

"I understand," said Remo.

"And that you trust me," Blaise added.

"I trust you," said Remo.

Blaise Perrin gave Remo a fatherly clap on the back. He brought his hand away, the fingers stinging.

"What do they feed you back home, anyway?"

"Anchors," said Remo, and Blaise Perrin didn't know whether to laugh or not. He just hoped the commandant was ready at his end.

Otherwise the whole master plan was going to blow back in their faces, like second-hand smoke.

22

Harold W. Smith got the word directly from the President of the United States.

"Yes, Mr. President?"

"Smith, I have the official National Transportation Safety Board report on the California crash, and the news isn't good."

"I'm listening."

"It was sabotage."

"The board is certain?"

"I'm not up on all the technical details, but from what they tell me, somebody tampered with the pressurization system on that jet."

"That alone would not insure a crash. The plane was off course at the time of the disaster."

"That's where we come to the truly insidious part. The official report lays it all out chronologically. And let me tell you, it's chilling to read. Just chilling."

"Go on," Smith prompted.

"Whoever sabotaged the plane knew that the captain would have to descend to what's called a 'low-altitude airway.' When they do that, they rely on special charts. There are two to a cockpit. A set for the captain and a set for the copilot."

"I follow you so far, Mr. President."

"They had a hell of a time extracting the charts from what was left of the cockpit. It was mashed tighter than Congress in a phone booth. But they found them. Both charts were counterfeit."

"Counterfeit?"

"Doctored to lead them off course," the President said tightly. "Somebody with a lot of money and organization pulled this off. When that plane lost pressure, those poor guys dug out those two false charts and flew themselves right into Mt. Whitney. And that's exactly where some-body wanted them to end up. Exactly."

Smith let out a pent-in breath. "Then there is no escap-ing it."

"No," said the President grimly. "General Nogeira ar-ranged the assassination of the governor of California and the lieutenant governor."

"And engineered this special election," Smith added.

"Well, whatever he was up to, he's not going to get the benefit of it."

"That does not mean his organization—and I agree with you that he must have had one, in order to accom-plish this audacious scheme—is not still operating, pursu-ing his vicious ends."

"I heard about the Ripper woman. The press aren't buying the inflicted-by-a-staffer story. The public thinks it's another attempt on a gubernatorial candidate. My God, it's like a banana republic out there in California. Is this what the future holds for the rest of this fine country?"

"Not if CURE has anything to say about it," Smith said firmly. "My people are on top of the situation. There will be no more political assassinations."

"I'm going to have this NTSB report suppressed until the election is done with."

"That is probably for the best," said Harold Smith. "I will keep you informed of developments."

Harold Smith replaced the well-worn red receiver. The President had offered no advice on the handling of the California situation. Smith appreciated that. Not that he would have listened to the President, but the way matters were going, this was shaping up to be an unprecedented situation. And Harold W. Smith, for all his experience in unraveling the Gordian knot of national security, wouldn't have known the best outcome to engineer— even if it had been in his power to engineer it.

23

The sun was setting as Remo tooled his rented car through the Santa Monica Mountains west of Topanga. The area was quiet. Here and there, the mountainsides were decorated with tar-paper shacks and cardboard condominiums that undocumented aliens had erected on the slopes. The sight reminded Remo of the mountains that ring the Valley of Mexico and Mexico City. Their sheer sides was a beehive of homeless people, too.

"If this keeps up, this state is going to be unlivable," Remo pointed out.

"What did you say?" asked Blaise Perrin, his head snapping around. He had been watching the pursuing van, now following at a decorous thirty miles an hour.

"The homes up there," Remo said. "That's no way to live."

"Change your attitude. Rona Ripper's hard work helped make it possible for the underprivileged to enjoy the bounty of this great state. She sued the county when they tried to displace those people."

"I heard cooking fires they've started have burned people out of their homes."

"And *I* heard it was spontaneous combustion."

Remo said nothing. He wondered what he'd do when they got to wherever it was they were going, and Cheeta Ching descended upon him. Her face, reflected in the rearview mirror, made him think of a remorseless harpy chasing a field mouse.

Remo got the answer to his question when they came to a barbed-wire perimeter fence. A black-and-yellow-striped guard rail was lifted by a sentry in a black Spandex jogging outfit.

They were waved through. So was the TV van, Remo saw in the rearview mirror.

"Now," Blaise Perrin said gleefully, "they're trespassing."

"Looked like they were welcomed with open arms," Remo pointed out.

"Trespassing," repeated Blaise Perrin. "Take this next left."

Remo went left. Around a low hillock appeared a scattering of quonset huts, surrounded by a hurricane fence. There was no sign to indicate what the complex was supposed to be. It made Remo think of a POW camp.

Two sentries in Spandex pushed open a tall gate topped by razor wire, and Remo drove through.

"What's this?"

"Education center. All Ripper volunteers are processed through this facility. It insures correct political attitudes."

"Uh-huh," Remo said, putting the car into a designated slot. He got out. Blaise Perrin emerged, buttoning his suitcoat and inhaling the mountain air greedily.

"Ahhh! Isn't this great? Fresh air! When we're done, all California will smell like this."

To Remo, whose sensitive nostrils now detected trace elements of airborne zinc and sulphur, that was hardly an enticing thought, even if it was an improvement over city smog.

He watched as Blaise Perrin stepped into the headlights of the approaching van and waved the driver into the adjacent parking slot.

"Just shoot her right there!" he called.

The van coasted to a stop, and the headlights were doused. The doors on either side popped open and out popped Cheeta Ching and her driver.

"Vito!" she called.

As if that were a signal, the ground came alive with men in olive drab, toting Colt automatic rifles.

"What's this crap?" Cheeta demanded.

"You're trespassing," Blaise Perrin said.

"I'm a major network anchorperson!" Cheeta spat. "I

don't trespass. I investigate. Look it up in the Constitution."

"In this case, you're trespassing," said Blaise Perrin, snapping his fingers coolly. The Colt rifles were cocked with military precision.

"This isn't a good idea," Remo warned.

Blaise Perrin smiled broadly. "Oh. I forgot to tell you. You're a prisoner, too."

Two rifle muzzles shifted from Cheeta Ching and her driver to Remo's white T-shirt.

Remo looked down the weapon's barrel and suppressed a smile. He was making progress. Already.

"Okay," he said nonchalantly, throwing up his hands. "I'm a prisoner."

"How can you just surrender like that?" Cheeta Ching said hotly.

"Because he doesn't want to be shot," Blaise explained.

"Because I don't want to be shot," Remo echoed, knowing it would put Blaise Perrin at ease and annoy Cheeta Ching.

"I hate you," Cheeta hissed. "What did I ever see in you?"

"A cute guy with an unforgettable name," Remo said.

Blaise snapped, "Let's go. Inside. All of you."

Remo allowed himself to be marched into the main building, a long, low, barracks-like structure in the center of the quonset huts.

The sign on the entrance door said POSITIVELY NO SMOKING.

So did the sign on the first inside wall they came to.

They were marched down a rough, unpainted corridor. On either side there were other signs:

SMOKING IS PUNISHABLE BY FLOGGING
NO IFS, ANDS, OR BUTTS
SAY NO TO NICOTINE
REMEMBER YOUR PATCHES

"Patches?" Remo asked. He was ignored.

A man with a blondish mustache, and a powder-blue paramilitary uniform that looked like it had been pilfered from the Universal Studios prop department, greeted them with a salute.

"I remand these antisocials into your custody, commandant," said Blaise, returning the salute.

"Commandant?" asked Remo.

"Antisocials?" said Cheeta.

"Shut up," said Blaise.

They were escorted past rows of cells. The cells were heavily barred, and all were empty except for piles of straw on the floor. Remo noticed white electronic devices attached to the ceiling of each cell. So did Cheeta Ching.

She demanded, "What are those? Burglar alarms?"

Blaise Perrin laughed.

At the end of the narrow corridor was a blank wall. On either side were facing cells. The commandant opened one cell, and Cheeta Ching and her driver were frisked at rifle-point.

"Are you crazy?" he snapped. "We aren't carrying weapons."

"We know," Blaise said smugly.

"Ah-hah!" said the commandant. "Contraband!"

A pack of menthol cigarettes was brought to light.

"Take a good look," Blaise told the unhappy driver. "Those are the last coffin nails you're going to see."

"You're going to kill us?" Cheeta blurted.

Blaise Perrin laughed without answering. Remo thought it was a crazy laugh.

Cheeta and her driver were pushed into a single cell, and the bars clapped shut.

The second door was opened and Blaise said to Remo, "In you go, sport."

"How am I supposed to get out the vote from behind bars?" Remo wanted to know.

"You don't," said Blaise Perrin.

Shrugging, Remo entered the cell. The door banged shut.

"Welcome to the wave of the future," said the powder-blue commandant in a hearty voice.

"A prison?" Remo asked.

"A reeducation camp."

Cheeta Ching exploded, "But I'm a summa cum laude journalism major!"

"It's not that kind of reeducation," said Blaise, smiling.

"What kind is it?" Remo asked in a cool, unconcerned voice.

"You'll find out in the morning."

"What if I don't want to wait?"

"In Rona Ripper's California, you wait if the Ripper organization tells you to wait."

"So I wait," Remo said.

Blaise Perrin stepped up to the bars and looked at Remo's high-cheekboned face.

"You're an awfully cool customer. Mind telling me why Rona wants you kept under wraps?"

"She thinks I'm a pain in the ass," Remo said.

Blaise frowned. "Is that a joke?"

"Not if nobody laughs."

Nobody did, so Blaise Perrin backed away from the bars and stormed off. His guards followed.

In the silence that followed, Cheeta Ching said, "I don't believe this."

"Believe it," Remo said.

"I've always admired Rona," Cheeta said unhappily. "She's a role model for aggressive women everywhere."

"Maybe if we ask nicely, they'll give us absentee ballots," Remo said.

Cheeta began pacing her cell. "We can't just sit here and let our First Amendment rights be trampled on. Even by a progressive woman."

"Not if we sleep instead," Remo said, throwing himself onto the straw in one corner of the hardwood floor.

Cheeta surged to her bars and glared at Remo. "What kind of man are you?"

"A sleepy one."

Remo willed himself to sleep. It was not easy. Cheeta Ching continued to carp and complain for the better part of an hour. That came to an abrupt halt when a guard came in with a pail of cold water and dashed it through the bars of her cell.

After that, Cheeta Ching got very quiet and eventually fell asleep. She used her driver for a pillow. He didn't complain in the least, but he didn't close his eyes either.

Remo woke up precisely at midnight. He had told his body to come awake at exactly midnight. He didn't know how he knew it was midnight when his eyes snapped open, any more than he understood the biological mechanism that brought him to full consciousness without any logy transition. It was Sinanju. It was a natural ability all members of *homo sapiens* possess, if only they could access it.

Remo rose to his feet, like an apparition from a fresh grave.

He took hold of the bars, testing them for strength. They were sunk into holes drilled into the floor and ceiling. He found they could be rotated. That meant they weren't sunk into anything more solid than the natural earth under the wood flooring.

Remo grinned. This was going to be easy. He grasped the two center bars and began twisting them. As he twisted, he applied downward pressure.

He took his time. Silence was more important than speed. And he didn't want to wake Cheeta Ching and her leather lungs.

It took a few minutes, but the tops of the bars dropped out of the ceiling holes. As he kept turning the bars, they sank further and further into the soft earth below, making soft grumbles of complaint.

When they were knee-high, Remo stepped out of his cell.

He moved down the narrow corridor, passed through an unguarded door, and paused at the juncture of two intersecting corridors.

Approaching footsteps warned him of a patrolling guard. Remo slipped into a storeroom and waited until the guard had passed. The storeroom was cramped for space. In the dark, Remo allowed his visual purple to adjust to the pitch-darkness until he could see shades of gray.

He picked through a box of what seemed to be medical supplies. Inside the box were smaller boxes and in them, flesh-colored circular patches resembling Band-Aids sealed in cellophane packets. They didn't smell like ordinary bandages, so Remo pocketed a bunch of them.

The guard's footsteps had moved to another part of the building, and Remo slipped out.

Remo stopped and let his senses open fully. His entire skin became a giant sensory organ. He counted heartbeats. There were eight people in the building, not counting himself. That meant four potential enemies, since Cheeta and her driver were locked down tight.

Remo resumed his search. He wasn't sure what he was searching for, but he knew he would recognize it when he found it.

What he found, when he turned the next corner, was a light framing the edges of a door, and Blaise Perrin's anxious voice coming through the veneer panel.

Perrin was saying, "They'll be secure here. And guess what? One of them's a smoker. We'll run him through the pilot program and see if he can cut it."

Remo went through the door. On the other side Blaise Perrin sat with his back to the door, his feet propped up on a desk.

"One second. I'm talking to Rona," he said impatiently.

"Give her my very best," Remo said pleasantly.

"Oh my God!" said Blaise Perrin. "Rona! He got loose!"

Through the receiver diaphragm, Rona Ripper's twisted voice could be heard barking, "Do your duty and cover my ass!"

Blaise Perrin came out of his seat without remembering to let go of the phone. He pulled it out of its base, lunging for a red lever mounted on the outside wall.

The lever was behind glass, and white letters said IN CASE OF FIRE, BREAK GLASS, PULL LEVER. There was a red metal hammer hanging from a silver chain.

Blaise Perrin got his hand on the hammer. But Remo's steely fingers got him by the wrist.

"I don't smell any smoke," Remo said, grinning fiercely.

Sweating, Blaise attempted to move his hand. It wouldn't budge. Effortlessly, Remo pried his fingers loose and guided the director of the Ripper campaign back to his seat. He then pried the phone receiver from his other hand and sat him down. Hard.

"Talk," Remo said.

"I have nothing to say."

"Rona Ripper is behind the attacks on the other campaigns. Am I right?"

Blaise Perrin actually looked startled. "Are you kidding? Why would she do that?"

"Because she wants to get elected."

"Rona is a pacifist."

Remo gestured around him. "Then explain all this."

Blaise Perrin hesitated. He swallowed. Finally, he said, "I'll tell you."

"Go."

"I could use a cigarette first," he said, gesturing to the pack of menthols that had been taken from Cheeta Ching's driver.

Remo laughed. "You political hacks are all alike. Say one thing in public, and practice another behind closed doors." He extracted a single cigarette and stuck it between Blaise Perrin's sweaty lips.

"No lighter," Blaise said, throwing out his hands.

Remo sighed, took a sheet of paper from the desk's out basket, and rubbed it between his palms briskly. First it became a ball, and then under the friction pressure, it became a ball of fire.

Blaise Perrin's eyes went wide. He got control of himself and pushed the tip into the blaze until it caught.

Remo blew out the burning paper and dropped blackened scraps into the wastebasket.

Blaise blinked. "How'd you do that?"

"Home magic course," Remo said. "And I haven't all night."

Blaise Perrin leaned back in his swivel chair and took a deep drag. He threw his head back and let out a long stream of bluish tobacco smoke.

"You're an idiot, you know that?" Blaise said with a smile.

There was something in the confident tone of the man's voice that made Remo look up. He saw the tobacco smoke billowing toward a white device bolted to the ceiling. It was identical to the ones that were mounted in the cells.

When it started to beep, he knew it was a smoke detector.

"I don't smoke," Blaise sneered.

All over the building other smoke detectors started beeping, sounding like arguing computers.

"The guards will be here any second now," Blaise said smugly. "Why don't you put up your hands now, and maybe they won't shoot you?"

Remo took the cigarette from Blaise Perrin's loose lips and returned it, lit end first.

While Blaise was dealing with a mouthful of hot ash and a burnt tongue, Remo went to the door.

"I'm in here," he called.

Running footsteps converged on the office.

Remo went to meet the first arrival. The man came around the corner with his rifle held at hip level. Remo took the muzzle and used it as a lever, slamming the man against a wall and stunning him.

"That's one," Remo said.

The commandant came from the opposite direction.

Remo flattened against the wall at the point at the corner. The man came in fast. Too fast to see Remo's foot trip him. He turned a somersault, and Remo caught him in mid-flip and used his head to make a hole in the wall.

The commandant ended up on his knees, his entire body loose, his neck joined to the wall.

"Two," Remo said.

The two remaining guards happened along then. They skidded to a stop, took one look at Remo, saw their commandant on his knees as if about to be guillotined by a wall, and changed their minds. They doubled back.

Remo decided there was time to interrogate Blaise Perrin before they got reinforcements. He went back to the office.

He heard the sharp breaking of glass, and remembered the fire alarm. A lot of good that's going to do, he thought.

Remo entered the room just as Blaise grabbed the lever.

"Don't waste your time," Remo said.

To Remo's right, the head of the commandant poking through the wall screamed, "Don't! Blaise! Don't!"

Remo started forward. Blaise pulled the lever.

Then a wave of concussive force blew out every wall in the office, and there was a hot yellow sheet of fire directly in front of Remo's astonished eyes.

Through the darkness that came next, he could hear echoing detonations. He counted seven. One for each of the buildings in the reeducation camp.

24

There was nothing to hang on to. And even if there had been, the shock wave would have been too strong to resist.

Remo let it carry him. His body, reacting to free-fall, went limp. He could feel the heat on his bare arms, smelled the hair singeing off, and prayed he wouldn't be scarred for life.

Most of all, he thought of how stupid he had been. He had taken the fire alarm at face value. It had been wired to a detonator. The entire complex had been rigged to self-destruct when that lever was pulled.

A tree branch slashed at Remo's face. Blindly, he grabbed out, snared another. It groaned, snapped, and Remo slammed into a nest of branches that lacerated his face and arms.

After that, he dropped straight down. He rolled upon impact and kept rolling, in case he was on fire.

Remo only stopped rolling when his back slammed into a boulder and blew the air out of his lungs.

He lay there a moment, taking inventory. His eyes came open, and he found his feet. The hair had been burned off his exposed skin and he'd lost a little off his head, but there were no broken bones, no internal injuries. He looked around.

The fires were everywhere. They crackled and snarled like trapped animals. The heart of the conflagration was like looking into a fallen sun.

"Cheeta," Remo croaked, climbing to his feet. "Chiun will kill me if she buys it."

Remo moved toward the flames. A man came running

out, his mouth open in a silent scream, his flaming arms beating like mad phoenix wings.

He ran and ran and then just flopped on the ground and kept burning. He stopped flapping his burning arms, though.

The heat made it impossible to enter the flames. Remo circled the blaze, which was so hot the perimeter fence had begun to wilt.

There were screams coming from the different burning structures. They sounded like they were being ripped out of the throats of their authors. They didn't last long at all.

Remo was forced to retreat.

He found Blaise Perrin draped across a boulder, his spine broken in three places. Remo grabbed up a fistful of hair and pulled his head back.

Perrin groaned. "You . . . can't . . . prove a . . . thing."

"What was that place?" Remo asked harshly.

"Reeducation. . . ."

"For political enemies?"

"No . . . for . . ." Blaise closed his eyes slowly.

Remo shook him back to consciousness.

"For . . . smoke . . ."

"For smoke?"

"Smokers," Perrin hissed.

"This is a concentration camp for people who smoke?" Remo said incredulously.

"It was . . . completely . . . humane. We had . . . whole program. Nictone . . . transdermal patches. Aerobics. Shots."

Remo pulled out one of the Band-Aids he had found in the storeroom. "Is this one of the patches?"

"You . . . put it on . . . person's skin and . . . it makes them allergic to . . . tobacco. By the year two thousand California would be smoker-free."

"Smoker-free? What about people's rights?"

"Smokers . . . have . . . no . . . rights," coughed Blaise Perrin. His head went limp. This time, no matter how much Remo shook him, he didn't come around. He would never come around again.

Remo used a heavy boulder to scoop out a fire trench, so the blaze wouldn't spread, then reclaimed his car, which was intact. The TV van had protected it. Its tires were smoking and melting slowly.

As Remo drove away the gas tank caught, and the van shot ten feet in the air and came down with a rattling thud.

Remo found a phone booth at a gas station in the Santa Monica foothills. He called the local fire department and reported the fire. Then he called Folcroft.

"Smith. Bad news."

"What?"

"Rona Ripper has a secret plan, too."

"Is it legal?" Smith asked.

"Definitely not. Her secret plan insures a smoker-free California."

"You mean smoke-free."

"That too. I just came from a concentration camp for smokers her people had built in the Santa Monica Mountains. Once she was elected, if you smoked, you'd go through the program."

"That's insane," Smith said sharply.

"This is California."

Smith's ragged breathing came across three thousand miles of telephone line.

"Remo, as you know we do not interfere with elections."

"Right."

"It is against everything CURE stands for. We are above politics. Above the process. Outside the Constitution, yes. But only because the Constitution has been subverted by elements which wish to repeal it."

"Right."

"I myself do not vote."

"Right."

"I personally do not care who governs California so long as they are legally elected."

"Right. Right," Remo said impatiently. "Cut to the chase, will you?"

"Remo, we are forced to take sides. Barry Black, Junior is committing voter fraud. Rona Ripper intends to force her personal beliefs on the citizens of that state, without recourse to lawful legislation. Neither candidate can be allowed to assume the governorship under these circumstances."

"So we help Esperanza get elected?"

Smith's tone was flat. "I see no choice in the matter."

"I'm not looking forward to facing Chiun."

"I would think he would be pleased."

"Not when I tell him Cheeta Ching just went up in a ball of fire," Remo said wearily.

"What is this?"

Remo explained the circumstances leading to Cheeta Ching's apparent demise.

Smith was thoughtful. At last he said, "Is there any trace she was in the camp when it exploded?"

"Not unless they dig up her blackened shark's teeth."

"Say nothing of this to Chiun. Or anyone. The election is less than a week away. After that, the chips can fall where they may. Our task will be done."

"Gotcha. I'm on my way. Where is Esperanza now?"

"San Diego." Smith's tight voice softened slightly. He sounded tired. "Good luck, Remo," he said.

25

FBI Forensics specialist Dick Webb hated the Everglades. Even with his legs encased in crotch-high fisherman's boots, he hated the Everglades. It was too hot. It was too humid. It was too muddy. And then there were the alligators.

It was because of an alligator that the central lab in Washington had sent him down to this hellhole.

An alligator had eaten no less than General Emmanuel Alejandro Nogeira, while in FBI custody. It was a major embarrassment. And it landed right on the Bureau's lap.

Which is why agent Webb was stuck with body-recovery duty.

The Bureau had managed to find most of· Nogeira's bloated carcass. Even the head, which had to be cut out of the stomach of the offending alligator. It was pretty well digested. They found a number of finger bones, too.

The problem with this was that the fingerprints had been digested away. They had the guy's toes, but nobody, not even the FBI, kept toe prints on file. Agent Webb planned to write up a memo on that subject as soon as he got back to Washington.

Anything, to make sure they never sent him to the Everglades again to search for a missing hand.

The other Nogeira hand had been bitten off. It was not in the alligator's stomach. The Bureau, to cover its bureaucratic ass, needed that hand to positively establish the identity of General Nogeira. Not that anybody doubted the corpse's identity. It was just that including a paragraph affirming a positive fingerprint ID was essential to perserving the Bureau's tattered reputation.

"Why can't we just go with dental records?" Webb had asked, when the problem was dropped in his lap.

"Nobody has them," he was told. "They can't find them down in Bananama, and Nogeira never saw the prison dentist. We need those prints, Dick."

Which left Dick Webb to wade through the malodorous Everglades in search of a hand that was probably alligator shit by now.

"I just hope I don't end up the same way," he grumbled to his alligator-spotter.

"Not as long as I'm here," said the firearms instructor on loan from Quantico, who was hunkered down on a spongy isle. "Uh-oh," he added suddenly.

Webb froze. "Gator?"

"No," said the marksman, bringing his sniper scope to his eyes. "I think it's a jellyfish."

"Jelly— Wait!"

Dick Webb's frantic shout came to late. The first shot got off.

"Miss!" The marksman said in disgust.

"Hold your damn fire!" said Dick Webb, wading like mad, no longer caring if gators lurked under the surface or not. He didn't know much about the glades, but he did know they didn't exactly swarm with jellyfish. Webb spotted the translucent white thing as it turned in the lazy current.

With a stick, he lifted it clear of the water. Delicately, he opened the flimsy thing. It dripped. Dripped from every limp appendage. Webb counted five—four long and one short.

"This is it! This is it!" he crowed.

"What?"

Webb turned. "It's a skin glove!" he cried, wading back. "It's a perfect skin glove!"

"What the hell is a 'skin glove'?" the marksman wondered.

"We find them in waters where floaters turn up," Webb explained. "A body in the water a long time will shed its outer skin layer, like a snake. This is Nogeira's hand skin. We call it a glove."

The marksman scratched his head. "Can you get prints off it?"

"Abso-fucking-lutely!" chortled Dick Webb, relieved

now that his chances of becoming alligator excrement seemed to have dropped into negative numbers. "It's all over. This will close out the case."

Agent Dick Webb waded back to dry land, with no idea how wrong he was.

26

Harmon Cashman was panic-stricken.

He had opened every drawer, and found none. He had checked the hotel room minibar. He had looked under the bed and between the rumpled sheets.

It was three A.M., and he had been up poring over polls and focus-group studies all night. The night had started on an up note. His candidate, the candidate of hope, Enrique Espiritu Esperanza, was riding high in the polls. He was not a shoo-in yet, but he looked good. It was great to be honchoing a major campaign once again—even if it was just a statewide run.

But once it was over, Harmon told himself, the sky was the limit. Where was it written that an Hispanic couldn't be President?

But that would be later. First he had to satisfy his bodily craving, before it drove him mad.

Hurrying down the hall to Esperanza's hotel room, he banged on the door, yelling, "Ricky! Ricky! Wake up!"

Hastily gathering a terry-cloth robe about his generous frame, Enrique Esperanza appeared in the door, his smooth brown face disturbed, like a cherub with hemorrhoids.

"Harmon! *Amigo!* What is it?"

Harmon Cashman grabbed the terry cloth with both fists. "We're out of cookies! Completely, totally, unforgivably out!"

"Come in, come in."

Harmon paced the room, saying, "This has never happened before! I must be losing my touch. You know how I manage everything to the last decimal. And now this!"

"Calm yourself, my friend. Sit. Please."

Harmon sat. His eyes skated around the room. His hands shook.

"You are nervous," came the soothing alto voice of Esperanza. "It is understandable. The election nears. All of your hopes are riding on the outcome."

"How can you be so calm at a time like this!" Harmon shrieked.

"I have been thinking. It is time to adopt new tactics."

Harmon Cashman's eyes cleared. "You nuts? We're doing great! Black is hiding in his attic, and Ripper's flat on her can. She's a laughingstock. They're both laughing-stocks."

"A lot can change in a week, my friend. Listen, we have been conducting a retail campaign to date."

"Yeah. Personal appearances. A lot of glad-handing. Pure grassroots politicking. Word of mouth is our best friend."

"I now wish to go wholesale," said Enrique Esperanza.

"TV ads? I don't know. I mean people respond to you in personal appearances. And the radio spots are doing well. . . ."

"I wish to appear in my TV ads."

Harmon Cashman gulped. "Ricky, no. It's not the same. You've got charisma. It's pheromones, or something. But I guarantee you, it won't work over the air. Radio interviews, sure. But not TV. Let's face it, it'll still be a trick get a Hispanic into the governorship."

"It is a trick I am convinced we can accomplish," Enrique Esperanza said forcefully.

Harmon Cashman shook his head stubbornly. "No chance. I'm campaign manager, and I say no. That's final."

"I have something for you."

"What?"

From a writing-desk drawer, Enrique Espiritu Esperanza brought out a colorful printed box, sealed in clear plastic. He brought it over and laid it before Harmon Cashman.

Harmon Cashman's eyes fell upon the clear plastic top. Staring back at him were the blank, black orbs of a row of fist-sized Oreo cookies.

"For you," said Enrique Esperanza warmly.

"What the hell . . ."

"They are new. They are called Big Stuf. Triple the size, and many times the creme filling you love so much."

Harmon Cashman ripped at the plastic top. He discovered that the giant Oreo sandwich cookies contained inside were encased in individual packets. Tears came to his eyes as he fought one open. He fumbled the sweet-smelling cookie into his hands.

Before he could pry the filligreed chocolate wafers apart, Enrique Esperanza grasped his wrist.

"You must first agree to the TV spots," he said firmly. "It is important."

"No chance."

"I will not allow you to indulge yourself with this matter unsettled. It would not be seemly. I am sorry."

The box was removed, and with it the giant cookie in Harmon's hands.

Harmon Cashman looked from the kind face of his candidate to the inviting, oh-so-near and yet-so-far Oreo cookie. Esperanza smiled. The Oreo seemed to smile, too. Both smiles promised the same thing. Hope.

"Please don't make me choose," Harmon said, tears coming to his eyes. A little dab of saliva appeared at the corner of his anguished mouth.

"There is a time for indulgence and a time for choosing," Enrique said sternly. "You must choose. Now."

"I gotta have that cookie," blubbered Harmon Cashman, the tears now streaming, his head nodding in spite of his better judgment. "I just gotta."

"Excellent," murmured Enrique Espiritu Esperanza, returning the cookie and releasing his wrist.

And Harmon Cashman fell to gnawing the sweet creme filling like a voracious animal, thinking, "The hell with the TV spots. The future can take care of itself."

27

The Master of Sinanju knew sadness. He tasted despair.

The word had come from no less than his patron, that very day.

"Cheeta Ching is with child," had said Enrique Espiritu Esperanza. "It has been announced. I am sorry to give you this sad news."

The Master of Sinanju withstood the blow without flinching. He excused himself and put on his white mourning kimono.

It was not to be. The Gods had willed it. There would be no second chance to bring forth a perfect son, a possible successor to Remo, one who would continue the proud line of Sinanju and continue the bloodline of Chiun. Now, in his declining years, his magnificent heart would carry two tragedies. The long-lost Cha'mnari, and now the beauteous Cheeta.

The sun had set while Chiun sat looking out at the many-towered city called San Diego, and with it had gone all hope.

The Master of Sinanju did not sleep that night. There was no comfort to be found in sleep. He took up parchment and quill and began composing an Ung poem to describe his innermost feelings. It would be a short one. He had no stomach for more.

It lacked but two hours before dawn when there came a knock at the hotel room door. Chiun ignored it. The knock was repeated.

"Chiun? You in there? It's me."

It was Remo.

"I am not in here," said Chiun, scratching out a careful ideograph that completed stanza three hundred and twelve.

"Don't be like this. I came a long way to talk to you."

"Be gone. I am disconsolate."

"Can you be consolate long enough to open the door?" Remo called.

Chiun sighed. There would be no peace with the white forever at the door. Laying aside his quill, he drew himself up on his feet and padded to the door, throwing it open with a curt gesture.

Remo came in, his face strange of cast.

"What is wrong?" Chiun demanded of his pupil.

"That's what I was going to ask you," Remo said. "You said you were disconsolate."

"And I am. For I have heard the terrible news about Cheeta Ching the beautiful."

At that, the face of the pupil of Chiun paled. "Look, it wasn't my fault," he said quickly.

"I did not say that it was," Chiun said suspiciously.

Remo's shoulders relaxed. "Good," he said, "because I had nothing to do with what happened."

"So you say," Chiun said in an arid voice. His almond eyes squeezed into slits of suspicion.

"It was an accident," Remo added.

Chiun's eyes became flowers of steel. "You have been with Cheeta!"

"Yes," Remo admitted, shame-faced.

"Knowing what she meant to me, you allowed this to happen?"

"I said it was an accident," Remo hurled back.

Chiun lifted tiny fists to the sky. "She carries your child, and you call it an accident!"

"Child? What are you talking about?"

Chiun shook his fists in his pupil's ignorant face. "I speak of the horrid news that Cheeta the Incomparable is fat with child."

Remo hesitated. His eyes went around the room. Chiun's eyes narrowed at his pupil once more.

"Well?"

"Yes," Remo admitted glumly. "I'm responsible for the child thing." He looked away with proper shame.

" 'Thing'! You call it a 'thing'! I call it a tragedy!"

"I said it was an accident," Remo said evasively.

Chiun composed himself. His face set, he folded his hands in the tunnels of his kimono sleeves. "It is done," he said, averting his injured face. "There is no way it can be undone."

"That's for sure," Remo said.

"We must make plans."

"For what?" Remo wanted to know.

"The upbringing of the child, of course."

Remo looked blank. "Upbringing?"

"He will be my pupil. You are hardly prepared to sire a male child, much less train one." Chiun hesitated. A sudden gleam came into his hazel eyes. "It *is* a male, isn't it?"

"How would I know?" Remo said in a miserable voice.

"It was your seed!" Chiun exploded. "Do not tell me you did not bestow upon Cheeta your best male seed."

"I said it was an accident. Now lay off."

Chiun took the puffs of hair over his ears in hand and cried, "Unbelievable! If you have sired another worthless female child, I do not know what I shall do!"

"Look, we've got nine months to sort this out. In the meantime, I've dug up a lot of dirt on Barry Black and Rona Ripper."

"Yes?"

"Black's pretending to be a Republican," Remo said.

"All republicans are pretenders," Chiun sniffed. "There have been no true republicans since Rome fell."

"And Rona Ripper's out to snuff every cigarette smoker in the state," Remo added.

"What is wrong with that? It is a worthy goal."

"Smith says it's against his edicts."

"Then it is bad, and this woman must be punished," Chiun sniffed.

"Smith says we throw our weight behind Esperanza and get him elected," Remo added.

The Master of Sinanju lifted a lecturing finger, saying, "My awesome weight is already pledged to that cause. It is your weight that has been absent."

"Well, I'm in the camp now. Where do we start?"

"We must eliminate the false candidates who pose a threat to our patron."

Remo shook his head. "Uh-uh. That's not the American way. First thing is we protect Esperanza. The rest can take care of itself."

"Nothing takes care of itself," Chiun snapped. "Especially children. You must remember that, now that you are to be a father."

Remo winced. He was only getting himself in deeper,

but he had no choice. If Chiun knew the truth about Cheeta Ching, he'd go ballistic.

"Black won't be a problem," he said flatly. "He's unelectable."

"Why do you say that?"

"He has two strikes against him. He's a former liberal, and he has a record."

"And the other?"

"There's a good chance she's behind these political attacks."

"Then we must repay her in the coin of her own choosing," Chiun said firmly.

"Not the way to go. Look, Little Father. The election isn't far off. Smith thinks we should just sit tight and protect Esperanza."

Chiun turned to face the glass balcony doors. He looked out upon the blazing San Diego night skyline, his bearded chin high.

"My loyalties are torn," he said, bleak-voiced. "I do not know what I should do. I serve Smith, yet Esperanza has promised me the treasurership of California. It is in my interest to eliminate his enemies before they grow too powerful."

"Little Father, you owe me a boon."

Chiun nodded.

"The boon I request is that you be satisfied with protecting Esperanza, not hurting the other candidates."

"You are certain you wish this?" Chiun asked thinly.

"Actually, I'd like to save my boon for a time I might need it more, but I'm on the spot here."

The Master of Sinanju turned, his wrinkled face Then wreathed in a smile. "Then you may step off your spot, for I agree to this."

"Good," said Remo.

"It is better than good," Chiun cackled. "Because it was my intention to do this all along. Heh heh. You have what you wish, and I have your boon. Heh heh."

Remo Williams didn't join in the Master of Sinanju's cackle of mirth. He was thinking ahead to the time when Chiun learned the truth about Cheeta Ching. He was sure to need that boon then.

He had planned to ask Chiun not to kill him.

28

It was called the Conference on Multiculturalism.

It was supposed to be called the California Gubernatorial Debate, but the Barry Black camp had insisted on the new name so that Enrique Espiritu Esperanza couldn't claim the multicultural high ground for himself.

"Done," said Harmon Cashman, through a mouthful of chocolate wafer. "This is easier than I thought!" he chortled, after hanging up on the Black campaign.

Rona Ripper's demand was much simpler.

"My candidate insists that this be a standing debate," said her campaign director.

"You got it," Harmon told the man, who had mysteriously taken the place of the former campaign director, Blaise Perrin. The press was still trying to figure out what had happened to him. He'd simply dropped out of sight, along with Cheeta Ching. Not that anyone missed her.

Harmon took the good news to Enrique Esperanza.

"Both camps have agreed," he said. "Black's people are going to jump on the multicultural bandwagon."

"This is fine. Multiculturalism should not belong to one man."

"And Ripper's people say we gotta stand, because Rona's rear end hasn't healed yet."

Esperanza shook his head. "The poor woman."

"Any demands you want to make before we finalize this?"

"Yes, I wish that Miss Ripper stand between Mr. Black and myself."

"Why?"

Enrique Esperanza shrugged. "It is merely whim. They

have demands, so I must make one. We do not wish to show weakness at this late stage."

"I'll run it past the others. But I'm sure they'll go along. Hell, the fact that they're willing to debate you means both camps are running scared."

"My polls are good?"

Harmon grinned. "The numbers are running our way, all right."

"Good. I think this is one time the dark horse will run in the money."

And both men laughed, Enrique Esperanza through his broad grin and Harmon Cashman through a mouthful of black-and-white cookie crumbs.

On the day of the Conference on Multiculturalism, an auditorium at Stanford University—the birthplace of Multiculturalism, according to the press releases issued by all three campaigns—was packed with representatives of the press and an audience of business and civic leaders from all over the state.

An unusual precaution was a long sheet of bulletproof Plexiglas that ran the length of the stage. This was to protect the candidates from any would-be assassin.

The press complained about the reflections their camera lights created, but no one demanded it be taken down.

Bulletproof limousines brought the candidates to the debate hall. Rona Ripper arrived first, and was escorted to a waiting room behind the curtain by state troopers.

Barry Black, Junior arrived in a pastry truck. His staff carted him in concealed in a balsa-wood pyramid covered with almondine frosting, on the theory that no one would shoot a giant cake, especially one they didn't know held the candidate.

Enrique Esperanza was the last to arrive. State troopers were not needed. His entourage consisted of inner-city gang members, who waved Oreo cookies at the cameras.

Remo and Chiun were forced to enter through a service door.

"This is an insult," Chiun huffed, as they slipped past the state trooper posted at the door as if he were an insensate statue, which by Sinanju standards he was.

"We are reduced to skulking, when we should be in the lemonlight, as befits our exalted station."

"Limelight," Remo hissed. "And if we show up on TV, Smith'll pull us both off the detail."

Chiun sniffed. "There will be sufficient lemonlight when I am Lord Treasurer of California," he allowed.

They worked their way unchallenged to the reception area, where the state troopers and the former gang members were making faces at one another.

"Have a cookie, Jack," one told a stone-faced trooper. "This stuff's proper."

The invitation was declined.

A trooper moved toward them, but Harmon Cashman, spotting Remo and Chiun, said, "There you are!" The trooper backed off.

"Glad to see you back on the winning team," Harmon told Remo.

"Any team we belong to automatically wins," Remo said.

In one corner, Enrique Esperanza was waving away the makeup man, saying, "I need no such artifices. I am Esperanza."

This was reported to the press and to the other campaigns. They too decided to go on sans makeup.

"Are you sure this is wise, Ricky?" Harmon asked doubtfully.

"I am sure of it."

And so was Harmon Cashman, when the three candidates stepped out from behind the curtain.

"They look awful!" he said gleefully, watching a direct feed on a backstage monitor. "Ricky looks perfect, but the other two look like a bobcat's dragged them in through the back door. The debate's practically won!"

"Don't count your chickens," warned Remo.

But Harmon Cashman wasn't listening. His nose was practically pressed to the video screen as he munched away on a foot-tall stack of Oreo Big Stuf cookies.

"That guy's headed for diabetic shock," Remo said to Chiun, as they went to another monitor to watch.

"You Americans would eat rubber, if it were sweet," Chiun sniffed.

*   *   *

The debate began with a short statement on multiculturalism from each candidate.

Rona Ripper promised that, if elected, she would not only outlaw smoking throughout California, but work diligently to prevent the tobacco companies from exporting their products to less sophisticated third-world markets.

"I will also propose a fifty-percent tax on tobacco products, and repeal the snack tax," she added. "If people can't kick the nicotine monkey on their own, we'll tax it off their backs!"

She was applauded.

Barry Black, Junior pointed out the hitherto-unnoticed fact that most of the actors playing aliens on *Star Trek: The Next Generation* were people of color. Especially the ones playing Klingons.

"Those of you who watched the original program know that it wasn't like this back in the wonderful sixties," he said with righteous indignation. "I say to you that this is racism, pure and simple. If elected, I will propose emergency legislation to integrate the imaginary Klingon planet once and for all."

This too was applauded.

Then Enrique Espiritu Esperanza took his turn. He was in his habitual white suit, which made him look like a pious adult celebrating his First Communion.

"I represent hope," he said. "Hope for all people. I am a brown man. A brown man running for a white office. All over the world, offices such as I aspire to are held by white men. Even in the countries to the south of us. You need only look at them. The President of Mexico, leader of a nation of brown men. Yet he is quite white. A *blanco*. In Paraguay, in Chile, it is the same. Why is it that only white men can hold office? I look to a new day, a day in which a brown man can lead a white people. A brown man who stands for white people, as well as brown. I am that man."

The crowd, some five hundred people, took in his words, their eyes rapt, their mouths busy. They had been given minipacks of Oreo cookies as they walked in the door.

"I am that man," Enrique Espiritu Esperanza repeated.

Seated at his monitor, Harmon Cashman had begun to weep bitter tears.

"He blew it! The stupid spick blew it! Now it's a racial campaign!"

And then the crowd began to chant.

"Esperanza! Esperanza! Esperanza!"

Harmon Cashman could not believe it. His candidate was up there committiing political suicide, and the crowd was cheering him on, white, black, brown, and yellow alike.

Somehow, some way, they saw his message of hope as relating to them all, regardless of skin color.

"This is incredible," he muttered.

In homes, in bars, in offices all over the state, the reaction was not as unanimous.

In Thousand Oaks, Al Bruss, a retired schoolteacher, decided he'd had enough. He was tired of the homeless and the illegals, who urinated in the formerly pristine streets and choked the streets as they wandered in search of jobs that often didn't exist even for legal citizens.

In the middle of the debate, he called his real-estate broker and said, "I've had enough. Put this place in your listing. I'm moving to Seattle."

In Santa Ana, in the heart of conservative Orange County, real-estate office phones rang off the hook. It was the same in San Francisco, San Diego, Sacramento, and elsewhere.

Unions, business groups, and activists, who had supported Esperanza before this, suddenly saw the future of California in stark terms. A future that did not include them. And they also saw the alternatives to Enrique Espiritu Esperanza as hopeless fringe candidates. They decided to put their energies into relocation, not voting.

Those who remained for the rest of the debate heard Rona Ripper and Barry Black, Junior give evasive, timid responses to questions about the future of California.

Each time he responded, Enrique Esperanza gave a forthright reply.

"The California past is Aztec," he said. "The California future is Aztec, and Filipino and Japanese. And of course, whites will be welcome to stay. We will find a place for them."

He was applauded after every statement. The cheering was reproduced all over California. A sea change that had been building for decades had taken human form.

America was on the threshold of having a Third World state within its borders.

At the end, the three candidates came forward and stood side-by-side in multicultural solidarity, taking in the thunderous applause that each thought in his heart of hearts was meant for him or her, but which in fact was still reverberating from Enrique Esperanza's last statement.

The audience came to their feet.

And it was during this cannonade of a standing ovation that it happened.

Every camera recorded it.

Positioned between the two male candidates, Rona Ripper suddenly jumped in place. She stiffened, her eyes going hot. And without any other warning, she turned and slapped an unprepared Barry Black, Junior in the face, screaming, "How dare you pinch me there, you flake!"

A great gasp broke the applause. Stunned silence followed. Barry Black, Junior turned a flustered crimson and seemed not to know what to do with his hands.

With his mouth he said, "I support your right to do that, even though I disagree with the doing of it." Then he added, "Ouch!"

Backstage, Remo said, "Did you see that? He goosed her. In front of the camera."

Harmon Cashman snorted. "Everybody knows Black is a complete flake."

"It wasn't Black. It was Esperanza," Remo said flatly.

"Remo!" Chiun flared. "Do not speak nonsense."

"I saw it," Remo insisted. "Black never moved. But Esperanza's shoulder bunched up just before Rona jumped. He reached across from behind and goosed her on the opposite cheek, so she'd think Black did it."

"Ricky wouldn't do that," Harmon insisted. He paused, adding, "But if he did, it was a masterstroke. And probably just won him the election. Black looks like a dip, and Rona Ripper just showed that she's a temperamental bitch. Ricky's in like Flynn!"

The overnight polls the very next day showed Esperanza nearly twenty points ahead of the other campaigns.

"But we're showing softness in the usual white voter blocs," Harmon Cashman confided to his candidate over a working lunch that very afternoon.

"I am not worried about the *blancos*. They are the past. I am the future."

"If this keeps up, they'll be deserting in droves by election day."

"It is their right. It is a free country."

The white people, in fact, didn't run from Enrique Espiritu Esperanza. They ran from California. Houses went up for sale. White voter registration fell off. Support for the Ripper and Black campaigns already had fallen sharply among white middle-class voters. Their campaign staffs were in ruins, owing to the repeated political arsons and assassination attempts.

The only alternative candidate, the interim governor, had dropped out for lack of funding.

And all over California, the homeless and illegal aliens and other disenfranchised potential voters saw the future in the dark-horse candidate named Esperanza.

And they saw hope.

Harmon Cashman saw more than hope. He saw certainty. Three days later, holed up in a Hollywood hotel, basking in the afterglow of a star-studded fund-raiser, he shouted it to the ornate chandelier.

"We're gonna win! We're gonna win! We're gonna win!"

"I believe this too," Esperanza said calmly. "This is why I am not going to campaign any further."

Harmon stopped dancing. "What?"

Esperanza shrugged. "There is no need. My opponents are reduced to making accusations and counter-accusations against one another. I, they cannot criticize. I am the multicultural candidate and they have come out in favor of multiculturalism. What is there to criticize? Oreo cookies and hope?"

"Pretty slick. Say, Ricky. You didn't really goose Rona up there, did you?"

"In politics, as in war, a little rear-guard action at the optimum moment can alter one's destiny," Esperanza said.

"For a guy who was growing grapes until a month

ago," Harmon said admiringly, "you sure know the ropes of this business."

"I am Esperanza. I know a great many things. For instance, I know that we are now a shoo-in."

"That's what I've been saying."

"Once in the governor's chair, I will control the largest economy in this hemisphere, one greater than most other nations'. And its people will be my people. People of color. They will trust me. They will do anything I ask."

"Anything?"

Esperanza nodded. "Even, if I suggest it, secede from the union."

Harmon Cashman blinked. "Secede?"

"Who is to stop me?"

"Well, the Federal government, for one thing."

Esperanza smiled beneficently. "Not if I have the President under my thumb."

Harmon's face acquired a stung look. "How would you get him under your thumb?"

"By informing him that I have knowledge of his employment of a professional assassin, the greatest assassin in human history, on his payroll."

Harmon Cashman blinked. "The little Korean?"

"No. *Our* little Korean."

"You really mean it? You want to make California a separate country?"

"If the people will have it. And I believe they will."

Harmon Cashman went bone-white. He felt a chill coursing up and down his spine. Woodenly, he stood up. "Excuse me, Ricky. If we're going to be in Sacramento soon, there's something I gotta do."

Enrique Esperanza looked up. "And what is this?"

"Work on my tan," said Harmon Cashman, leaving the room on leaden feet.

29

The next morning, Harmon Cashman awoke to find that an envelope had been slipped under his hotel-room door. He opened it and read the hand-written note.

Harmon:

I have returned to my home in the Napa Valley, to rest. I suggest that you do the same. For we shall need all our strength after the election.

Ricky

P.S. Help yourself to cookies.

Harmon found a package, neatly wrapped, standing out in the hallway. It looked big. Whistling his disappointment away, he carried the box back into the room.

The box was a literal smorgasbord of chocolate-and-white creme-filled treasures. There were mini-Oreos, regular packs, the Double Stuf kind with extra filling, and Harmon's current favorite, Big Stuf.

Putting a pot of coffee on the hot plate, he settled down to breakfast.

By noon, Harmon Cashman was feeling pretty good. So good, he ignored the knock on his door.

"Harmon. You in there?"

"Go 'way."

"It's Remo. Chiun and I are looking for Esperanza."

"He's gone to Napa Valley. Doesn't want to be disturbed. Doesn't need us. The election's in the bag."

"You sound drunk," Remo said suspiciously.

"I feel great," Harmon shot back.

After a minute they went away, and Harmon returned to building a cone of white creme filling on the breakfast nook table. He wondered if he should save some to sweeten his coffee. Regular sugar just didn't have the kick it used to.

After some thought, he decided to add a splash of coffee to the pile of creme filling. Coffee had lost its luster, too.

By three o'clock Harmon was feeling so confident of his prospects, he decided to share it with a certain someone. He put in a long distance call to Washington, D.C.

The President of the United States, after some thought, decided to take the call from his old campaign aide.

"Harmon, my boy! How're you doing?"

"Great, jus' great," Harmon Cashman said slurringly.

"Are you all right?"

"I am great. Jus' great. And after next week I'm gonna be greater. Gonna be on top of the world."

"Happy to hear it," said the President. "After that little chief of staff flap, we kinda fell off one another's Christmas card list. I was afraid you had hard feelings."

"Well, I do. And I'm gonna pay you back. As soon as we're in office."

"Harmon, do you know what you're saying, fella?"

"I'm saying I know your dirty lil' secret."

There was silence on the line to Washington.

Harmon began shouting, "I know about the lil' Korean! Well, he's *our* Korean now! That's right, Mr. Commander-in-Chief! The greatest assassin that ever was doesn't work for you anymore! He works for *us!*"

The President's voice became chilly. "Us?"

"Enrique Espiritu Esperanza, alias Ricky the Spic."

The President cleared his throat. In a tight voice he said, "I'm afraid I don't know what you are talking about. I'm sorry to hear that you're in such an agitated state, Harmon. I must go. Staff meeting. You understand. Good-bye."

"It's *adios*, now!" Harmon Cashman shouted into the dead line. "Better work on your tan, White Bread! Multicultural Fever is just starting in California, but it's gonna roll east real soon! Real soon!"

After Harmon Cashman had slammed down the phone,

he stood up. He was full of coffee and Oreos. He felt it necessary to release some biological ballast.

Harmon never made it to the bathroom. His overburdened stomach rebelled, and he vomited an unholy blackish bile all over his shoes, his clothes, and the floor.

And most importantly, all over his last box of cookies.

"No problem," Harmon said groggily, after he had emptied his stomach and rinsed out his mouth. "I'll just go buy some more."

There was a Japanese convenience store on the next block.

"What do you mean you sold out!" Harmon said, aghast, upon finding the cookie shelves bare of Oreos.

"Sold out. People buy. Much demand."

Harmon hurried to the next store. They were also sold out. It was unbelievable. There wasn't a solitary box of Oreos to be found in all of Hollywood.

"What's this damn country coming to?" he said, as he walked, sweaty-faced, back to the hotel. His hands shook. Cold, clammy perspiration trickled down the gully of his back. It was a very warm day.

As he crossed Melrose to the hotel, a red convertible came screeching around a corner.

Harmon barely noticed it. Not even when an Uzi was poked out of the backseat and began spraying bullets in his direction.

A stitching of lead caught him in the legs. Harmon Cashman went down. He screamed.

"God! Doesn't anyone have any Oreos?" he cried, as the convertible screamed away and a frightened crowd gathered around him.

Remo and Chiun found the surgeon who had removed four bullets from Harmon Cashman's legs on the twelfth floor of Cedars Sinai.

"He'll live," the surgeon told them. "But he'll need long-term rehabilitation."

"Will he walk again?" Remo asked.

"Of course. That is not what I meant. That man is suffering from a serious cocaine addiction."

Behind the doctor, through the closed door of Harmon

Cashman's hospital room, a shrill voice cried, "Take this slop away! I want my Oreos!"

"As you can hear," the surgeon said quietly, "he is suffering from a cocaine-induced psychosis. "Regression to childhood. It happens."

As they left the hospital Chiun said, "The cowardly attacks have resumed. Our place is with our patron."

"No argument there," said Remo.

Outside, Chiun paused. He looked up and down the street expectantly. Then, his face wrinkling in disappointment, he continued toward their waiting car.

"Looking for someone?" Remo asked, as he held open the car door for the Master of Sinanju.

"Yes. Cheeta. She is always the first to arrive when there is news. I wonder why she has not?"

"Search me."

Chiun gathered his bright skirts about him and slipped in. "It is too early for her to be burdened with your child," he said thoughtfully.

"Way, way too early," Remo agreed, slamming the door.

30

Harold W. Smith looked at the clock. It was after six in the evening. The day had been quiet. It was almost time to go home. The setting sun was painting Long Island Sound—visible through the picture window at his back— a gorgeous vermilion, a color the newspaper attributed to the eruption of a Philippines volcano.

Smith pressed the concealed stud that returned the CURE terminal to its desktop reservoir.

Getting up on creaky knees, he prepared to go home. His gray eyes rested on the closed desk drawer. It had been many weeks now. Smith had not been tempted to ingest Maalox, imbibe Alka-Seltzer, or resort to a single aspirin.

Perhaps, he thought, it's time to empty that drawer of its freight of pharmaceuticals.

Smith brought a green metal wastebasket around to the back of the desk and opened the drawer. One by one, he removed and dropped various bottles and cans into the basket. The last to go was a tiny canister of foam antacid he'd never gotten the hang of using.

It clanked into the basket, and Smith kneed the drawer closed.

He was on his way to the wooden clothes tree where his briefcase sat when the red telephone rang.

Smith returned to his desk with all the speed his old bones could muster. He caught the call at the third ring.

"Yes, Mr. President?" he said.

The President's voice was a flat, dry croak. "Smith."

"Is there something the matter?"

"I have just received a call from Harmon Cashman,

my former campaign aide," the President said in a strange voice.

"Now handling the Esperanza campaign."

"The man sounded positively high, Smith. He was babbling. I never knew he held such a grudge over losing the Chief of Staff job, but—"

"Yes?" Smith prompted.

"He threatened me, Smith. Actually threatened to expose what he called my 'dirty little secret.' "

Smith, getting a premonition, quickly took to his swivel chair. This was something he wanted to be seated for.

"I am listening, Mr. President," said Harold W. Smith, his voice cracking.

"Smith, he said he controls the greatest assassin in history. He called him 'our little Korean.' "

"My God!" said Smith.

"Could your people have been seduced by—"

Smith cut in sharply, "Impossible, Mr. President!"

"But—"

"Did Cashman mention CURE?"

"Well, no."

"Then organizational security remains uncompromised."

"Still, Cashman knows too much."

"I agree," said Smith.

"And likely Esperanza, too," added the President.

"It is possible," Smith said guardedly.

The President's tone sank to a hushed whisper. "Smith, right now Esperanza looks like he's gonna make it. That might not be a good thing for us. If you catch my drift."

Smith swallowed uncomfortably. His tie suddenly felt too tight, his skull too small to contain his brain.

"I am not convinced of that," he said. "There is nothing we can do at the moment. The election must go ahead as scheduled."

"You think this can be contained?"

"I do," Smith said crisply. "Now if you will excuse me, I must look into this further."

Harold Smith hung up. Going to the blue contact telephone, he attempted to reach Remo. None of the numbers brought results.

Smith, feeling his stomach rumble in complaint, brought his system back online.

Out in California, he discovered, Harmon Cashman lay recovering from surgery. His condition was described as "stable." Details were sketchy, but it appeared that the most recent political attack had been directed at him. Smith frowned. Was someone trying to nullify the election? If so, why?

He settled back in his chair, massaging his tired eyes, as he attempted to put the pieces together.

It was known that the late General Emmanuel Nogeira was almost unquestionably behind these attacks. It was also known that some of the attackers were tools of the Medellin Cartel. Nogeira and the cartel had past history together. Sometimes troubled history, but history nonetheless.

The most likely candidate behind these events is Rona Ripper, Smith reasoned. Black was a notorious but harmless flake. Ripper, however, was out there building concentration camps. There had already been violence, when the one Remo had discovered was destroyed to conceal its discovery.

It kept coming back to Nogeira. Had he been funding the Ripper campaign? What would Nogeira want with a vehement no-smoking candidate?

Then it hit Smith. "Outlaw tobacco! Stimulate cocaine sales!"

It fit. It made perfect sense.

All Harold Smith had to do was prove it before election day.

He began inputting the name "Emmanuel Alejandro Nogeira" into his terminal. Somewhere, he knew, there would be a kernel of datum that would connect the two. He just hoped he could find it in time to send Remo and Chiun in the right direction.

31

It was growing dark by the time Remo reached Napa Valley. On either side of the undulating road, tractors were pulling yellow gondolas through the grape vines. Migrant workers paused in the act of dumping crates of champagne grapes into the gondolas to wave greetings. All around them, brown hills enclosed the lushness of the valley in a protective ring.

"You really plan to take this treasurer's job?" Remo asked after a period of protracted silence.

"*Lord* Treasurer," Chiun said. "And I have not yet decided. I have many things on my mind."

"Well, I hope you don't," Remo said quietly.

Chiun turned, his eyes interested. "Yes?"

"But I'll understand if you do."

"You will, Remo?"

"Of course," Remo added. "I expect *you* to understand if I ever do anything you don't like."

"What have you done to displease me now?" Chiun snapped.

"Who says I have?"

"A father can tell," Chiun sniffed. "It is about Cheeta, is it not?"

Remo swallowed. There was never going to be a good time to break the news, but it seemed unavoidable now.

Remo opened his mouth as the car rounded a hill and the Esperanza mansion came into view. It was breathtaking, a Spanish-style hacienda perched on a verdant hill.

"We will discuss this later," Chiun said aridly.

"Deal," Remo said, relieved. "I'm going to pull off the road."

"Why?"

"We might as well test Esperanza's security while we're barging in," Remo said, easing the car to a stop.

"An excellent idea," said Chiun. "We will show him once again that he needs no others than us at his side."

They got out of the car and walked along, the heavy smell of grapes in their nostrils. The air was good here.

From the other direction, a car slithered up to the open gate, and through it unchallenged.

"Did you see that?" Remo said. "There's no one at the gate!"

"And I recognized the man who was driving," Chiun said, low-voiced.

"Yeah?"

"He is a member of a rival camp."

"Yeah? Whose?"

"The loud fat woman."

"I knew it!" Remo said, breaking into a floating run. "I knew it!" Chiun followed, his pipe-stem arms pumping.

They entered the grounds, which were lavish. An arbor-shaded circular driveway wound up to the looming mansion.

The car had pulled into the shadow of a guest house in the shadow of the great hacienda, and two men got out. They slipped up to the guest house door.

"Recognize the other one?" Remo asked.

"No," said Chiun.

They reached the house and found a window that was spilling light.

Remo snapped the driver's-side mirror off the car and, hunkering down under the window, used it to spy on the house's interior.

"Saw this in a movie once," Remo said, grinning.

"What do you see?" asked Chiun, standing off to one side.

"The other guy," Remo said. "Hey! I know him! He was a Black campaign aide. I saw him at debate."

Remo and Chiun exchanged dumbfounded glances.

"They're both in it together!" Remo hissed in surprise.

The Master of Sinanju frowned. "In political intrigues," he said slowly, "one plus one does not always equal two."

"Let's take them, and they can run the numbers for us," Remo suggested, dropping the mirror.

They slipped around to the front. Remo knocked the door off its hinges with a simultaneous kick to the lower hinge and a hard bat to the upper one. The door ripped free of its deadbolt lock.

"Tremble, amateur assassins!" Chiun shouted. "Your betters have come for your worthless heads!"

Feet scrambled up a flight of steps. Chiun surged in, Remo following.

They came around the bannister in time to see a pair of feet disappearing from view. Upstairs, a door slammed loudly. They went up the stairs, making virtually no sound at all.

"We were followed!" a frightened voice called out.

At the top of the stairs, Remo and Chiun hesitated. Remo's eyes raced along a row of closed doors. One still vibrated infinitesimally, from having been slammed shut.

"That one," Chiun hissed, pointing.

They hit the door running. It popped inward.

Inside, three startled faces looked in their direction.

Two were brown faces. Hispanic. Their eyes were widely luminous, and frightened.

The third face was also Hispanic in complexion.

"You are just in time!" cried the owner of the third face, Enrique Espiritu Esperanza. "These men are attempting to assassinate me!"

"No we're not!" protested the other two, fumbling machine pistols from under their clothing.

It was the last words they were destined to speak.

Remo and Chiun moved in on them. Remo shot between the pair, took Enrique Esperanza by his terry-cloth robe and pushed him behind a long, low item of furniture that was awash in bric-a-brac.

Remo turned, saying, "Don't kill—"

The sound of two grinding spinal columns cut off the rest. The two Hispanics fell from the Master of Sinanju's inexorable grip, their heads lolling crazily, their eyes bulging and glassy.

They gurgled once after they collapsed on the rug. That was all.

"Nice going, Little Father," Remo complained. "They could have told us something."

"Their faces told all," Chiun said coldly. "They were conspirators. In league with our political enemies."

Enrique Esperanza stepped up, adjusting his disordered robe on his broad shoulders.

"You did well to come here," he said softly, "for you were just in time to save me from certain death."

Chiun bowed. "When you have Sinanju, you need nothing more."

Looking around the room, Remo asked, "What kind of setup is this?"

32

Harold W. Smith stared at the computer screen. It was dark now. It was very dark.

Smith had searched his database all night for any connection between Nogeira and Rona Ripper. He had found none. Not one.

It was during this scanning that his computer had beeped an alert. Key buzzwords were routinely input into the system on a regular basis, and the CURE mainframes constantly scanned all databases within their telephonic outreach for new information on those mission-sensitive key words.

Smith pressed a key. In the corner, the screen displayed: TRACEWORD: NOGEIRA.

Smith called up the new data.

It was off an FBI mainframe. The final autopsy report of General Nogeira had been input into the FBI mainframes, making it available to Smith's roving data search. It was flagged TOP SECRET.

Smith scanned the report, first with curiosity, then with growing horror.

The official FBI autopsy on the body pulled from the Florida Everglades had reached an inescapable conclusion. A conclusion that sent Harold Smith scrambling for his green wastebasket and fumbling to his desktop an assortment of aspirins, antacids and other remedies. As he read along, he began unscrewing childproof caps and extracting pills. He didn't bother to identify them before they entered his mouth.

He popped an aspirin as he read that the body had lacked certain distinguishing marks known to have

marred the real body of General Nogeira, dictator of
Bananama.

One was that the dictator was known to have had five
general's stars tattooed to his naked shoulders, so that
even in disguise he would be identifiable to his allies.

The Everglades body had only four such stars on each
shoulder.

"Tattoos can be chemically removed," Smith said, in-
gesting a Dramamine.

There were other discrepancies. Body weight, height,
and an appendectomy scar that should not have been there.

"Inconsequential," Smith said, popping an antacid.

In the third paragraph, the report noted that fingerprints taken from the skin glove did not match those of
Nogeira.

"Easily explained," Smith told himself. "The skin
glove was from a drowning victim. Someone not connected with this."

The FBI report concluded in the final paragraph that
the body believed to be that of Nogeira was in fact that
of another person entirely.

"Premature," Smith scoffed, taking another aspirin.

At the bottom of the report was a notation that the
FBI had run the fingerprints through its extensive files
and produced no positive match.

Harold Smith logged over to the computerized FBI
fingerprint records and brought up a digitized copy of
the skin glove prints. They looked like ordinary fingerprints. He initiated a cross-match program that ran those
prints through various other files at his disposal.

It took an hour, but in the end Harold Smith had a
perfect match.

A second row of fingerprints showed beneath the first.
They were labeled. The name of the individual to whom
those fingerprints belonged made Smith blink wildly, as
if his eyes sought to reject the indisputable facts before
them.

The name was that of Enrique Espiritu Esperanza.

"Oh my God," croaked Harold W. Smith, his stomach, head, and eyes one great throbbing network of pain.
"I have instructed them to install the most brutal dictator
in this hemisphere as governor of California, and I have
no way to reach Remo and Chiun."

33

In the guest house of the Esperanza vineyard, Remo Williams frowned at the strange piece of furniture behind which he had pushed Esperanza to safety.

"It looks like an altar," Remo said, eyeing the assortment of statuary, portraits, and knickknacks. There was a wooden gourd set in the center of the feather-bedecked altar, and its bowl was dark with a brownish-red crust that could only be blood.

"Yes," said Esperanza. "One of my servants, he is from the Caribbean. An island man. You know, they practice strange beliefs on those islands."

"Looks like Voodoo stuff," Remo remarked.

"Santeria. Not Voodoo, but very much like it."

"This servant of yours," Chiun asked slowly. "Does he know of love potions?"

Esperanza blinked rapidly.

"Love potions?"

"Yes. I have a . . . friend who has need of such a thing." Chiun looked at Remo out of the corner of his eye. Remo looked away. Esperanza looked at them both and smiled with veiled understanding.

"Ah, I see," he said, gesturing. "Come, come. I will talk to him on your behalf. It may be that I can do something for this . . . friend."

As they were leaving the room, Remo said, "Cashman was hit this afternoon."

Esperanza laid a broad brown hand on his white-suited chest and turned, his face aghast. "No! Not Harmon!"

"He's not dead. The doctor says he'll recover."

"Ah, good," said Esperanza.

"Once he kicks his cocaine habit," Remo added.

Esperanza stopped again. "Harmon? Not Harmon."

Remo nodded. "The doctor confirmed it."

"How strange. You know, I have never known him to speak of drugs."

"Yeah, all you ever saw him do was wolf down Oreo cookies by the fistful."

"I understand those addicted ones often experience strange pangs and hungers," said Esperanza sadly.

They resumed walking down the stairs.

"What is that smell?" Chiun asked, sniffing the air doubtfully.

Remo answered. "Smells like Oreos."

"I keep a goodly supply here," explained Esperanza. "Once the election is over, I will donate the remainder to charity."

"Yeah," Remo said sourly. "A lot of starving people want nothing better than to sit down to a heaping bowl full of chocolate cookies."

"Remo!" Chiun admonished. "Watch your tone. This man is our patron."

"Sorry," Remo said, frowning. Something was bothering him. Something that danced along the edges of his memory. He couldn't think what it was.

Down in the parlor, Enrique Esperanza said, "My servant is away. Why do you not take this fine house for the duration of your stay with me?"

"Suits me," said Remo.

"A protector should always be at his patron's side," said Chiun flatly.

Esperanza considered. "I know: You may come with me, and your friend may remain here."

"It is proper," said Chiun.

"Okay," said Remo.

At that, the face of Enrique Espiritu Esperanza broke into a broad smile. It was a benevolent, almost angelic smile. His large teeth glowed like luminous pearls.

And then it hit Remo. Suddenly. The man had smiled just moments before, but quietly. Still, the way his mouth muscles had quirked tripped a dormant memory.

Now, with the radiance of that hauntingly familiar smile washing over him, Remo knew where he had seen it before. In the Florida Everglades. On an entirely different face. Not the smooth brown face of Enrique Espiritu Esperanza, but the ugly, reptilian, acne-cratered face of General Emmanuel Alejandro Nogeira.

As this was just sinking in, Esperanza and Chiun turned to go.

"Chiun, wait," Remo called.

The Master of Sinanju paused. "What is it?"

"I gotta speak to you." Remo eyed Esperanza. "Alone."

Chiun touched his wispy beard thoughtfully. "I have no secrets from my patron. Speak freely, Remo."

"Never mind," Remo said unhappily. "It can wait."

Chiun frowned. Esperanza's face was placid.

"Then let us go," he said.

They left. At the open door, Remo watched them start up to the big hacienda-style mansion.

Esperanza was saying, "I am certain we can concoct for your friend a suitable potion. I will call my servant. He will not mind a small interruption of his vacation."

"My friend will only need a weak dosage," Chiun put in. "His attractive powers are quite strong, it is just that the woman in question is very stubborn of will."

"Damn," Remo said after they'd disappeared into the house. "This can't be happening. I gotta call Smith."

He went in search of a phone. There was one on the kitchen wall. But when he picked it up, the line was dead.

Remo went through the house. He found no other phones. The smell of Oreo cookies was strong. It seemed to be coming, not from within the house, but through an open kitchen window.

Remo stepped out into the night. Yes, the smell was stronger out here. It was a hot smell. It overwhelmed the grape scent that made the air so heavy. The smell was cloying but unmistakable.

Moving stealthily, Remo followed it.

It was coming from some kind of long, low outbuilding on the opposite slope of the hill. A thin pipe of a smoke stack gave off the fresh hot smell.

There were no windows, so Remo simply went in the door.

A blast of hot air hit him in the face. It was thick with different smells—cooking chocolate, and other, more chemical odors.

No one noticed him enter, so Remo closed the door behind him and went to a pile of machinery. He crouched down, so he could see what was going on.

The place looked like a sweat shop. Hispanic workers toiled in the heat. One end was devoted to a number of brick ovens and other food-processing equipment.

Black chocolate wafers came rolling out of the open ovens, hot and malleable. They were stamped on one side by hand and flipped over like silver-dollar pancakes.

Remo saw what the stamping did to the wafers, and wondered why anyone would be counterfeiting Oreo cookies.

Nearby, giant vats bubbled with white matter. Over these, glassine packets were broken and their powdery contents shaken in.

Remo's nostrils detected their scent. The stuff looked like sugar, but it didn't smell like sugar.

"Coke," Remo said under his breath.

The white stuff was ladled off onto rows of black wafers set on long tables, making small, steaming mounds. Busy hands slapped identical wafers on top, and the finished cookies were set aside to cool before being packaged.

In one corner, there were boxes and boxes of Oreo cookies. Someone was opening them, tossing out the cookies, and replacing them with the counterfeit versions.

It's starting to make sense now, Remo decided. Cashman's addiction. The fervor with which the crowds cheer Esperanza's speeches as they munch on their give-aways. Everything.

Remo moved to the opposite end of the building. A different operation was under way there. Grim workers were doctoring long punch cards. They were adding extra punch holes.

Remo recognized them as voting cards. He wasn't sure how it worked, but he knew that every card was being fixed so that it registered a vote for Enrique Espiritu Esperanza when the voting lever was pulled.

He decided he had seen enough. Remo was on his way to the door when he spotted a cellular telephone lying on a work bench.

Unfortunately, the bench was almost completely surrounded by workers.

Remo decided it was worth any price to get that phone, so he simply straightened up and walked boldly toward it.

A sweaty-faced man shouted at him in Spanish.

Casually, Remo said, "No problem. Ricky sent me."

"*Que?*"

"Enrique," Remo repeated. "Carry on."

A varied collection of pistols and automatic weapons came out from under places of concealment as Remo laid a hand on the cellular telephone.

Remo smiled. No one smiled back. With his thumb, he activated the telephone and held down the one key.

In a moment, Harold Smith's tight voice was saying, "Remo! Thank God you called."

The voice spooked someone, because Smith's voice was suddenly drowned by a short burst of gunfire.

Remo twisted out of the way. He needn't have bothered. The bullets peppered the ceiling, making a hollow drumming sound.

Holding on to the phone, Remo faded back through the door, not bothering to open it. He simply bulled through.

On his way out, he batted the door back. It took its own frame back with it and slammed into three pursuing men.

Remo raced toward the mansion, the phone up to his face. He was shouting into the receiver.

"Smitty. You copy?"

"Remo, I hear shooting," came the anxious voice of Harold W. Smith. He burped.

"I'm at Esperanza's vineyard. Guess what? Esperanza isn't Esperanza. He's—"

"General Emmanuel Nogeira," said Smith bitterly.

"Huh? How'd you know that?"

"Fingerprints off the Everglade's body. They belonged to the true Esperanza."

"They must have kidnapped him and pulled the switch during the Baptism," Remo growled. "And I didn't see it because I was too busy ducking cameras. But can we prove it?"

A bullet track snarled over Remo's head. He cut off

to one side and kept zigzagging. Up ahead, lights were
going on all over the mansion.

"The real Nogeira has five general's stars tattooed on
each shoulder," Smith shouted.

"Tattooed?"

"He took his rank very seriously," said Smith.

"Yeah, well his smile gave him away to me," Remo
said.

"His smile?"

"Later," Remo said. "I just stumbled upon an Oreo
counterfeiting plant, and they're doctoring voter registration cards."

"Why would they counterfeit *Oreos*?" Smith shouted
over the growing din.

"They're loaded with coke!" Remo shouted back. "Instant voter support. Nogeira was turning California into
a land of cokeheads," Remo added.

"My God! It's Bananama all over again."

"Skip the anguish," Remo said quickly. "The bad guys
are hot on my heels, and Chiun's up ahead with Nogeira.
He doesn't suspect a thing. What do I do?"

"Nogeira must be eliminated. We have no choice."

"But Chiun'll kill me," Remo protested. "He thinks
Cheeta Ching is going to give birth to the next heir to
the House, and now this."

"Remo, we can deal with Chiun later. You have your
orders."

Up ahead a door opened, and from out of the house
a contingent of Crips, Bloods, and Los Aranas Espana
poured out. They had weapons in their hands and Oreo
cookies in their mouths, and their eyes were filled with
a crazy light.

"Nobody better shoot!" Remo warned them.

"Our man Esperanza says we gotta!" spat back a familiar voice. Dexter Dogget's.

And behind him, Remo heard the shout, *"Viva
Esperanza!"*

It was his pursuers. Probably Colombians or Ba-
nanamanians. Maybe both.

Remo threw himself on the ground as two fans of bullet tracks filled the air over his head from opposite sides.
Rounds actually struck one another in midair, making

short, ugly sounds and sending hot needles of lead spraying all around.

A few struck Remo's Hispanic pursuers. But only a few.

The pursuing Colombians did better. They chopped down about a third of the gang members in return. This brought further retaliation, and as he lay flat, cradling the cellular phone, Remo realized he had been forgotten. It was eye-for-an-eye time—which suited Remo just fine.

The firefight swelled into a crescendo of blood and bullets.

Moving low, Remo circled the mansion, the sound of firing covering him. He wondered why Chiun hadn't shown.

The Master of Sinanju listened thoughtfully as his patron explained the future.

"You will work for me. Exclusively."

"This is possible," replied Chiun. They stood before the dormant fireplace of the great parlor.

"I will pay you very, very well," continued Esperanza. "You will no longer need to work for the U.S. President."

"I do not work for him."

"Then who?"

"I cannot say."

Esperanza nodded. "I understand. I will expect the same loyalty."

Chiun inclined his head. "Of course."

"There is just one other matter," added Esperanza.

"Yes?"

"The one called Remo. He works for the government. He is CIA?"

"Possibly."

"He will be a hindrance to us. You must sever all ties with him."

Chiun touched his wispy beard in preparation before speaking.

Just then, the night exploded with the sound of automatic weapons fire.

Remo went in the back door. He brought it down with a flying kick and was past it before it quite hit the floor.

"Chiun!" he called. "Where are you?"

From a nearby room the Master of Sinanju's voice came, thin and unwelcoming.

"In here."

Remo veered toward the sound. He came up short, in a spacious parlor decorated in the Spanish style of old California. He pointed in the direction of Enrique Esperanza.

"That guy's a phony," he said hotly. "He's not Esperanza."

"It is true," admitted Enrique Esperanza. "I have taken the place of the real Esperanza, who had the misfortune to share a meal with a swimming reptile." He looked to the Master of Sinanju. "With your history, you must appreciate my cleverness. I had plastic surgery to make my face resemble his."

"Not to mention a dermabrasion," Remo inserted.

Esperanza smiled. "My new face is so much more photogenic, no?"

"No," said Remo flatly.

Esperanza shrugged and went on. "My plan is quite simply foolproof. I have recruited the very illegals I have helped to smuggle into this country in my—how you say?—previous life. The homeless will vote for me, too, because I have registered them under the names of the dead. Those who enjoy my cookies will also vote for me. Those I have frightened with my vision of the future of California will, sadly, not vote for Esperanza. But I think many of them have other plans for their own futures, which do not include California."

"Let's not forget the doctored voter punch-cards," Remo added darkly.

Chiun's wrinkled features acquired a questioning cast.

"Once I have my people put them in place," Esperanza explained, "they will insure that even those who vote against me will be casting a vote for Esperanza. Brilliant, no?"

The hazel eyes of the Master of Sinanju shone in appreciation. "Yes, it is very brilliant."

Remo shouted, "Chiun! What are you saying?"

"Merely the truth. This is a ruler after my own heart. He understands power. And he will achieve it."

"That mean you're sticking by him?" Remo demanded tightly.

"Only a fool would not," replied Chiun. "He is what is called 'a sure thing.' "

"Then call me a fool," growled Remo.

Chiun shrugged. "You are a child yet, Remo. You will learn that the true leaders are those who take power, not accept it from the fickle populaces."

Esperanza smiled broadly. "You are too late," he told Remo. "He is with me. There is no changing that."

"Too bad," Remo said. "Emperor Smith wanted him taken out."

Esperanza looked blank.

"Smith is my emperor no longer," Chiun said coldly. "Our most recent contract has expired. It will not be renewed. Better work has come along."

"He'll be sorry to hear that," Remo said. "Especially when he hears that you let a golden opportunity slip through your fingers."

Chiun cocked his head to one side. "What opportunity?"

"The one that atones for my earlier screw-up, when I let Nogeira get eaten by that alligator."

"What has that to do . . . ?"

"Because that's Nogeira right there," Remo said, pointing.

Chiun turned to the man he knew as Enrique Esperanza. "This is true?"

"Not at all," said a smiling General Emmanuel Nogeira. "I do not know what this man is saying."

"There's one way to prove the truth," Remo said. "The real Nogeira has five general's stars tattooed to each shoulder."

General Nogeira squared his shoulders.

"Nonsense," he said, tightening the cord on his terry-cloth robe. "CIA lies."

"Then you would not mind disproving this accusation," Chiun said slowly, his eyes going as narrow and steely as knife blades.

"Seems to me, I recall a clause in that contract that covers unfinished business," Remo said pointedly.

The man who called himself Enrique Espiritu Esperanza looked from Remo to Chiun, to Remo again. His mouth fell open like a hungry frog's. "I refuse," he said, sweat forming on his smooth forehead. "I am Esperanza. I do not need to prove anything. To anyone. And when my men finish shooting at shadows, they will deal with that pig of a CIA agent," he added, indicating Remo.

"I see," said the Master of Sinanju, turning away. His hands slashed back like the talons of a striking eagle. Nails ripped the terry cloth away, exposing the broad brown shoulders of General Emmanuel Nogeira—and five bluish-green stars on each shoulder, where the artist's needle had inscribed them.

Before anyone could react, in from the front door poured a knot of triumphant Colombians. They burst into the room, holding their weapons at the ready for instruction.

General Nogeira pointed at Remo Williams and said, "Kill that *blanco*!"

Then the blood erupted from his naked throat, as the right index fingernail of the Master of Sinanju opened it with a seemingly careless slice.

As the once-again-dead dictator of Bananama started to tip forward into a fountain of his own gore, Remo went to work on the Colombians.

They were handicapped by the need not to fill the parlor with flying lead and hit their own leader, so they began backing around for clean shots even as Nogeira's throat split open.

Remo danced in. He kicked high, and sent the jaw of one Colombian crashing up through his own palate. His foot had barely touched the rug on the rebound when the attached ankle twisted, and Remo's other foot went for a handy temple. The kick didn't tear the second Colombian's head off his shoulders. It only dislocated it. But the result was the same. The floor began to collect fallen Colombians.

The Master of Sinanju was more direct. He stepped up to each of his intended victims, batting their impotent weapons away, and punctured them at critical points. A paralyzing stab to a heart muscle here. A jugular-severing slice there.

It took less than two minutes. Nobody got off a single shot. When it was over, Remo and Chiun were the only ones left standing among the dead and dying.

They bowed once to one another formally. Remo bowed a second time. The Master of Sinanju returned it. But when Remo started a third bow, Chiun made a disgusted face and said, "Enough! Only a Japanese would indulge in such an unseemly display of emotion. Do not be a Japanese, Remo."

"Sorry, Little Father. It's just that I thought you had gone over to Esper— I mean, Nogeira's side."

"That," intoned the Master of Sinanju, "is a decision I would have made after the election, not before."

"That's a relief."

"Besides," Chiun added, "if I abandoned you, Remo, who would raise my grandson?"

"Uh, I hope that's not the only reason you made that decision," Remo said uncomfortably.

"Why do you say that?"

"Because there's something you need to know about Cheeta Ching. . . ."

And over the expanse that was the Esperanza vineyard, where men lay dead and dying, a piteous cry of despair rose up to the moon-burdened sky.

The blackened patch of ash nestled in the Santa Monica foothills was still being hosed down by fire apparatus when Remo pulled up to the fire-barrier sawhorses.

In silence, he got out. The Master of Sinanju, face still, hands concealed in the sleeves of his brocaded kimono, followed a decorous two paces behind.

A fire marshal stopped them.

"Sorry. Off-limits."

Remo flashed his secret service ID, and the fire marshal changed his tune.

"We're looking for a possible body," Remo told him.

"We got them all."

A low moan issued from Chiun's wattled throat.

"Find a female body?" Remo asked.

"No. All males."

"Then you missed one," said Remo, striding into the blackened area.

The smell of fire was like charcoal on the tongue. The sweet stink of roasted human flesh added to his discomfiture. Fire-scarred iron bars lay amid the burnt timbers and light gray ashes, like the bones of some metallic dinosaur.

Remo located the exact spot on the pile of ash that had been his cell, then walked five paces west.

"Right here," said Remo, standing on the spot where Cheeta Ching had been imprisoned.

He took up a bar and began to poke the ashes, which lifted into the warm air like snowflakes from some evil dimension.

Firemen gathered around, silent and curious. "If

you're looking for a body," one said, "those ashes you're stirring up may be all that's left."

Lifting a kimono sleeve to his pained face, Chiun turned away.

Remo kept poking until his bar struck something solid. Something that was not dirt and not rock. He got down on his knees and began scooping away ash.

A body was quickly excavated. Remo turned it over.

It was barely recognizable as Cheeta Ching's driver. His face was a seared mass of meat, and his right leg, under the split pants, showed raw bone where the meat and muscle had been torn loose, as if by a wild animal.

"Is it her?" Chiun squeaked, refusing to look directly at the corpse.

"No," said Remo. He continued digging.

Under his feet, the ash abruptly stirred. Feeling the ground move, Remo stepped away. Then the ash showered up, and, like a shark coming to the surface, the ferocious face of Cheeta Ching, face blackened, eyes blazing, mouth red with something redder than lipstick, emerged.

Cheeta sat up. Her head swiveled this way and that. Her barracuda eyes settled on Remo's astonished face.

"You!" she shrieked. "What took you so damn long to find me?"

"Cheeta?" Remo said in a dumbfounded voice.

"Cheeta!" Chiun said joyously, coming to her side. "My child! How you must have suffered!"

"Damn right I suffered," huffed Cheeta. "If it weren't for that stupid cameraman, I would have starved to death."

That statement sank in. Everyone, including Chiun, whose eyes went wide with horror, shrank away from the ashy apparition.

"You didn't . . . ?" Remo said.

Cheeta, spanking ashes off her arms, struggled to her feet, saying, "Why not? He was already dead. And he'd been roasted. I had to do *something* until somebody lifted him off me."

The fire marshal looked stunned. "She *ate* the guy?" Then, when it had sunk in, he threw up.

"Oh, look at him!" Cheeta blazed. "You'd think all *he* had to eat for two whole days was white meat."

The Master of Sinanju took his wispy hair in both hands and rent it savagely, crying, "My Cheeta! Forced to eat a lowly white to sustain herself!"

"Don't you *dare* tell anyone!" Cheeta spat.

"Don't worry," Remo said, backing away. "My lips are sealed."

"Good. This is my story," said Cheeta, looking around. "Where are the cameras? Are there any cameras here? I've got to tell my story! Legendary superanchorwoman's tale of courage and survival. Maybe I can interview myself on *Eyeball to Eyeball with Cheeta Ching*."

As Cheeta Ching stormed off, in search of a friendly lens and the alluring red light of air time, Remo said, "I'm sorry, Little Father."

Chiun let go of his hair. He watched Cheeta Ching storm down the mountain trail. "The poor child," he squeaked plaintively. "I must comfort her in her hour of travail." Lifting his skirts, he started off.

Remo called after him. "Chiun! Wait!"

"Do not follow us, Remo," Chiun called back. "You are not Korean. You would not understand. And the sight of your pale, un-Korean flesh would only disturb the delicate flower of womanhood that is Cheeta the Beauteous."

As the Master of Sinanju disappeared down the slope, Remo said, "Ah, the hell with it." He looked to the flabbergasted firemen. "Anyone got a phone hook-up? I have a call to make."

A week later, Harold Smith was saying, "The election has been postponed until a new crop of candidates can be fielded."

"What happened to Black and Ripper?" Remo wanted to know.

"Black sponsored an Indian rain dance and a sandstorm blew in, causing a chain-reaction freeway pile-up instead," Smith said flatly. "He was forced to drop out in disgrace."

Remo looked out from the Los Angeles hotel room. The smog formed a yellowish-black curtain over the San Gabriel mountains. "And Ripper?"

"It was leaked that Ms. Ripper is a former three-pack-a-day smoker who became addicted to Red Man chewing tobacco attempting to keep her weight under control," Smith said.

"There goes her credibility," said Remo.

Smith paused, then said, "I have a report that Harmon Cashman suffered cardiac arrest while convalescing."

"According to Chiun, that heart-stopping blow I used was a favorite around the Japanese courts," Remo said, examining his knuckles approvingly.

"The President has sent a sympathy card to the family," Smith said. "But he is nonetheless relieved. And there is the matter of the Ripper and Black campaign staffers Chiun removed, thinking they intended to assassinate Nogeira."

"What's the mystery?" Remo asked. "They were spies Nogeira had planted in the other campaigns."

"Ballistics tests on their weapons match the bullets that struck Harmon Cashman," Smith explained. "It is clear that Nogeira ordered that attack, as he had all the others. The idea was to stir up additional sympathy for his camp as close to the election as possible."

Remo whistled. "For a banana-republic politician, he knew how to run a campaign. Fake attacks on himself to draw attention, then order real ones against his opponents to demoralize them and throw suspicion off himself."

"Yes," said Smith. "It is fortunate that he did not acquire the services of the Master of Sinanju. How is Master Chiun, by the way?"

"I don't know," admitted Remo. "He hasn't said much since he came back from wherever he was with that Cheeta barracuda."

"Remo, I understood you to say that the report of Cheeta's pregnancy was a concoction of yours."

"It was. I made it all up. Why?"

"Cheeta's manager confirmed today that she is expecting."

Remo gripped the phone tighter. "When?"

"In nine months, more or less," replied Smith.

Remo's eyes went wide. In the other room, he could hear the Master of Sinanju. Humming. It was a very contented hum.

"He didn't!" Remo blurted. "I mean, he couldn't!"

"It is possible," Smith said blandly.

Remo closed his eyes, as if in pain. "With Chiun, anything is possible."

"Are you going to ask him directly?" Smith asked.

"No. Absolutely, positively not. I am never raising this subject again," Remo vowed, "and I hope it goes away. Forever."

"I hope so too," said Harold W. Smith fervently.

And from the other room, the humming of the Master of Sinanju continued unabated.